JUN 1 7 2014

I Love You More

I Love You More

More

A NOVEL

JENNIFER MURPHY

DOUBLEDAY
NEW YORK LONDON TORONTO
SYDNEY AUCKLAND

WITHDRAWN

BLOOMINGDALE PUBLIC LIBRARY
101 FAIRFIELD WAY
BLOOMINGDALE, IL 60108
630 - 529 - 3120

This book is a work of fiction. Names, characters, businesses, organizations, places, events, and incidents either are the product of the author's imagination or are used fictitiously. Any resemblance to actual persons, living or dead, events, or locales is entirely coincidental.

Copyright © 2014 by Jennifer Murphy

All rights reserved. Published in the United States by Doubleday, a division of Random House LLC, New York, and in Canada by Random House of Canada Limited, Toronto, Penguin Random House companies.

www.doubleday.com

DOUBLEDAY and the portrayal of an anchor with a dolphin are registered trademarks of Random House LLC.

Jacket design by Rex Bonomelli
Jacket photographs: women (from left to right):
© Izabela Habur/Getty Images, © Zoonar GmbH/Alamy,
© Larysa Dodz/Vetta/Getty Images; gun © moodboard/
Alamy; veil © ramirez/Alamy

LIBRARY OF CONGRESS CATALOGING-IN-PUBLICATION DATA
Murphy, Jennifer, 1956–   February 17
I love you more/by Jennifer Murphy. — First edition.
pages   cm.
1. Teenage girls—Fiction.   2. Betrayal—Fiction.
3. Domestic fiction.   I. Title.
PS3613.U737245.I3 2014
813'.6—dc23
2013045338

ISBN 978-0-385-53855-8 (hardcover)
ISBN 978-0-385-53856-5 (eBook)

MANUFACTURED IN THE UNITED STATES OF AMERICA

1 3 5 7 9 10 8 6 4 2

First Edition

For David and Madi

Rumors

(The Events Surrounding the Murder)

. . .

Who brings a tale takes two away.

—IRISH PROVERB

Picasso

The rumors started before my daddy's body got cold. I'd made my peace with the lies by then—lies I've learned are a necessary evil—and, being from the South, I'm used to *cloying* (that means sickeningly sweet) smiles, but I hadn't figured on the sideways glances, hushed talk, loud silence. Feigned ignorance. I mean someone's dying had always made the front page of the *Hollyville Herald*. Even Mrs. Morgan's twenty-year-old cat got a paragraph, but not my daddy. The particulars of Oliver Lane's funeral were tucked in the ad section between an upcoming gun show, an irony I'm sure was lost on the editor, and a JESUS LOVES YOU, standard filler for slow news days. Thankfully there was no mention of murder, or of the fact that the police suspected Mama or one of those other two ladies. It wouldn't be polite to put such things in writing.

My name is Picasso, like the artist. Mama said she named me Picasso because he painted about truth, but I think Mama misinterpreted his words. What Pablo Picasso said was this: *Art is a lie that makes us realize truth.* What I think he meant is that great art is born from skillful lying, and something else, something much more profound, that lying is okay as long as its end goal is altruistic. Well that's how I read it anyway, and that's how I've been able to justify what happened that day.

Looking back, it all started three years ago when the first lady showed up at our house. I was ten years old at the time. Daddy was out of town on business; he'd been traveling a lot. Mama was sticking a couple of chicken pies in the oven when the doorbell rang. It was August and hot, the kind of hot it gets in North Carolina in the dead of summer. The kind of hot where your skin melts and your tongue swells the minute you walk out the door, and the last chore you want to do is take out the trash because the smell's so bad. Mama's long, straight blond hair was tied up in a ponytail, her face and neck covered in sweat beads, her mascara running.

"Run and get the door, Picasso," she said.

The lady had blue eyes like Mama and me, and skin as pale as an onion. She was tall, but not as tall as Mama, and skinny. The navy blue suit she wore looked like it was painted on, it fit so perfect. I figured she was selling religion.

"You must be Picasso," the lady said, and forced her bright peach lips into a big smile that displayed perfect white teeth. "You're even prettier than your picture."

Funny, how I didn't think much about that statement at the time. Shouldn't I have wondered how she'd seen my picture? But there's so much I didn't wonder about back then, at least not right away.

Mama had come up behind me. "Can I help you?" she asked the lady.

"I'm Jewels. I know your husband." Her voiced cracked. "We have two children. Twin boys."

She tried to unzip her handbag—I saw that it was the exact same handbag Daddy had gotten Mama for Christmas that year. Its strap got twisted with that of her briefcase. Both fell to the ground. Files spewed across our front porch. She kneeled. Her shoulders shook. While choking out a couple of sobs, she gathered the papers, stuffed them back in the briefcase, stood, and rearranged the bags on her shoulder. A tear trailed from her eyes, removed a crooked line of makeup from her face. She straightened, wiped her cheek with the palm of her hand, smearing her caked foundation even more, pulled a picture from her handbag, and handed it to Mama.

Mama's face went white. I couldn't tell whether she was scared or angry. Daddy used to say that Mama was an expert at covering her emotions. "Picasso, go upstairs and do your homework," she said, sternly.

"I don't have any homework, Mama," I said. "School doesn't start until next week, remember?"

She raised her voice. "Don't you have summer reading?"

I'd finished my reading two months earlier, but I knew she didn't care about that one way or another.

"Come in," I heard her ask Jewels as I climbed the stairs. "Would you like some iced tea?"

"Yes," Jewels spluttered. "Thank you."

It was a couple of months before Jewels showed up again, this time with another lady. That morning, the light through my window was duller than usual. Rainwater drooled on the windowpane. The alarm went off just as I looked at my clock. I took a shower, brushed my teeth, put on my school uniform, and went downstairs to prepare my breakfast: a glass of orange juice and a cinnamon Pop-Tart.

I was in the kitchen scraping butter on the Pop-Tart when I caught a whiff of perfume. Mama was wearing her favorite low-cut, form-fitting black dress, and she'd done up her face like she did when she and Daddy were going out on one of their "adult nights." The dress was also one of Daddy's favorites. Whenever Mama wore it, he would run his hands over her hips and breasts, and usually the two of them would end up kissing their way up the stairs and into their bedroom, and sometimes they wouldn't go out after all.

"Do you have a meeting or something?" I asked.

"No," she said. "It's raining."

Mama liked to sleep in, so usually I walked to school, but on rainy days, like that one, she'd drag herself out of bed, throw on a pair of jeans and a sweatshirt, not even brush her teeth, and drive me to school.

She turned on the teakettle and opened the kitchen blinds. "Looks like it will clear up later."

I rinsed my glass and plate, put them both in the dishwasher, and started gathering my books.

"You forgot to put the butter away," Mama said.

Just then, the doorbell rang. Mama rushed to open the door.

"I know we're early," I heard a lady's voice say.

"I was just getting ready to drive Picasso to school," Mama said.

"We can wait in the car?" the lady asked more than said. "Oh, hi Picasso. Don't you look pretty today?"

Now, you can see the kitchen clear from the front door because our house isn't that big and has what Mama calls an open floor plan, but I was still startled when I heard the woman say my name. Like the last time, Jewels wore a tailored business suit, this one beige. The suit and her hair were wet from the rain. It crossed my mind that it wasn't very smart of her not to bring an umbrella, but mostly I started wondering why she showed up again. She carried the same handbag, the one like Mama's, but not the brief-case. Another woman stood next to her. I learned later that her name was Bert, short for Roberta. She wore a stretchy green dress, also wet, and Birkenstocks. Her belly stuck out so far it looked like it would burst any minute. She was shorter than both Mama and Jewels and chubby, and in my opinion not very pretty. Her hair was a mousy brown, her eyes that muddy color that some people call hazel, and she had a mole on her cheek that was the size, and shape for that matter, of a small beetle.

Mama turned around. She looked surprised, as if she'd forgotten I was there. "Can you give us a minute, Picasso?"

I wasn't sure what she was asking, so I sat down on one of the island stools.

"No, I mean, will you go upstairs? And brush your hair. It's sticking up all over the place."

When I came back down, Jewels and Bert were gone.

"Much better," Mama said, looking at my hair. "You ready?"

"Who were those ladies, Mama?"

"Oh, they're just members of a committee I'm working on."

"What committee?" I asked.

Mama was busying herself in the coat closet. "Where is that raincoat of mine? Oh, here it is."

"How does that one lady know Daddy?"

She messed with her zipper. "What did you say, Picasso?"

"That one lady said she knew Daddy."

"I don't remember her saying anything about knowing Daddy," Mama said.

"She did say it," I said. "Last time she was here."

"Last time?" Mama asked. "Those two women have never stepped foot in our house before."

"Not both of them, Mama. Just that one. Jewels."

"You're mistaken, Picasso. Now skedaddle. You're going to be late for school."

Mama had never lied to me, at least that I knew of, but it wasn't the lie itself that bothered me. It was the why of the lie.

Mama and I weren't big car talkers, so she turned on the radio and listened to some lady who was helping callers figure out how to decorate. Mama was forever changing stuff around in our house. Back then our house was mostly white: white kitchen cabinets, white trim, white sofa, and sort of white furniture (Mama called it distressed). Daddy always said Mama got a gold star in decorating. He also said she got a gold star in money spending so it was good he made a lot. The line for the drop-off circle wasn't very long, which meant I was close to being late.

"Hurry," Mama said, when one of the new teachers, Miss Chest (her real name was West), opened the door for me. "Remember, I'll pick you up if it's raining. Otherwise, just walk. Okay?"

Mama was rocking on the porch swing when I got home from school that afternoon. Daddy was right: Mama was the prettiest woman in the entire world. She wore a light pink sundress and black flip-flops. Her hair was hanging loose, catching the wind. I slid off my backpack, kicked off my shoes, scooted in next to her, and laid my head against her shoulder. Her hair smelled sweet, like flowers.

She kissed the top of my head. "How was school?"

"Fine," I said.

It wasn't. Ryan Anderson, the boy I'd had a big crush on since kindergarten, still hadn't noticed me, and those Think They're All That Girls had up and started calling me Pee-pee Picasso again, which wasn't too creative given the fact that it had been a very long time since that particular adjective made any sense at all. I didn't see any reason to tell Mama that. I tried not to share that kind of stuff with Mama; I didn't want to upset her. Mama's never been very good at hearing bad things. Back in kindergarten, when those girls first started calling me that name, I told Daddy about it.

"Everybody has accidents now and then, Partita (an instrumental piece composed of a series of variations)," he'd said.

Daddy never called me Picasso. He called me all kinds of different *P* words, so I would learn them. It might be an hour or it might be a week, but sooner or later Daddy would ask me what every one of my names meant. "You shouldn't worry about it. Those girls will forget before you know it."

"They're mean, Daddy," I said.

"Do you want me to talk to your teacher?" he asked.

"Will you?"

"Sure thing." He looked around to make sure Mama wasn't there, leaned in close, and whispered in my ear, "How about we drive into town and get you some of that homemade ice cream you like?"

"Mama will get mad," I said. "We haven't had dinner yet."

"I won't tell if you won't." He made his secret smile, the one where instead of showing his teeth, the ends of his lips went up just a little and his eyes widened.

Daddy had five smiles. On top of the secret smile, there was what Mama called his charming smile (or sometimes, usually when she was mad, his get-what-he-wants smile), where he opened his mouth wide, causing little dents to form in his cheeks and his nose to wrinkle, and twinkled his eyes at the camera or whoever he was looking at. He also had his private-time smile, which he used exclusively for Mama, and his proud smile, where on top of curling his lips, he cocked his head, squinted his eyes, and looked off in the distance. I didn't see the fifth smile very often. I called it the unsmile, not only because it wasn't a smile exactly (it was more like a cross between a smile and a glare), but because sometimes I wasn't even sure I saw it, it went away so fast.

Daddy never did talk to my teacher, Mr. Dork (his real name is York), about those All That Girls and their stupid name-calling. Daddy didn't do a lot of things he said he would.

"Why do I have such a dumb name?" I asked Mama as we swung back and forth.

"Picasso's a beautiful name," she said. "I told you it means 'truth.' You were the first true thing that ever happened to me, and the first and only thing I've ever truly loved. The moment you came into the world, I unzipped my heart, stuffed you inside, and zipped it back up real tight so nobody else could get in there."

"What's love got to do with truth?" I asked.

"Everything," she said.

"Didn't you put Daddy in your heart too?"

She stared at the air, as if something far, far away had caught her attention. "Promise me you'll never get married."

"Why not?" I asked.

She cupped my chin in her hand and looked straight into my eyes. "Promise me."

"I promise."

"Good. I love you, Picasso." She kicked the toe of her flip-flop on the porch's light turquoise, painted-wood floor to keep the swing going.

Daddy used to say that there was something about Mama that pulled him like a magnet. He said he felt it the first time he saw her. I was just a baby the first time I saw Mama, so I don't remember ever not feeling Mama's pull. I've always loved Mama more than anyone or anything, loved her so much that the fear of losing her was always just one step behind the love.

I was sleeping when Daddy got home that night. The fight woke me. I got out of bed as quietly as I could. The mattress springs squeaked when I lifted my behind. I stood there for a moment, still as a lamp, and then snuck out to the top of the staircase to listen.

"What is wrong with you, Di?" Daddy was saying. "You can't really just be upset that I forgot to put gas in your car. I'll fill it tomorrow before I go to work. Okay?"

"It's not just the gas, Oliver," Mama said. "It's everything. You're never home. A few nights ago, one of the smoke alarms malfunctioned. It was three in the morning. And there I was dragging a ladder in from the garage and fixing the damn thing. It's not that I can't fix stuff, when I was single I fixed stuff all the time, but I'm not single now. I'm married." I thought I heard her sniffle. "It's just that sometimes I don't feel married. You're gone so much."

Then she was blubbering, which surprised and worried me. I'd never heard Mama cry before. When I was little, Daddy once told me that Mama was born on an island called Ice, because that's what all its inhabitants were made of. In the middle of the island there was a big thermometer that was always set below zero so that the people wouldn't thaw out. Every hundred years a big refrigerated boat would stop at the island, and if you just happened to be eighteen years old when it arrived, like Daddy said

Mama was, which I thought was lucky, you could journey to the college of your choosing. Mama chose the University of North Carolina. When I asked Daddy why Mama didn't melt when she moved to the southern portion of the United States of America, he said, "People don't change just because they move to a different place."

"I'm sorry, Di," Daddy said. "You know I love you more than life itself. I promise I'll try to be home more. Okay?"

I heard that slobbering sound their lips made when they kissed.

"Do you want to go upstairs?" Daddy asked.

"No," Mama said. "Not tonight. I'm not feeling well. You go on. I've got some reading to do." Mama was a *domestic engineer* (that means she ran our home and family relations) so mostly she just read fiction books, or her Junior League stuff. Back then she held a pretty important position at Junior League. I guess she was also a Junior League engineer.

I scurried back to bed. Only seconds after I'd pulled up the covers and closed my eyes, Daddy came into my bedroom. I pretended I was asleep. He sat on my bed for a long time. Then he kissed my cheek and left.

As the months passed, Mama and Daddy talked to each other less and less. They stopped kissing and even hugging. Mama had so many bad moods it seemed like they were growing together into one big one, like our neighbor Mr. Buttons's eyebrows. She stared into the air more than she didn't. By Thanksgiving break, Ryan Anderson still hadn't so much as glanced in my direction, and although those All That Girls quit calling me Pee-pee Picasso, they figured out a new and better name for me: Plump Picasso.

When I told Daddy about that name, he said my being a little plump wasn't a bad thing at all. "Girls with a little fat on their bodies grow into shapely, attractive women. Just look at your mama."

"Mama was fat?"

"Not fat, just a little plump."

"How do you know that?" I asked, skeptically.

"I saw a picture of her when she was your age," he said. "I'll find it and show you. And look at your mama now. She's as beautiful as the goddess of love. Her Roman name was Venus. Do you remember her Greek name?"

"Aphrodite," I said.

"That's right. Ares, the god of war, fell in love with Aphrodite the first time he saw her. Just like I did with your mama."

"Was Aphrodite plump when she was my age?" I asked.

"She never was a little girl," he said. "She emerged from the ocean a full-grown woman. The gods found her standing on a seashell. Whenever we're at the beach and I watch your mama coming out of the water after one of her morning swims, and I see her long blond hair matted against her head and shoulders, the sun making her wet skin glisten, I swear she's Aphrodite reincarnated."

When Daddy talked about Mama, his face and eyes lit up, and sometimes he said things like that about her, gushy, embarrassing things, and usually, just like he did that day, he'd end the conversation by saying, "I love you and your mama more than life itself."

That day I still believed him.

I heard them laughing before I saw the bright blue convertible. The car was parked in the church parking lot at the end of our street. Since it was so pretty out, and I'd left home early enough, I decided to take the long way around to school. It wasn't quite spring yet, but it was warm and the sun was so bright that even the saddest people couldn't help but have minutes of happiness. So bright I couldn't see who was sitting in the car. I shaded my eyes with my hand. Two women with longish, straight blond hair and dark sunglasses sat in the car. Both wore red blouses with matching head scarves that tied under their chins. They could've been twins they looked so much alike. Even though they'd changed their hair color, I was pretty sure I knew who they were.

I crossed the street slowly, being careful not to make any noise. I was so busy watching the two of them and making sure they couldn't see me that I didn't notice the mess of dirt and gravel that had spilled from Mrs. Jesswein's newest flower bed onto the road's shoulder. My feet skidded; my heavy backpack shifted. I lost my balance. Stones shot through the air, sprayed on Mrs. Jesswein's lawn. Before I knew it, I was on the ground, my legs splayed out in front of me, my skirt hiked up, my behind and hand stinging. I stole a look in the blue car's direction. They hadn't seen me; they still laughed. I gathered myself and slunk away. Like Kinsey Millhone, my all-time favorite female detective, I ducked behind some tall bushes between Mrs. Jesswein's house and the parking lot, crouched down, and spied on them. I could see the two of them very clearly. One had a beetle-shaped mole on her cheek.

It felt strange listening in on their conversation. The air was still; I could hear them as clear as if I was listening from my spot at the top of the stairs.

"What's taking her so long?" Bert asked.

"You know Diana," Jewels said. "She's probably perfecting her makeup."

"You should talk," Bert said.

"I don't wear that much makeup."

"You wear enough."

"I didn't used to."

"You mean when you were three?"

In the distance, I heard a house door slam, then heels clicking in my direction. It was Mama, which confused me. She wasn't even dressed when I saw her last. She passed by my hiding spot and got into the backseat of the blue car, I saw that she was wearing a red head scarf and blouse too. Rather than turn to greet her, Jewels simply nodded as she repositioned the rearview mirror. Even though she wasn't looking in the mirror, Bert nodded too. The car backed out of its parking space and drove away, the tires screeching. Within moments all I could see were three sets of blond hair flapping in the wind like wings, and then they were gone.

Kyle

My first thought was: God, she was beautiful. It wasn't just her flawless features; it was also her elegance, fragility. Later, I wondered whether she always exuded that sense of vulnerability, or if its presence was a response to the situation. But I didn't think about that then. My second thought was: Lucky bastard. My third was: Sorry bastard. I'd always counted out my thoughts like that when I arrived at a murder scene. After the day was long over, I'd sit down at the rickety wood dining table in my small, sparsely furnished apartment with my nightly three fingers of Redbreast, and write each word on an index card. Then I shuffled them, laid all but the last facedown, and one by one turned them upright. With my practiced poker face, I challenged myself, attempted to solve the crime over and over, from different angles and varied perspectives. Although it had been awhile since I'd worked a murder case, the word list flew through my mind like a banner behind a plane.

Beautiful, lucky, sorry.

It was the Fourth of July weekend. The temperature, in the upper nineties and climbing, was the highest in recent history. Good for tourism but challenging for suit coats and ties. Mack and I had rolled down all the unmarked Buick's windows before we braved its scorching black leather seats, but that hadn't helped much. Even the wind was hot. We were complaining about the car's broken air conditioner when the call first came in. I thought we'd be responding to another drunken teenage party. We'd already answered six the night before and one that morning. Then the dispatcher gave the response code.

"Did she say 187?" Mack asked.

"Sure sounded like it," I said. I stuck the flasher on the roof, turned on the siren, and hit the gas.

We don't have many murders in the Outer Banks, and even less on Cooper's Island. A domestic disturbance or two, a barroom brawl, a cat caught up a tree is about the extent of it, except from mid-March to mid-April when high school and college kids head our way for their spring breaks, or during the holidays inside and around the lazy heat of summer: Memorial Day, Fourth of July, and Labor Day. The island itself is roughly eight square miles of sand and wild "brownery" interrupted by a small business district, clusters of houses and trees, and the occasional touristy gift shop. Driving can be a challenge. Most of the roads are ancillary, narrow passageways that accommodate only one car at a time, some paved, some dirt. Luckily Mack and I had been driving along Route 122. Paved and even partially striped, it runs through town and continues in one big circle around the island.

It had been two years since I'd been back and I can't say I'd missed working murder cases, but I did get that old rush. There's a smell to fear and blood. A stale, sour stench that doesn't only soak your nostrils; it gets into your skin, hair, clothing, and mind like bar smoke, and not even a change of clothes, shower, or solving a case will wipe it completely away. I used to hate that smell, but not that day. The minute I got that first whiff, I felt like I'd come home.

We parked. A steep sandy embankment covered with smatterings of tall grasses and weeds led down to one of the more deserted stretches of beach on the island. Less than ten feet of grade separated the dirt driveway from the edge of the drop-off. There was no guardrail and no streetlights, a standard characteristic of our eastern shores. Although it didn't happen often, an impaired driver or an accidental push of the gas pedal instead of the brake had led to more than a few cliff-hangers. Seagulls circled low over the shallow mid-tide water searching for small fish or crustaceans that might have washed ashore, their high-pitched squawks a battle song. The usual breeze off the ocean was noticeably absent, the air eerily still. The only sign of human life was a sand castle in the making and a child's red plastic pail.

The house was your typical Cooper's Island rental, a one-story shingled box, this one a shit-brown color, with a wraparound wood deck that had weathered to a silver gray. Three long flights of stairs, also weathered wood, separated by bench-lined landings led from the back deck down to the beach. Although I couldn't see it from where I stood, I imagined sliding glass doors opening onto the deck. A short set of stairs led to the house's side-entry door.

The door was wide open.

"I'll secure the perimeter," Mack said. Mack and I had been together since my return to the island. When I first laid eyes on him, I swore he'd just graduated from Cooper's High, not to detective third grade. He is boyishly handsome, with bushy dark hair and a well-earned six-pack. I'd just transferred from Detroit PD. When he asked me why I'd traded Motor City for Podunk, I told him I wanted to spend quality time with my ailing mother. That's been my story.

I knocked on the doorframe before I walked in. The swamp cooler drummed loudly; the heat pouring in through the open door had no doubt put it into overdrive. In addition to the vic, I counted three people in the tight space: a middle-aged woman with fiery red hair, a bald-headed man wearing a Cubs baseball hat, and *her*. She sat on the sofa wearing a red one-piece swimsuit, white towel held tightly over her shoulders, blond hair matted to her head and neck, her piercing blue eyes seemingly fixated on the picture above the fireplace directly opposite her, a cheesy deserted beach scene with a lone seagull flying in the sky. Like one of those replicants in *Blade Runner,* her profile was perfectly chiseled, her posture proud. I could've stood there looking at her forever. I've always been a sucker for a thing of beauty, and not just women. A Vermeer painting, Brioni suit, Aston Martin sports car.

The body was lying prone in front of a white-brick fireplace, head turned toward me, eyes open, right arm tucked beneath the stomach as if cupping it, the location and size of the blood pool suggesting a gunshot to the abdomen. The place was tidy, no obvious signs of a struggle. Like many of its kind, it was a mishmash of tacky and tasteful. Eating bar and wicker stools sporting pink-and-blue shell-patterned cushions immediately to my right. Small kitchen beyond it. White appliances. Bleached-wood cabinets. Gray laminate countertops with chipped corners. Hallway straight ahead, bathroom door open, probably bedrooms either side of it. Living room to my left. Surprisingly clean transition from the kitchen and entryway linoleum to Berber carpeting. Fireplace on the wall opposite the side entrance. Bookcases either side of it. Just as I thought, sliding glass doors—why were they closed?—leading out to the deck. Two chairs upholstered in the same shell fabric as the barstools, one in the far corner opposite the fireplace and one almost blocking the side-entrance door. Coffee table and woven taupe sofa between them.

The red-haired woman spoke up first. Your usual beach retiree type. Expensive salon hairdo and manicure. Sixtyish. Too-tan skin. Floral swimsuit cover-up. Bright pink lipstick. Plump around the middle, but otherwise well kept.

"I'm Clara Butterworth," she said. "My husband and I were first on the scene." She looked over her shoulder. Mr. Cubs leaned back against the kitchen cabinet, his arms crossed, eyes closed like he was napping. In addition to the hat, he wore a short-sleeved plaid shirt and just-over-the-knee-length khaki shorts, making him appear shorter and rounder than he probably was. "And before you ask, yes, just like the syrup." She let out a little laugh, but caught herself. "Oh, I am so sorry. This isn't any time for jokes, is it?"

"Detective Kyle Kennedy." I reached into my breast pocket, took out my notebook, handed her my card, extended one toward the wife (at least I thought it was the wife). "Ma'am?" She didn't acknowledge me.

"Oh, she hasn't said a word since we got here, Detective," Mrs. Butterworth said.

"You say you arrived first Mrs.—um—ma'am. How long ago was that?"

"Fifteen minutes? It was seven forty-five, right Melvin?" Melvin was as unresponsive as the woman on the sofa. "Well, anyway, you could probably verify that. I called 911 the minute we walked through the door."

"How do you know the victim?"

"I don't, Detective. He was lying there like that"—she pointed at the body—"when we came in. We're staying down the street. Same place we stay every summer. We're from Lake Forest." She looked at me as if she wanted acknowledgment. "Illinois?"

I walked past her to get a closer look at the vic's body.

"He's dead, Detective," Mrs. Butterworth said. "I already checked."

"You touched the body?" It was always the well-meaning witnesses that contaminated crime scenes.

"Just his wrist," she said.

Since the right arm wasn't exposed, Mrs. Butterworth would've had to walk around the body. I noted her shoes. Gold lamé slides with a short stacked heel. No apparent blood transfer or impressions on the tightly looped carpet.

"Did you touch anything else?"

"I don't think so, Detective. Did we, Melvin?"

Mack came through the door carrying the crime scene kit that we kept in the trunk of the Buick. "Brass and CSIs are on the way."

"How far out?"

"Depends how backed up the ferries are. Thirty minutes max I should think."

"Half an hour?" Mrs. Butterworth asked. "That seems awfully excessive, Detective, don't you think? Even for here."

I stood, cleared my throat. "Detective Jones, this is Clara Butterworth. She and her husband were first on the scene."

"Ma'am," Mack said and nodded, then headed to the body.

"I'll need to ask you a few questions if that's okay, ma'am," I said. In Detroit, I would have ushered her to a private room and questioned her after the scene was properly secured—body inspected and outlined, evidence bagged, photos taken, site sketched—but this wasn't Detroit. This was Cooper's Island where the homicide division boiled down to Mack and me, and proper procedure was a luxury.

"Of course, Detective." Before I'd even crossed the room the woman's tongue launched into motion. She and her husband had just sat down to breakfast when she heard the shot. Quarter after seven, she said. No she didn't check the time on the clock because she didn't think much of it. Thought it was fireworks. But she and her husband always ate breakfast at seven fifteen. "My husband is very punctual."

"What made you come over if you thought it was just fireworks?"

"We went to get the paper after breakfast like we always do— the doctor says Melvin needs his exercise—and we saw that the door was open." She leaned through the doorframe, pointed. "Everyone within a quarter mile of here gets their mail and paper from that same bank of mailboxes across the street. If Melvin had his druthers we'd get the paper before breakfast, but it doesn't get delivered until—"

I interrupted. "Did you say the door was open?" I'd just assumed it was left open by the Butterworths.

"Yes. Very open."

"Go on," I said.

"Well, as I was saying, the paperboy like everyone else on this island, including your crime scene investigators I should say, is slow as molasses. At home our paper is on our stoop by five thirty; that's when Melvin rises. He prefers to do his exercise and shower before breakfast, but here he has to wait until after. Anyway, we were almost to the box when I saw the open door. I asked Melvin if we ought to check it out, and he said we should go right over. Didn't you, Melvin?"

Not even a cursory nod.

"There was this odd smell as we approached. I can't quite say why, but I had this strange feeling that something was wrong, and I must say I was a little scared of what I might find, but I said to myself, Clara, you need to get over your fears and get in that house, now."

"You said it was seven forty-five when you arrived. You sure about that?"

"On the nose," she said. "It takes us twenty minutes to eat, another five for me to clear the table and rinse off the dishes, and five to walk to the mailboxes. I do the dishes when we get back while Melvin reads the paper. He likes to sit out on our deck with his second cup of coffee. Two's the limit, you know."

"Do you remember seeing anything or anyone out of the ordinary either on your walk over or when you arrived at the scene?"

"Do you mean like someone leaving the scene or sniffing around the house?" she asked. "Like an intruder? I don't think so. But maybe it'll come back to me later, you know like those witnesses on TV. Do you want me to close my eyes and recount my entire morning? What I heard and smelled and all that? I'd be happy to do that."

"Thank you, ma'am, but that won't be necessary." I hate TV crime shows. "What happened when you entered the house?"

"I saw her first." Mrs. Butterworth indicated the woman on the sofa. "I introduced myself, but she didn't say a word. Then I saw the body . . . well, him." She pointed at the victim. "He looked pretty dead, but I thought I better make sure. So I marched right over and felt for his pulse."

"Two shots," Mack said. "See here? Exit wounds. I don't want to flip the body until the CSIs get here, but I'd say one to the chest and one to the abdomen. Looks by the trajectory of the bullet holes in the wall"—he pointed at two dark spots near the wall's corner between the fireplace and sliding glass doors—"that the shots came from the direction of the side door."

Beautiful, lucky, sorry, gun.

I was just about to bring up the gun when Mrs. Butterworth scolded us for talking in front of the child. Child? There she sat right next to her mother, fingers tightly laced in her mother's. How had I not seen her before? She looked about the age of my nephew, my sister's son. Was he ten now? Eleven? All I could see beneath the towel that enshrouded her was a pair of spindly white legs and a thick head of curls. She had her mother's blue eyes and the dead man's dark hair (Mediterranean descent?), but her skin tone was much lighter than both of theirs. Her eyes and cheeks were damp, as if she'd been crying, and there was something about the way she looked at me, something beyond sadness, beyond pride or defiance or even protectiveness that I knew I'd seen before but couldn't quite place.

"What's your name, sweetie?" I asked.

She looked down at her feet.

"I'm real sorry about your daddy," I said. "I know you must be sad."

Nothing.

"I saw this really cool sand castle on my way in. Did you make that?"

"My daddy and me," she said, without looking up.

"Wow, cool. My dad used to build sand castles with me too." A lie. Not the sand-castle building part, the dad helping me part. "Maybe you could give me the official castle tour?"

She eyed me suspiciously. Progress at least.

"If you don't want to, that's okay." I addressed Mack. "Do me a favor, will you? Take this young lady to her bedroom and keep her company for a while. Play a game or something." I had no idea what girls that age played with. Mack's face wasn't the only one that registered disapproval.

"Fine," the kid said. "I'll give you a tour." There was no mistaking her defiant tone.

I looked through the sliding glass doors just beyond the vic's body. The sand castle was within eyesight. It looked safe enough. "Why don't you go on out. I'll meet you there."

"Mama, I'm going down to the beach, okay? I won't be far." She pried her mother's hand loose, set it gently down on her lap, rose, took a step, hesitated—

"Don't worry about your mama," I said. "Detective Jones and I will take good care of her."

She exited through the side door, her expression blank as she passed by me. I could barely hear her footsteps on the wood deck as she rounded the house and headed down the stairs.

"I'll do a quick check of the rest of the house," Mack said.

I gave my attention back to Mrs. Butterworth. "We'll need you to sign your statement once we get it typed up, but otherwise I think we're done here. We'll be in touch if we need anything else." Mrs. Butterworth didn't seem too keen on leaving.

"Clara," a deep, commanding voice said from behind me. So Melvin had lungs after all. "Time to go." An order. Ex-military?

Her body shot to attention. She extended her hand to shake mine. I didn't take it. There's nothing cordial about a murder scene. "Oh, well, all right then. I have your card if I think of anything." She smiled conspiratorially. "Thank you, Detective."

"Thank *you*, ma'am."

Melvin all but dragged his wife out the door.

Mack emerged from the hallway. "Vic's name is Oliver Lane. Thirty-eight years old. Business card says he's some sort of law-yer. Wife's name is Diana." He nodded toward the sofa. "Thirty-six. She's carrying a passport but I couldn't find a driver's license. Looks like they live in a small town called Hollyville. My phone says it's over there by Cape Fear."

"What about the kid?"

"Picasso, according to this mystery book. *I Is for Innocent*. My wife loves Sue Grafton."

"Picasso? Like the artist?"

"Spelled the same way."

"Any luck on the murder weapon?"

"Nope. Once the CSIs have done their job and the body's gone, we'll get some boys in here to tear this place up."

"Maybe the intruder took it with him or dumped it. Make sure they search any nearby trash receptacles and bushes. There's some high grass in that field across the street."

When I turned my head in her direction, Diana Lane's eyes met mine. It wasn't that I'd forgotten she was there, a man could never forget a woman like that was in the room, but her despondence had fooled me into thinking she wasn't listening. Tears ran down her face. She leaned forward, put her head in her hands, started to sob. Her entire body shook. The towel fell from her shoulders. Her wet swimsuit didn't do much to hide her curves, her breasts, her erect nipples. Goose bumps rose on her arms. I took off my suit coat, wrapped it around her shoulders. She leaned into me, closed her eyes, dipped her head slightly forward. Without thinking, as if

I'd been doing it my entire life, I sat, took her in my arms, held her while she cried. Mack's expression was blank, controlled, but however hard he was trying to hide his disapproval, it was palpable. I released her, straightened, stood, nodded at Mack, as if to say, *I know, I know, I lost it there for a moment.*

"Is there somebody I can call?" I handed her my handkerchief.

She dried her eyes, blew her nose. "I don't have family here. I don't have family at all. Just Oliver and Picasso."

"Are you okay to answer a few questions?" I asked, trying to regain my business voice. "Or we can talk later. After—"

She shook her head. "No, I'm fine."

"Do you have something you can take? To calm you?"

She pointed toward the kitchen. "Windowsill above the sink."

I found some Aleve and two prescription bottles with Oliver Lane's name on them: zolpidem and lorazepam. The lorazepam was the same dose my mother used to take for panic attacks; I figured it was safe enough. I made a note of the doctor's name and filled a glass with water.

"Here," I said when I got back to her. "Take this. It might help take the edge off."

She washed down the small white pill, drank the entire glass of water. "Where's Picasso?" she asked as if she'd just noticed her daughter wasn't there. The kid was stealth.

"Outside," I said, glancing through the sliding glass doors. "Building a sand castle. We'll need to question her as well. I need your permission to do so without your presence, or I could ask her to come back inside."

"No," she said. "I don't want her here. Picasso has seen enough already."

"Mack, I'm going to head outside and talk to the kid. Why don't you take over from here?" Given my brief lapse in judgment, I thought it was best that way.

"Sure thing," he said.

Diana Lane's eyes met mine again.

"I won't be long," I said.

The crime scene van was already parked in the driveway when I walked through the door. The bloodsucking media wouldn't be far behind. Out of the corner of my eye, I saw Mrs. Butterworth bustling toward me.

"Oh, Detective," she called. "Can I have a brief word?"

"How can I help you, ma'am?"

"Well, it may be nothing, but I thought I should at least say something."

"What's that?"

"Well, when I came into the house, the child was talking to her father."

"Talking?" I asked.

"Yes," she said. "She was kneeling next to him. She seemed very upset. I don't know exactly what she was saying, but I thought I heard something about her mother being sorry."

"Did she say what her mother was sorry about?"

"No, not that I heard anyway."

"What made you think she was upset?"

"She was crying, and it was like she was pleading with him."

"Pleading?"

"Yes, you know, like begging him not to die. Oh, and just one more thing. I told 911 that a man had been shot, but that I thought he was still alive. Since the child was saying something to him and all. So I hope I'm not in trouble for giving them false information."

"I'm certain you aren't," I said.

"Oh, I hope not. Will you tell them that it was an innocent error?"

"I'll do that," I said. "Thank you, Mrs. Butterworth. You've been most helpful."

"My pleasure," she said. "And you know how to find me." She smiled and began walking up the drive.

"Mrs. Butterworth," I called after her.

She turned. "Yes, Detective."

"Where is it that you're staying exactly?"

She pointed at a thicket of trees at least three hundred yards west of the crime scene—all I could see was a portion of red roof—and continued on her way. No wonder she and her husband hadn't seen anything.

I descended the weathered beach steps, all the while watching the kid gather sand in her hands, meticulously pat it onto the wall of her sand castle. So concentrated. So vulnerable. So screwed. Poor thing. Her father was dead, and there was a good possibility that her mother had killed him. Although I loved my sister's kids, I'd never really wanted any of my own, never wanted to bring children into this fucked-up world. When I was a few feet away, the kid stopped working and gave me that same look, the one I'd seen inside, like she was staring into my soul, and I remembered where I'd seen it before. It was in an affluent Detroit neighborhood, a house robbery gone wrong. We arrived at the scene to find a man and woman dead on the living-room rug; they'd been shot in the back of their heads execution style. A low growling sound came from somewhere upstairs. A German shepherd paced before a closed closet, blood dripping from a wound in his chest, his eyes wild, fiercely protective, posture vigilant, a dead six- or seven-year-old boy maybe a foot in front of him. We thought that was the end of it until we tranquilized the dog and opened the closet door. A baby no more than three months old lay sleeping in a pink blanket. I found out later that the dog didn't make it. It was weeks before I could get the look in that dog's eyes out of my mind. I never did find out what happened to the baby.

As I walked toward the kid, I thought about what Diana Lane had said just before I left the house: *Picasso has seen enough already.*

What *had* Picasso seen?

Picasso

I remember feeling grateful for my sand castle. It was taking longer than I thought it would for Detective Kennedy to show up and "get his tour," and the whole thing—the salty scent of the ocean, the sound of crashing waves and squawking seagulls, the feel of the sun beating on my shoulders and the wet, gritty sand running through my fingers—was helping keep my mind off Daddy's dead eyes. The thing is I wasn't just thinking about Daddy's dead eyes. I was thinking about his dead eyes in relation to his unsmile eyes, which is hard to explain unless I share an actual unsmile event. As it turned out, Daddy made a bunch of unsmiles while we were at the beach in those last few days before he died, more than I remember him ever making in such a short amount of time before, but I think it's best to share the very first one, the one he made the morning after we arrived, the one I shouldn't have questioned because, if I hadn't, maybe everything would've been different. I would've had time to warn Mama. She might've listened to me. Daddy wouldn't have died. And I wouldn't have been sculpting away at my sand castle, alone, in a less than fully and artistically absorbed manner while waiting what seemed like forever for Detective Kennedy to show. But, as usual, I didn't question that unsmile, or the ones that followed it, until it was too late.

So, rewind forty-eight hours.

It's probably best to start with the heat. It was hot that summer on Cooper's Island—the kind of hot that makes your throat hurt when you breathe too deeply, melts your body and mind, and makes folks irritable. People in those parts were calling it a heat wave. Daddy called it "stupid hot." He said intense heat numbed the brain and that's why there were more crimes in the summertime. He said he knew the statistics because of his job; he was a lawyer. As it turns out, it was ironic he said that being that two days later *he* became a statistic. We'd been working on my sand castle nonstop for hours—well, with the exception of wave riding and Coca-Cola breaks now and then. We'd gotten the bottles from the Cooper's Island General Store—they even came in an old-fashioned-looking red Coke machine—and were using the empty ones for smoothing and sculpting sand.

"Where do you want the moat?" Daddy scrunched up his face and squinted his eyes against the brightness. Sweat dripped off his forehead, hairy chest, and armpits.

"How about here?" I asked, pointing to a spot between the castle and the ocean. "There's already a big hole here anyway, from all our digging."

"I was thinking the exact same thing," Daddy said. "You're so smart, just like your daddy." He made his proud smile.

We dug the hole bigger and bigger until it was at least three feet wide in each direction. It was hard work, the digging, mostly because the water kept softening the sand and the side kept caving in, so periodically Daddy made a show of sitting back to rest, but what he was really doing was watching Mama swim, even though she was so far out in the ocean that she looked like a red dot. After a while, the dot turned into a spot, then a shape, and when it was almost to shore, I could make out Mama's arms and hair.

"Isn't your mother a vision, Peanut (the oval seed of a South American plant, widely roasted and salted and eaten as a snack)?"

Mama had swum in far enough to stand; she was pushing through the water in our direction. When she reached the shore, she grabbed the towel she'd left on her sunning chair, shook all her hair to one side, and wrung it with her hands just like she always did with wet washrags. Mama was always getting on me for leaving too much water in washrags. "Makes them smell when they dry, Picasso," she'd say. Mama looked surprised when she saw Daddy and me, even though we'd been sitting in the same exact spot all morning. Mama is like that; she lives in her own world. Sometimes I'll be sitting right in front of her, and she'll walk right by me without noticing I'm there. "Lost in her head," Daddy always said.

"Did you put on sunscreen?" Mama asked. She asked me that a million times a day—well, maybe not a million, but close. "You could get third-degree burns on a day like this."

"Number thirty," I said.

"Didn't I bring some forty-five?" she asked.

"I didn't see any."

"Well, just make sure you put it on after every time you go in the water. Okay?"

"Okay," I said, even though I already knew to do that.

"I think this is the biggest sand castle yet," Mama said. "It looks like a Gaudi." Gaudi is an architect who made drippy-looking buildings. Mama said that about every sand castle Daddy and I made.

"We're not done yet," I said. "We haven't even started the fortress or the drawbridge, and Daddy says maybe this time we'll try to make a gatehouse."

"That's quite an ambitious undertaking. What are you working on now?"

"The keep," I said.

"Keep?" Mama asked.

"The central tower," I said. "You know, where the people in the kingdom barricade themselves when enemy soldiers get past the moat."

"Did you learn that in school?"

"No, Mama," I said, wanting to add, *castle architecture isn't exactly a school subject,* but that would be sassing. "I found it in my dictionary."

For my tenth birthday, Daddy had gotten me the fourth edition *American Heritage.* In the introduction, it said it had "nearly 10,000 new words and senses that reflect the rapid pace of change in the English language today."

Daddy put his hand on his belly to stop it from growling. "Should we take a break, Pineapple (a large juicy tropical fruit consisting of aromatic edible yellow flesh surrounded by a tough segmented skin and topped with a tuft of stiff leaves)? I'm feeling kind of light-headed."

"I made tuna salad this morning before I came out for my swim," Mama said. It was Mama's second swim, her right-before-lunch swim.

Daddy looked at me. "We love Mama's tuna salad sandwiches, don't we?"

"Best in the world," I said.

I'm almost to the unsmile part.

Daddy and Mama left first. I waited for Mama to call me in for lunch, but after what seemed a long time, I started wondering if maybe I hadn't heard her above the sound of the waves, so I decided to head on up. I looked around to make sure I didn't see any bratty little kids that might wreck my castle, which had happened more than once in the past, but there wasn't a soul on the beach, and only one house anywhere close, at least that I could see. That's why Mama had chosen the place. She said she wanted total privacy. I remember sliding into my flip-flops so the bottom of my feet wouldn't burn, and trudging through the sand and up the wooden stairs. I was just getting ready to rinse off at the spigot when I saw Mama and Daddy standing inside the open sliding glass doors. They were kissing. I stood there for a while, watching them. It had been so long since I'd seen them kiss like that.

Daddy's eyes met mine. "How long have you been standing there?"

"I . . . I don't know," I said.

"What do you mean, you don't know?"

And then he made the unsmile.

Now remember what I said before when I was describing Daddy's five smiles? About the unsmile disappearing as fast as it came and me sometimes wondering if I even saw it? Well, that's what happened. The unsmile was gone by the time Daddy added, "Why don't you go back down and work on your sand castle, Peeper." I never did look up that word.

Now back to where I started: me waiting for Detective Kennedy to come get his tour while trying not to think about Daddy's dead eyes.

Here's the thing. First of all, I'd never seen dead eyes before, not even on a cat or a dog (Mama is allergic). Second of all, I was stunned by how similar Daddy's dead eyes looked to his unsmile eyes. They were the same kind of empty, like even though they were staring right through me there was nothingness behind them, which was creepy enough with dead eyes, but living eyes? Third of all, I realized I had never really thought about Daddy's unsmile eyes until I saw his dead eyes, and now I couldn't stop thinking about them. I wondered how Daddy had been able to make his eyes look dead when he wasn't and, most of all, what that meant about Daddy. Did Daddy feel dead inside when he made his unsmiles and that's why his eyes looked that way? Or was it the opposite? Were Daddy's unsmiles the real him? Had he always been dead inside and the other four smiles were him trying to make himself alive?

I was thinking about all this when I saw Detective Kennedy walking down the beach-house stairs.

"Nice keep," he said when he got to me.

Detective Kennedy wasn't very handsome, not like Daddy anyway. He was a little pudgy in the belly like me, and his nose was bent toward one side of his face, which made him look a little sinister. He had friendly eyes though, and thick, wavy, light brown hair. I wasn't exactly sure how old he was, but I figured around Daddy's age. He was wearing a suit and tie when he walked into the beach house; he'd taken off his jacket, but he still looked silly wearing his white shirt, tie, and trousers on the beach. I thought he'd just stand there trying not to mess up his shoes, but he didn't. He reached down, untied them, and kicked them off, and then he loosened his tie, rolled up his trousers and sat down next to me. I saw that his shirt was wet under his armpits.

"God, I hate wearing suits." He looked up at the sky. "It's an oven out here. I'd much rather be in my swim trunks. I burn though."

"Me too," I said, surprising myself. I hadn't meant to be conversational right off. Being that he'd said he made a lot of sand castles, I decided to test his credibility. "Do you know about castles?"

"I do actually. I won a blue ribbon for one once at the county fair."

"Not sand castles," I said. "Castles."

"A little, I guess. I went to Ireland once—that's where my ancestors are from—and I went to see some ancient castles."

"What do they look like? Inside I mean."

"Oh, you know, lots of red velvet and pictures of stiff-looking old men."

"No armors?"

"One or two."

"How'd you keep it from falling apart?"

He looked confused.

"The sand castle," I said. "You said you won a blue ribbon. I've never seen sand castles at fairs." Not that I'd been to any, but he didn't know that.

His smile was slow and crooked. One corner of his mouth went up higher than the other. "We took pictures. And I don't know about all fairs, but you can win ribbons for sand castles at this county's fair. I grew up here. Right down there." He pointed down one side of the beach, but I didn't see any houses.

"You lived on the beach?"

"Not on the beach," he said. "But not too far. When I was a kid, we went to the beach every day after school, and we practically lived on it during the summer. We probably made a gazillion sand castles."

"There isn't any such thing as a gazillion," I said.

"Sure there is," he said. "There's a gazillion stars in the sky, aren't there?"

I didn't know how to answer that question because I wasn't exactly sure how many stars there were in the sky.

"This sand castle is better than any one I ever made," Detective Kennedy said.

"Better than the one that won the ribbon?" I asked.

"Much better," he said. "Our standards aren't all that high here. Must've taken you and your daddy a long time to build this much."

"Only a couple of days," I said. "We started the day we got here."

"Did the two of you work on it this morning?"

"Just me. Daddy slept in. He and Mama were up late."

"Where was your mama when you were working on the sand castle?"

"Swimming," I said. "She swims three times a day here: first thing in the morning, right before lunch, and in the late afternoon before she starts making dinner. That's one of the reasons why we come. She likes the ocean better than pools."

"That makes sense. Do you come a lot?"

"Every summer since I was born."

"And you always stay here?"

"No. This is the first time. We used to stay someplace else."

"Different house?"

"Different island."

"Which one?"

"Bodie," I said.

"I went to school on Bodie when I was a kid," Detective Kennedy said. "Busier over there, huh?"

"How'd you get to school?"

"I took the ferry. You ever seen a sunset from a ferryboat?"

I shook my head.

"Most beautiful thing you've ever seen. When the sun dips into the sea, for a split second the water breaks into so many prisms of color it looks like the inside of a kaleidoscope." He looked at me. "You don't believe me? Well then, I guess I'll have to show you sometime."

I wondered why he thought he'd be knowing me long enough to show me sometime.

He fidgeted around, like a dog trying to make a comfortable spot, and then he laid his back all the way down on the sand, sprawled out his legs, stared into the sun, and closed his eyes. "Don't tell anyone," he whispered.

I figured he'd fallen asleep, he stayed like that for so long.

"Picasso—do you mind if I call you Picasso?" He turned on his side, propped himself up with his elbow.

"Why would I? That's my name."

He chuckled. "True. I'm wondering if you remember what time your mama went for her swim."

I knew that was it; his real questions were coming. I was a little nervous, but not as much as I thought I'd be. "It was still dark out. She always goes when it's still dark out."

"Do you know what time it was when you came out to work on your sand castle?"

"Not exactly, but pretty much as soon as it got light."

"Which door did you use?"

"The side door."

"Why the side door?"

"I'm not allowed to go in and out through the sliding glass doors because I might get the carpet dirty or wet."

"Do you remember if the sliding glass doors were open when you left?"

"No," I said.

"No they weren't open, or no you can't remember."

"No I can't remember."

"And when your mama comes back in after her swim, does she usually use the sliding glass doors or the side door?"

"She doesn't have a usual way. She hasn't swum here that many times."

"Let me see." He counted on his fingers. "Eight times, right?"

"Seven," I said. "She didn't swim the day we got here."

"How many of those seven times did she go back in through the side door?"

"Two, I think."

"So today and one other time?" He didn't wait for me to respond. "Why do you think she used the side door this morning, instead of going through the sliding glass doors?"

I bit my lip. "Because the sliding glass doors were locked?"

Detective Kennedy chewed on this for a while. He rose to a sitting position and looked into my eyes. The back of his shirt was covered with sand. "You seem like a brave kid, Picasso. The next few questions I'm going to ask you might be hard for you to answer, not because you can't but because they might make you sad. Do you think you're up to it?"

"I guess."

"Okay, then. Do you know about how long it was after you'd come out to work on your sand castle before you heard the shot?"

"It was right after I saw Mama starting to swim toward shore."

"What made you look at the ocean? Didn't you have your back to it like you do now?"

"I check a lot because Mama gets mad when I get sand all over the house. When I see her swimming back, I know I need to finish up pretty soon so I have enough time to rinse off real good at the outside spigot."

"Where's that?"

I pointed at the standing faucet at the top of the stairs.

"Does your Mama rinse off there too?"

"Sometimes."

"What happened after you rinsed off?"

"I went inside."

"And that's when you saw your daddy?"

Instead of looking at Detective Kennedy, I started smoothing out one of the castle walls. I figured that was a good time to do what Mama does when she doesn't want to answer questions, like when I asked about Jewels and she pretended she was fiddling with her zipper. I could feel Detective Kennedy staring at me. I stopped working and looked at him.

"*Yes,* that's when I saw Daddy."

"I'm sorry, Picasso. I know this must be hard. Just a couple more questions, okay? Are you absolutely sure your mama wasn't there when you saw your daddy—I mean found him like that?"

"You mean dead?" I said. "No. She wasn't there. She was still swimming."

"You're sure?"

"I'm sure."

"Where were you when she came in?"

"Over by Daddy. I didn't know that he was dead at first."

"Was he?"

"Yes."

"Did you say anything to him?"

"I can't remember for sure."

Detective Kennedy looked deep into my eyes. I couldn't tell whether he actually felt sorry for me or if he was just pretending to. Daddy pretended a lot. "You did a real good job, Picasso. I might have more questions later, but I think that's enough for now." He rose, started rubbing the sand off his clothes, looked at me, and laughed. "I think it's a lost cause. What do you think?"

In spite of myself, I laughed too. He looked like Gulliver with his hair all matted, his trousers rolled up, his clothes and toes full of sand.

"Finally," he said. "A smile. And a very pretty one at that. See you later, alligator."

"In a while, crocodile," I said.

I watched him walk toward the beach house. When he was about halfway there, he stopped, turned around, like he had eyes in the back of his head and knew I'd been watching him. He waved.

I waved back and started working on my sand castle again, only this time it felt different. I was grateful, but not because I was trying not to think about Daddy's eyes, which I'd pretty much forgotten about. I was grateful because my interview with Detective Kennedy was over. Awhile later, I saw that two white vans had parked in the driveway; one of them had a sign on it that read Channel 3 News. I realized I hadn't noticed them arrive. I stood, looked toward the beach house. Even though I could see people moving around inside, I couldn't really see them clearly. They were mostly just shapes. But still, it worried me a little.

Did someone see?

The Wives

We had decided to wait one year. We knew there would be a murder investigation and that the police would suspect all of us regardless, but if they found out that we knew one another, the risk of discovery would be greater. Once Oliver was dead, there would be no communication between us whatsoever. And there wasn't. Yet the events of that day, and the year prior, had wound us together as tight as the neck of a noose. It wasn't only that we knew one another's thoughts, felt one another's fears, experienced one another's pain, or saw our own reflections in one another's faces. It was as if we had been conceived by the same sperm and waited patiently in the same bloody womb to be born. Oliver's death would mark our rebirth. Although we knew our journey through the birth canal and into the world would be unpleasant, we hadn't anticipated how much so. Even with all our planning and preparation, none of us were ready for the cold slap of reality that greeted us, especially Diana.

At first—in between her bouts of extreme sadness over the loss of Oliver of course—Diana obsessed over what really happened that day. Had she or hadn't she called off the murder? The plan was to call Jewels the afternoon before, at five o'clock. If it was a go, she was supposed to say "The meeting is on," and if not, if something went wrong, she was to say "The meeting has been canceled." What had she said? Had she even made the call?

She recalled fretting over a credible excuse to leave the house, something we hadn't thought to discuss in advance, and, yes, that's right, telling Oliver she needed to run into town to pick up something she forgot for dinner. Oliver and Picasso sat either side of the coffee table playing Scrabble.

"Why don't you let Picasso and I go get it," Oliver said. "What do you need?"

"Salt," she said. It was the first thing that came into her mind.

Oliver laughed. "Salt? Don't they have any here?"

"Not that I could find," she said.

"We can get by without it. The doctor says I need to cut back anyway."

"No," she said, a little too frantically. She calmed herself. "I'm making shrimp and grits. It'll be bland without salt."

"We could grill up some burgers instead."

"The shrimp will go bad. You two stay here. I want to pick up another book anyway. I'm almost finished with mine. You can't get that for me. You know how I need to read the opening page first." She saw her book sitting on the sofa end table, the bookmark protruding not even a quarter of the way in.

"Anything we can do for you while you're gone?" Oliver asked.

The question relieved her. "No, I'm good. Everything else is ready." On her way out the door, she slid the book she was reading into her handbag.

Yes, she'd made the call, but what message had she left?

For a long while, Diana didn't remember much of what happened that day. She didn't remember her swim, or walking back to the beach house. She was just there. She had vivid nightmares. Sometimes Oliver was dead, but he began talking to her, told her how much he loved her and Picasso. Sometimes she felt the warm gun in her hand, smelled gunpowder, an unexpectedly smoky and tinny smell. Oliver, still alive, grabbed her ankle, held it tightly, cocked his head in disbelief, sadness, then fear. When she woke from these dreams, she felt nothing but curiosity. Curiosity about the look on Oliver's face. Curiosity about the measured saturation of the blood on the short-looped carpet. Curiosity about her reactions: power, calm, relief. Pleasure.

There were things Diana was certain about. She remembered standing in the doorway, and Picasso walking into the room from the hallway, wearing her purple swimsuit, the one Diana had seen hanging on the bathroom hook before she headed out for her swim. Picasso cast an incredulous look at her mother, ran to her father. Pled with him. A woman and man appeared. Then two men in suits. One caught her attention. He wasn't exactly handsome, but there was something about him. A commanding presence? He was tall but somewhat soft, especially around the middle, and his nose had obviously been broken. Diana chastised herself for being curious in *that* way while her husband lay dead just a few paces away.

She also remembered the younger detective questioning her, and how anxious and warm she'd become. Whereas once she'd shivered, sweat oozed from her pores. We had playacted that scene several times, but as Diana found out, reality was always more complicated than imagination.

"I apologize for this, Mrs. Lane," the detective had said. "We were hoping to ask you these questions before the crime lab showed. But this'll only take a minute. Can you tell me what happened?" He pulled a small spiral-bound notebook and pen from a pocket inside his suit coat.

"Who are you again?" Diana asked.

She was doing what we discussed, attempting to take control from the start.

"Oh, sorry, ma'am," he said. "I'm Detective Jones. Detective Kennedy and I are with Cooper's Island PD."

"What do you mean what happened?" she asked.

"Your husband was shot, ma'am." He pointed at Oliver. "We've ruled out suicide. So that leaves—"

"Why have you ruled out suicide?"

"Was your husband depressed, ma'am?"

She pondered the question. Though Oliver hadn't officially been diagnosed with bipolar disorder, he had mood swings and took medication for them. Like all of us, Diana had been seduced by the happy Oliver but fell in love with the brooding, misunderstood Oliver. "Sometimes, but not lately. I was just wondering how you know it was murder."

"I don't recall saying it was murder, ma'am," he said. "It could've been an accident."

"Do you think it was?" she asked, with perhaps a little too much interest.

"Doubtful," he said. "Do you know anyone who might want to hurt your husband?"

"No," Diana said. "Everyone likes—I mean liked—Oliver. What about burglary?"

"Is anything missing?"

"I haven't checked," Diana said. "Oliver usually traveled with several thousand dollars in cash."

"Where did he keep the money?" Detective Jones asked.

"His wallet."

"Nowhere else?"

"Sometimes he put part of it in a drawer."

Detective Jones made some notes. "You're sure he brought the money with him?"

"If you mean did I actually see it? No, I didn't."

"We'll look into it," Detective Jones said. "May I ask where you were at the time of the murder?"

"Swimming. I saw him when I came back inside."

"You came back in through the side door?"

"Yes," Diana said.

He wrote something in his notebook.

"Why does it matter where I came in?"

"It doesn't," Detective Jones said. "Just seems a little strange with the sliding glass doors being right there. That nice little deck set up for ocean watching. And it's right at the top of the stairs. I'd probably come in that way. Especially since you went out that way. But that's just me."

"Why do you think I went out that way?" Diana said.

"I thought you said that earlier." He made a show of looking back through his notes.

"I . . . I might have. I don't remember."

Just stick to our story, Diana.

"Do you usually lock the doors behind you?"

"Well, no," Diana said. "Were they locked? If they were, then I must've gone out through the side door."

But Diana was certain she left through the sliding glass doors. Or was she?

"Where were your husband and daughter when you left for your swim?"

"Sleeping. I swim early."

"How early?"

"Sixish."

"You a good swimmer, ma'am?"

"I swam competitively in college."

He wrote. "Do you swim out pretty far?"

"A mile or two, depending."

"Depending on what?"

"How long I plan to swim."

"How long is that?"

"An hour, hour and a half, sometimes longer."

He paused, tapped his pen. "How long did you swim this morning?"

"Until seven thirty."

"So an hour and a half? Not an hour?"

"Yes."

"How do you know that? Do you wear a watch when you swim?"

"No." The writing made Diana nervous. She didn't like the thought of everything she said being recorded. Even though we had rehearsed many times, what if she forgot something? What if some of his questions confused her? Like the ones about which door she'd used.

Take a slow, deep breath, Diana.

"Do you need some time, ma'am?"

"No, I'm fine. What did you ask me?"

"I asked how you know you swam for an hour and a half."

"I don't need a watch. I can tell by my routine. I did the longer routine today. I count it out. Breaststroke, then backstroke, then sidestroke, then breaststroke again, and so on."

"Mrs. Butterworth says that she and her husband heard the shot at seven fifteen. According to you, your husband was lying there when you walked in, so why didn't you call an ambulance?"

"Mrs. Butterworth?"

"Your neighbor. The woman who was here earlier."

"Oh, yes," Diana said. "I don't know. I guess because he was dead."

"Did you check?"

"What do you mean, check?"

"To make sure he was dead."

"No." Now her heart was pounding.

"Why not?"

Pounding louder.

"Mrs. Butterworth says you were standing by the door when she came in around seven forty-five. So you just stood there for fifteen minutes without feeling for a pulse? Without calling 911 to report that he was dead? Why not, Mrs. Lane?"

"I don't know," was all Diana could say.

She couldn't tell Detective Jones about the mix of emotions she'd felt, that she'd wished the entire thing—Jewels showing up on her doorstep, the plan, the murder—was all a bad dream, that any minute she'd wake up, go for her swim, come back into the house, and make breakfast for Oliver and Picasso. She couldn't say that her husband had admitted his infidelities the night they arrived at the beach house. That he'd apologized. Told her that he loved her and Picasso more than his other families, *more than life itself.* That he'd break off his other relationships—she still couldn't say *marriages.* She couldn't tell the detective the real reason she hadn't checked Oliver's pulse: She *knew* he was dead.

"Just one last question, ma'am. Is there any particular reason you're carrying your passport with you? You aren't planning on leaving the country anytime soon, are you?"

"No. It's just that I misplaced my driver's license, so I thought I might need some other form of identification. You know, just in case . . ." She paused. Had that sounded incriminating? "I mean, I'm sure I'll find it. I'm always losing it."

Diana waited for Detective Jones to ask what she meant by "just in case," but he didn't. He closed his notebook and put it in his breast pocket. Then he addressed a uniformed woman who was standing near Oliver's body.

"Maggie, we'll need to get a swab of saliva from Mrs. Lane and check her hands and swimsuit too." He looked back at Diana. "Is that okay?"

"Check for what?"

"Gunshot residue, ma'am, and blood splatter."

Diana's heart dropped. She felt faint. "Am I a suspect?"

"Everyone's a suspect, ma'am, until we eliminate them. Sit tight. It won't take long. The wolves will be arriving soon. Let's hope you and your daughter are out of here before then."

"Where will we go?"

"I'll get an officer to drive you to the station until things calm down. Then you can pack and we'll get you home."

Detective Kennedy returned just as Detective Jones was rising. Diana looked at Oliver's body one last time, shuddered, and then, clasping Detective Kennedy's coat tightly around her shoulders, she walked past her dead husband and looked through the sliding glass doors. Down by the ocean, a young girl was building a sand castle, and though the girl was too far away to be distinguished as her own, her Picasso, Diana could still *see* her. Her stomach sank. What if someone had been on the beach?

What if someone saw?

Picasso

I never did finish that sand castle. Mama and I packed up and left Cooper's Island that very afternoon. Detective Jones offered to get somebody to drive us home being that Mama was upset and had taken one of Daddy's pills, but she said she didn't want to wait, that it had been several hours already, definitely long enough for the medicine to wear off, and she'd be fine. I kept expecting the police to say something else to Mama, like "Don't leave town" for instance, or some other TV-crime-show-type warning, but they never did. It was like she wasn't even a suspect, which meant, as far as I could tell, that they'd believed Mama's and my answers. I remember feeling relieved about that, like I'd cheated on a math test and gotten away with it.

Mama and I didn't talk much on the way home, which, like I said, wasn't unusual, but she didn't even turn on the radio, or the air conditioner for that matter. I noticed how quiet it was first, quieter than an empty house, and then I started getting hot, and before long I was sweating so bad my thighs were sliding around on the leather seat.

"Do you mind if I open my window," I finally asked.

Without taking her eyes off the road (Mama never takes her eyes off the road when she's driving), she reached over and turned on the air conditioner. Then she started crying. Not loud crying, or even tears-running-down-her-face crying. It was more like these short broken breaths, almost like she kept seeing stuff that startled her.

Funny thing was, I didn't feel at all like crying. The best I can describe how I felt on that ride home, and in the days immediately following, was "dull," like all my feeling edges, inside and out, had been smoothed over with fine sandpaper, leaving me without any emotion whatsoever. I wasn't thinking much on Daddy, about him lying there like that, still and bleeding, or worrying over how he got himself that way. But through all that not thinking and not worrying, I admit I was doing some major wondering, which specifically had to do with the "whys" of things. Why didn't I feel anything? Why wasn't I balling my eyes out? Why didn't I feel guilty about lying to Detective Kennedy? And most of all: *Why was I so hungry?* I mean that had to be sacrilege. I remember thinking that right at that moment, sticky thighs aside, while Mama and I were enjoying our ride home in the comfort of Daddy's V-8-powered BMW 7 Series, which the marketing brochure had described as a full-size luxury sedan and likely the benchmark for large sport sedans on the market today, Daddy was probably zipped in a body bag and bouncing around on some stiff cot on his way to the morgue. My daddy, who had only hours ago been scooping wet sand out of my sand castle moat, would soon be rotting in moist dirt forever. *And I was hungry?*

Mama went upstairs as soon as we got home. I thought she'd come back down and ask me what I wanted for dinner, but she didn't. After a while, I went to check on her; she was asleep. I tiptoed to her money drawer, grabbed a twenty-dollar bill, went back downstairs, and called Pizza Palace. The pizza was delivered in less than thirty minutes just like the man on the phone said. I got a Coke from the refrigerator, turned on the TV, and buried myself in the sofa.

I must've fallen asleep because when I woke up I saw Daddy's face on the TV. It took up the whole screen. Then there were pictures of the beach house, Daddy lying dead on the floor with a light blue sheet covering him, and Mrs. Butterworth talking into a microphone.

The next day, Mama got a call from a lady on her Junior League committee. I was surprised she actually answered it. I shot upstairs as fast as I could to pick up the phone in her room.

"Is it true, Diana?" the lady asked. "Is it true that Oliver is dead? That he was murdered? I just got a call from Rhonda Little."

"The police don't know for sure," Mama said.

"You poor dear," the lady said. "Is there anything I can do? I could bring dinner by tomorrow night."

"Thank you, Joan," Mama said. "But I think I need some time alone to digest all this."

"Of course," the lady said. "Please don't hesitate to call me if you need anything at all. And don't you worry over the summer bazaar. We've got it covered. That's not saying we won't miss you. Of course we'll miss you. You're committee chair. Do you want me to take over for you for a few weeks? I'd be happy to."

"That won't be necessary," Mama said. "And Joan, I'd appreciate it if you wouldn't tell anyone about the police suspecting it might be murder. No one knows anything yet for certain, and, well, you know how people can be."

"Why, of course, Diana," the lady said. "I won't tell a soul."

And just like that the rumors began.

Kyle

Beautiful, lucky, sorry, gun, motive.

It was the day before Oliver Lane's funeral. I'd told Mack that attending our vic's funeral was strategic, but the truth was, strategy was an excuse. Diana Lane had gotten under my skin. A small part of me thought it was possible my brain had fabricated her. Sure she might be a looker, but the rest of it, the chiseled perfection, the helpless fragility, the innocent yet seductive stare, was an overactive imagination at work. Seeing her again would cure me. I'd start sleeping again. Mack would quit asking me whether I'd heard what he just said. A fifth of Redbreast would last longer than a week.

Mack and I were at our local precinct, a three-room space with six holding cells and a bathroom in a blue-shingled, white-trimmed, awning-graced building that matches every other building in downtown Cooper's Island. In addition to Mack and me, there are two other officers, a part-timer we call Hawkeye, because he's a dead ringer for Alan Alda, and an easy-on-the-eyes female rookie named Quinn. Our administrative staff includes a front-desk person, Sharon, who looks like a sweet old lady but chain smokes and has a voice gruffer and deeper than most men; our hippie, weed-smoking IT guy, Jake; and two girl Fridays, Bonnie, a hell-raising, buxom brunette in her early thirties, and her younger half sister, Klide (their mother obviously had a sense of humor), a shy, introverted, extremely diligent petite blonde. Klide had recently graduated with an economics degree from Duke and decided to intern with us for a few years before pursuing her MBA. I hate the idea of losing her; whenever I want something done right I give it to Klide.

As part of Dare County, we do a lot of business at the sheriff's office over in Manteo, but each island has its own police department. Ours is sandwiched between a Laundromat and a bowling alley. Cooper's Alleys doubles as a dance bar during tourist season, and is generally loud and jam-packed. A small grocery store, a drugstore, a hardware store, a bookstore, some tacky touristy shops, and a greasy spoon that makes a mean fish-and-chips rounds out our block of Main Street, which includes three full cobblestone-paved blocks, one either side of us, and a couple of dwindling ones either end of those. Somewhere in either direction Main Street turns back into Route 122. It's hard to know for certain since Cooper's doesn't believe in street signs.

I was on the phone when the other line rang. It had been busy like that all morning. Thank God for Bonnie and her gift of gab; she could make even the most self-important of folks forget they had somewhere else to be.

"He sounds official," Bonnie said, after forwarding the call to me. "And rich. Think he's single?"

"Is this Detective Kyle Kennedy?" Bonnie was right. His voice had that gracious gentlemanly lilt specific to wealthy gentleman of the northernmost states of the South, particularly Virginia and North Carolina. The farther south you got, the less lilt and more twang.

"Speaking," I said.

"This is Captain Benjamin Mercy. I'm with the homicide unit here in Raleigh. Our office is in the process of e-mailing you a report and some photographs, but I thought you might want to hear this firsthand. It's about that vic of yours. Oliver Lane?"

"I'm listening," I said.

"Well it appears he had another life here in Raleigh."

"What do you mean, in Raleigh?" I asked. "I know his law firm has an office there."

"He also had a residence here. Shared it with his wife and sons."

"Wait a minute," I said. "You sure we're talking about the same guy? Our vic lived in Hollyville with his wife and—" I was going to add *daughter,* but my mind had finally gotten itself around what Captain Mercy was telling me. The brain can be slow sometimes, even dense. A wise friend of mine, my teacher and mentor at the police academy in Detroit where I got my training, once said that there are three worlds: the world we know, the world we are yet to know, and the world we don't even know exists. He said a good cop is always looking for that third world.

"Same guy," Captain Mercy said. "Wife reported him missing two days ago. Looks like he did a good job of covering his tracks. Condo deed and mortgage are in the wife's name alone. Same with electric and gas bills. Not many photos. Wife, name's Julie by the way, says he was camera shy. Only thing I could find in his name is a BMW 7 Series, but we haven't been able to locate the actual vehicle."

"I think I know where it might be," I said.

"Thought that might be the case," Mercy said. "How's the weather over there?"

"Hot," I said.

"Here too. But at least you've got the ocean. My wife's been after me to take her to the Outer Banks for a few weeks now. I apologize. I must admit I hadn't heard of Cooper's Island until this all happened."

"That's okay," I said. "Nobody has. Let me know if you make it over here. I'll buy you a cold beer."

"You take care now," Mercy said. "And let me know if you've got any questions after you read the report."

"Will do," I said. "And thanks."

"No problem. Happy to be of service."

"Change of plans," I said to Mack after I hung up the phone. I caught him up on my conversation with Captain Mercy while I downloaded the police report, which included Julie Lane's statement and a few photos of our vic. "We need to split our resources. I want to get to the second Mrs. Lane as soon as possible. You good with interviewing her alone?"

"Sure thing," Mack said. "Anything specific you want me to ask her?"

"Just get a sense of her. Too bad they already told her about her husband's other life. Would've been helpful to see her initial reaction."

Picasso

Daddy's funeral was at Saint Paul's Episcopal Church, the same church where I'd seen the blue convertible in the parking lot four months earlier. Even though at least twenty big fans were blowing, it still felt just as hot inside as it was outside; everybody was talking about the heat. On the way in, I'd overheard this conversation.

First lady: "It's like Dante's *Inferno* in here."

Second lady: "Well, you know what they say."

First lady: "What's that?"

Second lady: "Hell hath no—"

I couldn't hear the rest.

Mama had asked that Daddy's casket be closed, which I remember thinking was a good choice. Daddy wouldn't have liked people seeing him wear makeup. Mrs. Cleary played Pachelbel's Canon on the piano as pretty much the whole town filed in. Pastor Mike gave Daddy a nice eulogy, even though he hardly knew him, while folks fanned themselves with the remembrance pamphlets Mama had somebody make. Then Polly Anderson, Ryan Anderson's mom, sang a solo, some hymn about dying and being welcomed into heaven's gates that I didn't recognize, but our family was never much on church. I spent most of the service looking around for Ryan, but as it turned out, he wasn't there, which was probably good. The black dress Mama had bought for me looked like something a kid would wear, what with its white Peter Pan collar and empire waist. If it were up to Mama, I'd be stuck in preadolescence forever. When the funeral service was over, we got in a big black air-conditioned limousine, rode out of our neighborhood, through the Hollyville town square, which is basically a park with a big white pergola surrounding a platform that gets turned into a stage during the Hollyville Pride Festival and other major events, like the annual Christmas nativity play and Punxsutawney Phil Day (also known as Groundhog Day), then on past the Hollyville Golf Course where Daddy used to play, the Hollyville YMCA where Mama does yoga, and finally to the cemetery. I could see Daddy's gravesite before we got to it. It looked like an outdoor party was taking place what with all the flowers and the big canopy, except the canopy was black. I remember thinking that Daddy would've liked the burial plot Mama and I picked out. It was on top of a hill. Mama said it cost more than the ones that weren't on the hill, but she could pay for it over time.

It rained during the service; luckily the canopy covered Daddy's casket and the row of folding chairs where Mama and I sat. Most folks, including Mama and me, had brought umbrellas just in case, which I thought was resourceful. I don't know what got into me that I was so preoccupied. I knew I should be listening to what Pastor Mike was saying about Daddy, but for some reason I was much more fascinated by Daddy's coffin, how shiny it was, if it would stay shiny once it was deep inside the ground, whether earthworms could penetrate it and crawl into Daddy's mouth and eyes, how long it would take for his skin to dry up, if I would still recognize what was left of Daddy's face and body in, say, a year, exactly when he turned from a human prune into a skeleton, why nobody had ever thought to put a video camera inside a coffin to scientifically record the decaying process. I got so lost in thought that Mama had to nudge me when the service was over. Then we left. I remember being disappointed that I didn't get to see the casket being lowered into the ground. I'd never seen a casket being lowered into the ground. Not in person anyway.

After the limousine dropped us off at the church, Mama went inside to give Pastor Mike an envelope. On our walk home, I asked her what was in it.

"Money," she said.

"You have to pay for a eulogy too?" I asked. I had no idea that somebody's dying was so expensive.

"Well, not really pay for it. It's more like a tip." Then she explained about church being a business.

When Mama and I were in front of Mrs. Jesswein's house, we saw that someone was sitting on our porch swing. I squinted. We hadn't seen Detective Kennedy since the day Daddy died.

"What does he want?" Mama said. She sounded mad.

"Good afternoon, Mrs. Lane," he said as we approached. "Picasso." He nodded at me and smiled, and I did too.

There was something about the lazy curl of Detective Kennedy's lips that was catching. I mean Daddy's charming smile was real nice, definitely prettier than Detective Kennedy's crooked smile, but it didn't make me automatically want to smile back.

"May I offer you some iced tea, Detective? It's rather hot out here for a suit and tie."

"Thank you, ma'am. That would be most appreciated." He patted his forehead with a handkerchief, stuffed it in his pants pocket, and followed us inside. "It's nice and cool in here. Air-conditioning?"

"Oliver had it installed a few months ago. We just couldn't go through another summer like the last one."

"Seems to be getting hotter by the year," Detective Kennedy said. "What I wouldn't give to have air-conditioning in my place right now. My swamp cooler just isn't cutting it."

Mama had gone to the kitchen to get a pitcher of tea out of

the refrigerator. She always has a pitcher of tea ready and waiting, even in the winter. Mama is always saying that graciousness and politeness are two of the most essential and telltale qualities of a proper Southern lady. She also says that these qualities are even more important when dealing with your enemies, which, as far as Mama was concerned, meant Detective Kennedy, and, as far as I was concerned, meant I had no chance of ever being considered a proper Southern lady, because I had no intention of ever being gracious or polite to the All That Girls.

Detective Kennedy started walking around, looking out the window, at the furniture, pictures on the fireplace mantel.

Mama returned with the tea tray.

"Quaint neighborhood you live in, ma'am," Detective Kennedy said, as Mama put the tray on the coffee table. "When was this house built?"

"In 1910," Mama said.

"Looks like you've done some renovating," Detective Kennedy said. "Is that a Wolf range?"

Mama ignored his question. She'd only just bought the range the month before Daddy died on account of she was mad at him. She'd bought a bunch of other stuff too: new clothes and shoes, a Marc Jacobs handbag, a new dining-room set, and a bunch of paints and brushes and canvases.

"What can I do for you, Detective?" I saw that she'd poured the tea into the crystal glasses she only used for special guests.

"I just had a few more questions, ma'am," he said. "Is this a good time?"

"Picasso and I just came from her father's funeral," she said. "Would *you* consider that a good time?" I couldn't believe Mama was sassing a detective.

"I know," he said. "I was there."

"You went to my husband's funeral?"

"Yes, ma'am."

"Why?"

"I wanted to pay my respects."

"Sure you did," Mama said.

"I figured since I came all this way you wouldn't mind indulging me."

Mama set three coasters on the coffee table, transferred the glasses from the tray, and sat in Daddy's brown leather club chair. It didn't look right, her sitting in Daddy's chair. I sat on the fireplace hearth, which is about as close to the coffee table as the sofa is.

"Have a seat, Detective." She motioned toward the sofa. He looked a little scared to sit on it. "Don't worry. It's a slipcover. It's washable. How can I help you?"

He took a sip of tea. "Mighty fine. My mother put mint leaves in her tea. I lived in Michigan for a while, and one of the things I missed most was sweet tea. Up north they think sweet tea is Lipton from a machine with sugar packets. I thought I tasted mint in yours."

"You did," Mama said proudly.

"What do you think of your mother's sweet tea, Picasso?"

"Best in the world," I said, and for a minute I felt sad because that's what Daddy and I always said about Mama's tea and cooking.

"I think so too," he said.

He reached into the inside pocket of his suit jacket and pulled out his pen and writing pad, and what looked like pictures.

"Do you happen to know a woman named Julie Lane?"

Mama chewed on the question. "*Julie* Lane? No. Is she a relative of Oliver's?" Which was actually a strange question since as far as Mama and I knew Daddy didn't have any relatives.

"You could say that." He stuck a photograph faceup on the coffee table. It was Jewels.

"I've never seen her before," Mama said.

"How about you, Picasso?"

"Is it really necessary to involve Picasso in this?" Mama asked.

"Sorry, ma'am, but we have to follow all leads."

I looked at the picture and then at Mama. I thought she might be looking at me, but she wasn't. "No."

"You sure, Picasso?" he asked.

"I'm sure," I said.

"Who is she?" Mama asked.

Now, I thought Detective Kennedy was going to say something like "Oh, no one" or "No one important," but he didn't. What he said really surprised me.

"Your husband's other wife." He watched Mama's face.

"Other wife?" Mama asked.

"Your husband has—I mean had—another family, Mrs. Lane. I'm sorry to be the one to tell you."

Mama gasped, as if she was shocked. "You must be mistaken. Oliver would never—"

"Never what?" Detective Kennedy showed us the other picture. It looked like a church picture of Daddy, Jewels, and two little boys who looked exactly alike. I remember thinking about what Jewels had said that first time she showed up on our porch, about her and Daddy having twins. I didn't like seeing a picture of Daddy's other kids. Then I got worried that Detective Kennedy might have seen the church picture of Daddy, Mama, and me when he was looking at Mama's picture wall. We had it taken back when Daddy had decided our family should get more religious, which only lasted from the beginning to the middle of second grade.

"Is that your husband, ma'am?" He pointed at Daddy.

Mama didn't say anything.

"She's pretty shaken up," Detective Kennedy continued. "Her husband left for a business trip and never came back. Poor thing. She couldn't even bury him because her marriage wasn't legally binding. Can you imagine how awful it would be not even to have the closure of a funeral?"

"This is preposterous," Mama said. "My husband did not have another wife. Surely this is all a big mistake."

"Unfortunately it's not. We've verified that her husband and yours are one and the same. Did your husband travel a lot, ma'am?"

"But how, I . . . I mean *when* did you find out about her?"

"She reported her husband missing to the Raleigh Police Department a few days ago," Detective Kennedy said. "Seems she saw his face on television but didn't want to believe what she was seeing and then, well, she heard his name—" He paused, took another sip of his tea. "That's where she lives. Raleigh. Would you like her contact information?"

"That won't be necessary." Mama stood. "I'm very tired, Detective. If you wouldn't mind, I'd like to take a nap."

Detective Kennedy stood too. "Certainly, ma'am. I'll be in touch."

After Detective Kennedy left, Mama ran to the phone and started dialing.

"Don't Mama," I said.

She kept pushing numbers.

"Mama," I yelled. "The police have probably bugged our phone."

She stopped. "What did you say, Picasso?"

"They're watching us, Mama. And listening." I wanted to say more, like that she needed to keep to the plan that the three of them had agreed to, that Jewels was right about it not being a good idea for them to be in contact for a while, but I'd already said too much. As far as Mama knew, I had no idea what really happened at the beach house the morning Daddy died. As far as Mama knew, I had no idea what was supposed to happen.

Mama looked at me strangely and hung up the phone. I thought she might ask me something else, but she didn't. She just sat back down in Daddy's chair and drank the rest of her tea.

Kyle

Mack and I found out about Oliver Lane's third wife on Labor Day weekend, generally our busiest weekend of the year and usually the most memorable. One year, during a major storm, some hardy fools braved the choppy waters between Kitty Hawk and Ocracoke in a thirty-nine-foot Sea Ray and lost their lives. Back in the day, because of its notorious shipwrecks, that stretch of water had been dubbed the "Graveyard of the Atlantic" and now and again folks decided to test their balls against its. Another year, ferry operators strategically chose that particular holiday to go on strike. The Labor Day following Oliver Lane's murder was no different. A bunch of frat boys rented three houses in what we call our "cul-de-sac," basically a dead-end street, invited a group of girls from the fourth house over to party on Saturday night, and ended up burning one house to the ground and damaging the other three. Our lone fire truck had always been enough to handle any mishaps, but not that time. Three more had to be called in from the mainland. No small order. Not that there weren't plenty of fire trucks to go around. The problem was yet again with our greatest vulnerability: the ferries. Already inundated with tourists, and less than reliable even in the off-season, what started as a small, innocent bonfire turned into the largest fire Cooper's Island had seen in recent history. With the exception of some minor burns no one was seriously hurt. The bad news was, Mack and I were up all night calling parents and schools, carting kids to nearby medical centers and emergency rooms, and taking official statements. The good news was, on my last ride back to the island, I got to see one of the more glorious sunrises I'd ever seen, nearly magical enough to cast a Labor Day–forgetting spell on me, definitely wondrous enough to give me a second wind, which ended up being just the boost I would need to deal with what happened next.

After a very welcome shower, I headed to the office. Klide was hovering near my desk.

"This came in a little while ago," she said. "I thought you'd want to see it right away."

"What is it?" I asked. I was still wriggling my arms out of my suit jacket.

"It's from the police department in Boone. Apparently that Oliver Lane guy had another wife."

I hung my jacket on the back of my chair and sat. "We already know that, Klide. And what do you mean, Boone?"

"Boone, North Carolina," she said. "It's a different wife."

"A different wife?" I was aware I was being repetitive, but I hadn't even had my coffee yet, and none of what Klide was saying was registering.

"A *third* wife," she said.

"No shit?" I asked.

Klide handed me a police report with a fax cover sheet—*Who sends faxes these days?* I leaned back and started reading.

"You want me to run down to the Tiki Hut and get you some good coffee?" Klide asked. The Hut doesn't make the finest coffee but it definitely beats ours; Bonnie has a heavy hand.

"You are an angel," I said.

It wasn't surprising it had taken that long for us to hear about it. Connecting the dots was generally the job of the local authorities, and obviously Boone had been asleep at the wheel. What was surprising is that Roberta Lane had taken so long to report her husband missing.

Back in Detroit, we'd always made unannounced visits on Sundays because the chances of finding someone home were greater. The element of surprise was essential to solving a murder case. Holidays were a crapshoot, but I didn't want to wait. With all that had happened that morning, Mack and I got a later than optimal start, but we were able to make up some time on the road. We arrived midafternoon. The third Mrs. Lane lived in a small blue cottage with a rocking-chair front porch, white shutters, and stencil-cut window boxes. The house, like most of the ones nearby, sat on a hill inside a thicket of evergreen trees. We'd driven two blocks beyond it when we realized we'd gone too far. We doubled back. The house number was on the mailbox, but the house itself was completely obscured.

The first thing we noticed when we got out of the car was the drop in the temperature; there was already a chill in the mountain air. I saw a curtain move in one of the windows as Mack and I climbed the front steps. A woman opened the door to our first knock. She was short and plump, with muddy green eyes and thin lips; there was an unsightly mole about the size of a dime on her right cheek. I wondered why she hadn't had it removed; it was a simple procedure. She wore a long gray corduroy skirt and an oversized burgundy cardigan sweater over a white blouse. Other than the long, straight blond hair, she looked nothing like the other two wives.

"Mrs. Lane?" I asked.

"It's *Ms.* actually," she said. "Ms. Miles. I never took my husband's name. I'm assuming you're here about Oliver?"

"I'm Detective Kennedy and this is Detective Jones," I said. "We're with Cooper's Island PD. We'd like to ask you a few questions. Do you have a moment?"

"A moment?" She smiled. "I'm guessing this might take longer than a moment. Please come in, detectives."

If our surprise visit made her uncomfortable, she didn't show it. I scanned the room. Overstuffed bookcases of various shapes and sizes lined every available wall. The furnishings—sofa, easy chairs, coffee table—were all tones of beige and brown, and had obviously seen better days. She led us to the back of the house and a windowed-in porch that overlooked an unusually large back-yard with a well-manicured garden one story below. A territorial view of the town peeked through a row of arborvitaes. The dark, woodsy decor—cedar paneling, creaky unvarnished wood floors, stone fireplace, and leather sofa and chairs so worn that they looked like they'd lived through World War II—played second fiddle to the pungent scents of musty rugs and recently burned wood. I felt like a boy in a tree house.

"There's a walkout basement beneath us," she said. "From the front, you can't tell the house has two stories because it sits on a hill. Right now the space below is unfinished, but we'd hoped to renovate it one day, make it a large great room that led out to English gardens and perhaps some sort of water feature. We even joked of making a maze out of greenery and setting up a permanent croquet lawn for all the children we planned to have." She paused, smoothed her skirt. A nervous habit? "This was Oliver's favorite room in the house. He always said it brought back boyhood memories. You know tree houses and such." Had she said that with emphasis? "Please have a seat, detectives. I had just turned on the kettle when I heard the door. Would either of you like a cup of black tea or some hot cocoa?"

"Hot chocolate for me," Mack said.

"Tea is good," I said.

"Milk or sugar?"

"Both," I said.

I was thinking how perfect a douse of rum or brandy would be when Roberta Miles said, "I've got some Captain Morgan, Detective." This time she stared directly at me. There was obviously more to the woman than her outward appearance suggested. Was that what Oliver Lane had seen in her?

"No thank you, ma'am," I said. "We're on duty."

"Please, call me Bert, Detective. Ma'am sounds so condescending, don't you think?" She flashed me a sweet and unexpectedly pretty smile, and left to get our tea and cocoa.

"I'm sorry for your loss," Mack said when she returned. She set our cups on the wagon-wheel coffee table in front of us.

Her blouse fell open as she leaned into the chair, revealing a nicely defined collarbone and round, taut breasts. Her baggy clothing had fooled me into thinking she wasn't shapely.

"I haven't seen one of these since my college days." I indicated the coffee table.

"Isn't it wonderful?" she said. "It was my wedding gift to Oliver. We saw one at a café in town soon after we met, and I told him how my father used to have one just like it, and it was the strangest thing: his father had one too. Do you believe that? It was uncanny how much Oliver and I had in common."

"Like what?" Mack asked. Noting her questioning glance, he added, "I'd just like to get a better picture of who your husband was. It may help our investigation."

"Of course," she said. "Well, both of our fathers died from a heart attack, and at the exact same age. Consequently, we both preferred to eat healthy. No meat or poultry other than free-range chicken, fresh-caught fish, organic fruits and vegetables, nuts and seeds, almond butter. And we'd just started hiking more regularly. We both loved the outdoors. Financially we were perfectly matched; Oliver was very frugal. And reading. Oliver enjoyed reading even more than I."

I wanted to say something sarcastic like *What a great guy,* but decided against it. "I understand you have a child, Ms. Miles?"

"Yes. She's eleven months old. Her name is Isabelle. She's napping."

"Pretty name," I said.

"It was my grandmother's. Do either of you have children?"

"Not me," I said.

"One boy," Mack said. "Evan. He just turned three."

"Oh, I can't wait until three. Do you have a picture?"

Mack dug into his pocket, flipped open his wallet.

"He is so handsome. He looks like you."

"Do you think so?" Mack asked as he admired his son's picture.

There was something about Roberta Miles that made a man feel instantly comfortable, even special. She was warm, nurturing. She had a certain softness about her that made you want to bury your head in her lap, let her stroke your hair—tell me everything would be okay—

"You said you had some questions about Oliver's murder?" I was surprised how easily the word *murder* had rolled off her tongue.

Mack replaced his son's picture and adopted his questioning posture. Roberta Miles's responses were slow, thoughtful. She'd been at a writers' conference.

"Wildacres Retreat? In the Blue Ridge Mountains?" She waited for us to indicate we knew the place. We didn't. "Well, it lasts two weeks. The first week you just write, and the second you workshop some pieces. I only attended the last week, what with Isabelle and all."

"You took your daughter with you?" I asked.

"No, my mother stayed with her. She was visiting from Baltimore. I must admit I was quite exhausted, Isabelle was rather colicky, and I think I may have had a bit of postpartum depression. My mother's coming was Oliver's idea. The retreat was a last-minute decision actually. Pure luck it fell while she was here."

"Did you go for your job?" I asked. "You manage a bookstore in Boone, right?"

"Yes, Black Bear Books. But that isn't why I went, Detective. I'm a closet poet."

"What time did the conference start?" Mack asked.

"Check-in was between noon and three," Roberta Miles said.

"How'd you get there?" Mack asked.

"I drove," she said. "It's only an hour and twenty minutes from here. It seems I left the very morning Oliver was murdered; only I didn't know that then. Gave me the chills when I found out."

"What time did you leave?"

"I'm not certain. Seven, perhaps? I wanted to leave before Isabelle rose. You know, so she wouldn't cry when she saw me leaving."

"Why so early?" Mack asked. "Since check-in wasn't officially until noon."

"Like I said, Detective: Isabelle. But I also wanted to stop off for breakfast at the Woodlands. Do you know it?"

"Can't say that I do," Mack said.

"Well, you are missing quite a treat. The Woodlands Barbecue is down in Blowing Rock, a little out of the way if you're going to Wildacres, but it has some of the best barbecue in the state."

"Did you pay with a credit card?"

"Oh my, no. I'm not a big fan of credit, especially when it comes to inconsequential purchases. I did pay the conference fee with a credit card."

"So there's no way you can prove you were at the Woodlands."

"Well, not through an actual receipt, if that's what you mean. But I think the waitress will remember me. I gave her a twenty-dollar bill and told her to keep the change. Can you imagine, my entire meal was under twelve dollars? And I got the chicken and pig platter."

"Correct me if I'm wrong, but breakfast couldn't have taken more than an hour, so what did you do with the rest of your time?"

"I went into Little Switzerland and did a bit of shopping. It's a lovely and quaint little village just up the Blue Ridge Parkway from Wildacres."

"Did you buy anything?"

"I'm not much of a spender, Detective Jones. I just wanted to browse. I did have a cup of tea at the inn, but unfortunately I didn't pay for that with a credit card either."

"What time did you arrive at . . . uh"—Mack looked down at his notes—"Wildacres?"

"A little before noon, actually, but the director let me check in early. Would you like me to give you her contact information? So you can verify what time I arrived? I'll give you my mother's infor-mation as well." Before either of us could answer, she'd opened a drawer in the nearby end table, retrieved a notepad and pen, and started writing. "Here's my mother's phone number, and here is the website and e-mail address for Wildacres. I'm afraid I don't know the telephone number off the top of my head, but I'm sure it's listed on the website. Is there anything else you need? The address for the Woodlands?"

"I can look it up," Mack said. "Though there is one thing I'm wondering about."

"What's that, Detective?"

Mack leaned forward, rubbed his chin with his thumb and forefinger. "Seems odd you didn't touch base with your husband while you were gone. Wherever we are, the wife and I check in every day."

"That does seem a bit peculiar, doesn't it?" Roberta Miles said, and smiled. "Well, you see, detectives, there isn't any cell-phone service at Wildacres. With the exception of the retreat center itself, it's pretty undeveloped up there, mostly forest, dirt roads, even bears. It's barely accessible in the winter months. Oliver travels—I mean, traveled—a lot. It wasn't unusual for him not to contact me for a few days. When we were first married, I must admit I wondered about that, but then, well, I just got used to it."

"Makes more sense now, I should think," I said.

"What do you mean?" she asked.

"Well, since now you know about his other lives."

She didn't respond.

"When exactly did you contact the local PD?" Mack asked.

"You mean the police? The Wednesday after I got back."

"You arrived home on Saturday, right? So four days later?"

"Yes."

"Why four days? Why not, say, two, three, or even five?"

"It wasn't about the number of days. Oliver didn't come home. He always arrived home by dinnertime on Tuesday and left on Thursday afternoon. That's how his travel schedule worked. So when he wasn't home by Wednesday morning I knew something was wrong."

"And you never connected your missing husband with the dead man on Cooper's Island?" Mack asked. "His picture was all over the news."

"I don't own a TV," Roberta Miles said. "Nor do I subscribe to the local paper. I prefer not to surround myself with negative energy."

I could almost feel Mack trying not to roll his eyes. Mack is your regular, everyday guy. We'd actually had more than one conversation about his dislike of those *artsy-fartsy granola types.* "You were married to Oliver Lane for what, well over a year, and you didn't have any idea he had two other wives?" Mack asked. "You never once wondered where he was when he wasn't home with you and your daughter?"

She straightened. "You all might find this naïve, detectives, because your line of work breeds suspicion, but I am proud that I've always seen the good in everyone and anything. Why would I suspect my husband of something so distasteful as polygamy? Oliver was a good man, good husband, good father. Would you suspect *your* wife of such a thing, Detective Jones? Does it ever cross *your* mind that she's with another man while you're at work?" She paused. "I thought not."

Mack was staring at Roberta Miles with his mouth open, face flushed.

I jumped in. "You're right about our line of work, ma'am. It does, as you say, breed suspicion, but unfortunately somebody has to fight the bad guys so honest, trusting people like yourself can go on being that way."

"I appreciate your diligence, detectives." A hint of sarcasm?

"We should be on our way," I said, and rose. Mack followed suit. "Thanks for your time and frankness, and for so graciously inviting us into your home unannounced."

I gave her my card, told her again how sorry we were, asked her not to hesitate to call if she needed anything. She walked us to the front door, urged us to drive safely, watched us get into the car, drive away.

"Geez, do you believe that guy?" Mack said, when we were safely buckled in. "I mean she knows the guy had two other wives and yet she was still painting him as perfect. Sounds like he was some player."

"My bet is he'd been at it for a while. Hey, I'm hungry. You?"

Downtown Boone was as quaint and rustic as I thought it would be. The two-story brick buildings housed an array of mountain-type stores specializing in ski, bicycle, and hiking gear, along with specialty clothing and gift shops, an art supplies store, a gallery, Mast General Store, which looked like it carried the kitchen sink, and a number of restaurants. We found a place called Heavenly Diner. The neon sign and striped awnings were right out of Mayberry. My mother was a huge *Andy Griffith* fan. I smelled grease as soon as I walked in the door; I hadn't realized how hungry I was. A counter that backed up to the kitchen ran the length of the narrow restaurant. Several booths with red vinyl seats, Formica tabletops, and miniature jukeboxes lined the windowed wall. All, save one, were occupied.

The waitress, who may have been attractive had it not been for the cropped purple hair, nose ring, black lipstick, and green fingernails, wore a crisp white uniform and pink apron.

"Hi," she said. "I'm Belinda. Can I take your order?"

I'd expected her name to be something like Roxy or Gigi. "How're your burgers?"

She shrugged. "I don't eat meat, but customers seem to like them."

"I'll have a burger and fries."

"Cheese?" Belinda asked.

"Sure. And what about your malts?"

"What about them?"

"They any good? Oh, that's right, you probably wouldn't know since milk comes from a cow."

"Funny," she said. "They're called Heavenly Malts, aren't they?"

"Then I'll have a vanilla malt too."

"Same for me," Mack said.

"Just the malt?" Belinda asked.

"No, the burger too, but no cheese."

Belinda yelled our order to the cook, and then went back behind the counter where she seemed to be in deep discussion with a young man on one of the barstools. He sported a similar hairdo and nose ring, and very tight black jeans.

"So what do you think?" I asked Mack.

"Those nose rings look like they'd hurt," he said.

"I mean about the case," I said.

"Well, for one thing, unless we can verify that Roberta Miles was at the Woodlands, her alibi is weak. Wildacres Retreat is roughly the same distance from Cooper's as Boone is."

"You're saying she could've shot Lane and made it to the writers' retreat by noon?"

"Easy," Mack said. "If she didn't stop for breakfast and tea."

"But Lane got shot at seven fifteen. She would've had to leave a lot earlier than seven."

"Maybe she lied; I'll check with the mother. And I don't buy what she said about not knowing her husband was missing. I mean, who doesn't know their spouse, shit even their room-mate, is missing when they don't see or hear from him in nearly two weeks? I don't care how diligent she is about avoiding nega-tive energy, she can't avoid life. What? Does she live in a gopher hole?"

"It's a little like that up here," I said.

"You mean you believe her?"

"I didn't say that. What about the other two wives?"

"Julie Lane's alibi checks out. She was representing her archi-tectural firm at some meeting in Philadelphia. Called a 'design charrette.' Apparently everyone working on the project, includ-ing the local community, draws the building together. Can you imagine? Getting paid to sit around some table drawing pictures? Sounds like a junket to me. And, if we believe the kid's version of what happened the day of the murder, it lets Diana Lane off the hook."

"It's not like the two of them had time to get their stories straight," I said. "Not to mention her lab work came back negative for blood and gunshot residue."

"Funny, though, that she didn't call 911."

Belinda delivered our burgers and malts. She looked as if she wanted to ask us what we'd been talking about. She prob-ably didn't encounter a couple of suits driving an unmarked black Buick every day.

"Is there anything else I can get you?"

"Nope, looks good," I said.

She hovered for a moment, but then went off to take another order.

We devoured our burgers without speaking. After I sucked up the remaining drops of my malt, which had definitely lived up to its name, I asked Mack where we'd left off.

"Diana Lane not calling 911."

"Maybe she just didn't think to," I said. "She was obviously in shock."

"Or maybe she was buying time," Mack said.

"For what?"

"For her accomplices to get away."

"Accomplices?"

"The other wives."

"You think they did it together? That's a leap."

"I'm just throwing the idea out there. The blond-hair thing is pretty weird. I mean the exact same color, style, and length? What's up with that? And what about their answers? That whole 'don't call me ma'am' thing for instance. Julie Lane said something very similar when I talked to her. How about the other Mrs. Lane?"

"Which other Mrs. Lane?"

"The first one. Diana. Geez, this is confusing."

"What about her?"

"Did she say anything about not calling her ma'am?"

"Not that I remember. But even if she had, lots of women don't like to be called ma'am. It's some sort of feminist thing. I admit the hair stuff is strange. Maybe our vic asked them to wear their hair that way, and besides, if they were trying to elude us, wouldn't they have made an effort to look as different as possible?"

"Don't you find it odd that Diana Lane knew exactly how long her swim took? Or that she just happened to return to the beach house fifteen minutes after the murder. There was no gun; we tore that place apart. So obviously whoever pulled the trigger took it with her."

"Or him," I said.

"So you're still saying burglary?"

"I'm *saying* that things aren't always as they appear."

"How so?" Mack asked.

"Agatha Christie. *Murder on the Orient Express.*"

"Let me guess," Mack said. "Another movie analogy."

"Hear me out," I said. "A murder takes place on a train. The Belgian detective Hercule Poirot investigates and finds that the dead passenger, Ratchett, is really a notorious criminal named Cassetti, who kidnapped and killed the three-year-old heiress Daisy Armstrong. Turns out each of the twelve passengers had a connection with the kid, and one by one stabbed Cassetti in his sleep, but in the end, Poirot pins the murder on an unknown assailant who secretly boarded the train during the night."

"Wow," Mack said. "He let them get away with it?"

"He thought the guy deserved it," I said. "But that isn't the point."

"What is?"

"*We* knew the passengers had murdered Cassetti. We watched it. But if we hadn't, if the scene of the actual murder had been cut, we might have bought Poirot's theory about a thief boarding the train in the night. It was *plausible*."

"I don't get it," Mack said. "You yourself said it was the passengers, that Poirot made the thief thing up."

"The point is, you and me, we're each playing a different movie in our minds where this case is concerned. What we need to do is get rid of any of the scenes we've imagined but can't substantiate. I was thinking about what Diana Lane said about her husband always having cash on him when they traveled. Since we didn't find any at the scene, I decided to check that out. Turns out our vic paid for everything with cash. I'm betting the wives aren't the only ones who knew that."

"Who doesn't use credit cards?" Mack asked.

"Somebody who doesn't want a paper trail," I said. "And you don't think that's sketchy? There may be more to Oliver Lane than polygamy."

"I don't know," Mack said. "A robbery angle seems like a stretch."

"Maybe. Maybe not."

"So what now?"

"We do our job. We check into Roberta Miles's alibi. Recheck the other wives'. We find out if anyone saw a suspicious car either on the ferry or the island, or a woman matching either Julie Lane's or Roberta Miles's description near the beach house the morning of the murder. We keep looking for that gun. We do a deeper investigation into Oliver Lane's background. Talk to his therapist, or whatever doctor prescribed those pills I found at the scene. Check in with his work colleagues again; make sure we didn't miss anyone. See if any of his clients had it in for him. Seems he represented some mean dudes, Mafia types, wealthy bankers, shady politicians. And we don't make any judgments until we've got something concrete. At this point, all that other stuff—the timing of the murder, the wives' answers, Diana Lane's arrival at the scene—could just be coincidences."

"Since when do you believe in coincidences?" Mack asked.

Picasso

We didn't see Detective Kennedy again until he found out about Bert.

It must've been September by then. I remember I was wearing my school uniform, a plaid skirt, white shirt, and navy cardigan, so obviously school had started. I looked through the peephole when the doorbell rang.

"Hi, Picasso," Detective Kennedy said when I opened the wood door. I didn't unlock the screen door.

"Mama's not home," I said.

"Do you know when she'll be back?"

I shook my head. "She's at a Junior League meeting."

"Well then, I'll just wait on the porch."

Our house, which is yellow with black shutters, a red door, and a full front porch, sits farther back from the street than most of the ones around us, so the driveway is long. The garage sits back even farther and doesn't attach. Before I was born, it was just a garage, but Daddy had a second floor built on top of it where Mama could paint. If I think real hard I can still get a hazy image of Mama painting. I remember her holding the handle of one brush between her teeth while gliding another across the canvas, jars and jars of paints, cans of brushes of various sizes, the smell of the turpentine, the feel of the wet paint on my fingertips, the colors, gobs and peaks and squirts of color on the palette and canvas like a rainbow of icing on a dream cake. But that was so long ago. I watched Detective Kennedy from the picture window in the living room. He took off his suit coat, laid it carefully over the back of the porch swing, and sat on one of the rocking chairs for a while. Then he got up, fast, like he had just that second remembered something, went down the steps, and headed toward the driveway. I couldn't see him after that. In a few minutes, I heard the basketball hitting the backboard above the garage door. I went outside. Detective Kennedy was running back and forth dribbling the ball like Daddy used to do.

"Game of horse?" he asked.

"Okay," I said.

"Ladies first." He tossed me the ball.

I stood with my legs spread on the white line that Daddy had painted on the driveway, bent forward at my waist, pushed the ball back between my legs, aimed, and swung it into the air. Detective Kennedy caught the ball when it went through the hoop.

"Good shot," he said. "Do you always throw the ball underhanded like that?"

"Yes."

"Hmm," he said.

"What?" I asked.

"Well, it's kind of a girl way to do it, don't you think?"

"I guess."

"Do you want to learn how to do it the way the pros do?"

"Okay," I said.

"One free shot a turn. How's that sound?"

"Good."

I made most of the girl shots, but my free shots didn't even make it all the way to the basket.

"Hey," Detective Kennedy said when he saw my disappointment. "You just learned how to do it. Don't be so hard on yourself. You'll get better."

I was lining up one of my free shots when Mama drove up.

"To what do we owe this pleasure, Detective?" Mama asked when she got out of the car. She'd parked at the very end of the driveway. She looked annoyed like she always did when she couldn't pull the car into the garage.

"Ma'am," Detective Kennedy said and nodded. "You probably aren't going to believe that I just happened to be in the neighborhood."

"You're right," she said, "I'm not."

"Mama, watch." I repositioned myself and tossed the ball. It made a clean swooshing sound as it went through the net. I couldn't believe it.

"Yes," Detective Kennedy said. "That's what I mean." He ran to me and raised his hand for a high five. "Exceptional shot, Picasso."

We clapped.

"I suppose I don't have any choice but to invite you in," Mama said to Detective Kennedy.

"We can sit on the porch if you'd prefer," he said. "Your rocking chairs are quite comfortable. You can even take mine; it's all warmed up."

"I'd really rather not advertise your presence to the neighbors," Mama said.

Detective Kennedy looked at me, raised his eyebrows, and made a smile that looked a lot like Daddy's secret smile. "You got any of that sweet tea?" He grabbed his suit coat from the porch swing, put it on, and followed Mama inside.

"The Toyota you drove up in, is that yours?" Detective Kennedy asked, as Mama headed to the refrigerator.

"Yes, why?"

"I seem to recall you were driving a BMW on Cooper's Island."

"That was Oliver's. It's in the garage. Do you know anyone interested in an overpriced car?"

"So you're looking to sell it?"

"I certainly don't need it anymore," Mama said as she set the tray on the coffee table. This time she'd brought the entire glass pitcher; the lemons and mint leaves were clearly visible.

Detective Kennedy walked over to Mama's picture wall while she laid out the coasters and poured the tea.

"Is that you, Picasso?" he asked.

"Right after I was born," I said.

"You're much prettier now," he said.

I laughed. People were always saying how cute newborn babies were, even though they weren't. I was happy that Detective Kennedy told the truth. I remembered what he said about a sunset making the sea turn colors. I'd googled "watching a sunset from a ferry" and "sunset changing ocean into many colors," but other than information on sediment cores, fairies, and a page from some book that used a lot of pretty words, I couldn't find anything that proved what he'd said. I also couldn't verify the number of stars in the sky.

I saw that he was almost to the church picture of Daddy, Mama, and me, the one like he showed us of Daddy with Jewels and those little boys. I held my breath. Thankfully, all he said was, "Just this one picture of your dad?"

"Daddy didn't like having his picture taken," I said.

"Are you going to sit, Detective?" Mama asked.

"May I?" he asked.

She gave him an angry look. "Please. What can I help you with this time?"

I went and sat on the fireplace hearth again and watched both of them. I liked having Detective Kennedy in our house. I wished Mama liked him more, or at least was nicer to him.

"Oh, yes," he said. "I almost forgot. I have another photograph

I'd like to show you." He reached into the pocket inside his coat and put a photo on the coffee table.

Mama didn't look at it right away. I could see from where I sat that it was Bert.

"Am I supposed to know this woman?" Mama asked.

"You tell me," Detective Kennedy said.

"I have no idea who she is."

"Picasso?" Detective Kennedy said to me.

I shook my head.

"It was worth a try," he said. He put the picture back in his coat. "Picasso mentioned that you were at a Junior League meeting," he said to Mama. "Fine organization. What committee are you working on?"

"You can't tell me you're really interested in my Junior League commitments, Detective," Mama said. "That seems beyond thorough"—she paused—"even for you."

"You underestimate me, Mrs. Lane," he said. "My mother was president of the Cooper's Island chapter for five years. Maybe you knew of her? Alice Kennedy?"

"No, sorry. Is she still active?"

"She passed, almost a year ago now."

"I'm sorry for your loss, Detective."

"Thank you, ma'am. Are you okay with me calling you ma'am?"

"Why wouldn't I be?"

"It's just that I've heard some women find it condescending."

"I can't imagine why."

"I've been meaning to ask what you have in the oven. It smells great."

"Liver and onions," Mama said. "It's in the slow cooker, not the oven."

The look he gave Mama was genuine. It was a look of admiration. "I can't believe you make liver and onions. Nobody makes that anymore. It's one of my favorites." He looked at me. "How's your mother's liver and onions?"

"Best in the world," I said.

I wasn't surprised when Mama asked Detective Kennedy if he wanted to stay for dinner because that was the polite thing to do, and since Detective Kennedy was also from the South, I figured, like Mama surely did, that he would graciously decline.

"Oh, I shouldn't," he said.

"Well then—"

"But if you insist." This time, he shook off his jacket faster than a wet dog, and relaxed into the sofa. "Anything I can help you with?"

Mama didn't look too happy; she picked up the tea pitcher and went to the kitchen.

Detective Kennedy leaned toward me and whispered, "I don't think your mama likes me. Any suggestions?"

"Flowers," I whispered back. It always worked for Daddy.

"I've got a quick errand to run, ma'am," he said to Mama.

I was setting the table when Detective Kennedy got back. He winked at me as he snuck up behind Mama and stuck the flowers in front of her face. "Do you need me to get a vase down for you? From a high shelf?"

Mama cocked her head like she was surprised that he knew her vases would be up high, and then she pointed above the stove.

Detective Kennedy filled the vase with water, cut the stems, arranged the flowers, and put the vase on the table. I couldn't imagine Daddy arranging flowers.

Nobody was talking so I figured I'd start. "Why'd you become a detective?"

"My dad was a cop," Detective Kennedy said.

"On Cooper's Island?" Mama asked.

"No, ma'am. Detroit."

"Detroit?"

"That's where I was born. We moved to Cooper's Island when I was five and my sister was three. She's married now, has two kids. Matt and Molly. They live over in Wilmington." He looked at me. "Matt's about your age. I'll have to introduce the two of you sometime. He's pretty handsome."

He'd said that *sometime* word again, like he figured he'd be around for a while. I remember wondering if that was something he just said, to be polite, like Mama saying "Nice to *see* you" instead of "Nice to *meet* you," just in case she'd met the person before and forgot.

"Okay," I said, even though I was pretty sure that Detective Kennedy's nephew was nowhere near as cute as Ryan Anderson.

"What about you, ma'am? You from these parts?"

"Born and raised in this very house," Mama said.

"You don't hear that very often. You mentioned you didn't have family."

"Did I?" Mama asked.

"The day of your husband's murder." He watched Mama's face. I couldn't tell whether it was because he was concerned or was waiting to see how she'd react to his saying *murder*.

"Oh, yes, of course," Mama said. "My parents and younger brother died in a car accident."

"I'm sorry," Detective Kennedy said to Mama. "That must've been tough."

"It's fine," Mama said. "It happened a long time ago, when I was eighteen. I'd already left home, gone to college."

"Daddy's parents died in a car accident too," I said. "He was about the same age as Mama was."

"Wow," Detective Kennedy said.

"Yes," Mama said. "It was one of the things that brought Oliver and me together."

It was quiet for a while, and then Detective Kennedy started telling stories about growing up on Cooper's Island. He told this one about him and some friends trying to break into the Catholic church attached to his school by climbing up a bunch of ivy, and I committed the image of Detective Kennedy climbing that ivy to my mind so I could enter the story, and then I remembered another story, "Jack and the Beanstalk," and I saw Daddy reading it to me when I was very little, and I entered that story too, and found myself fading back and forth between Detective Kennedy's voice and Daddy's voice, between Detective Kennedy climbing the ivy and Daddy climbing the beanstalk, and then the two stories merged, and I stood on the ground between the ivy and beanstalk, and both Detective Kennedy and Daddy held out their hands to me, beckoned me to jump up and climb with them, and my heart started beating faster and faster because I didn't know who to choose, and then something happened. I heard Mama laughing—Mama *laughing*—I hadn't heard Mama laugh since even before Daddy died, and I followed the sound of her laughter back through that magical space that separates story from reality, back into Mama's and my house, back to the dining-room table, and there she was, her face and eyes bright, her smile wide, and I smiled too as I listened to Detective Kennedy telling us how when he and his friends finally got to the open window they'd planned to crawl through, the boy on top lost his grip causing them all to tumble down and land right in front of the priest's feet, and as punishment, the priest made them all altar boys, which, according to Detective Kennedy was not a fun job. By then tears were falling down Mama's face she was laughing so hard, and Detective Kennedy snorted—can you believe it, *snorted*? I had no idea Detective Kennedy was a snorter. And me? Well, I was still smiling, but I admit tears nudged at the edges of my eyes like annoying meerkats, and I remember wondering whether they were tears of happiness or tears of sadness, because in all honesty I felt both. And then the phone rang.

Mama jumped.

The laughing and snorting and wondering stopped. Mama looked at the phone but didn't answer it, which was awkward. After the third ring, Detective Kennedy stared at Mama, like the way Mr. Dork stares at kids when he asks them hard questions. "Why haven't you asked me about the picture I showed you, Mrs. Lane?" He sounded like a detective again, not somebody who'd be knowing Mama and me for a long time.

Fourth ring.

"What?" Mama asked.

"The woman in the picture. Aren't you curious who she is?"

Fifth ring.

Mama didn't say a thing. I didn't think that was very smart.

Last ring.

"Who is she?" I asked.

"Your daddy's third wife," Detective Kennedy said.

Kyle

My ride back to Cooper's Island was as wet and dark as my mind. I left the windows cracked just enough to let in some air but not soak me, or the car. There was something soothing about the sound of the wipers and the swirling patterns of the water on the windshield, and something eerie in its thick, meandering consistency, like the pooling of fresh blood.

Once I'd merged onto the freeway, I dialed Mack's number.

"Hey, Boss," he said. "What can I do you for?"

"Could you do me a favor and check the titles on Diana Lane's house and auto. Not the BMW. It's a Toyota crossover. License plate number is—"

"Already checked," Mack said. "Both are registered in Diana Lane's name. And both are paid for by the way. Same with Julie Lane's and Roberta Miles's homes and cars. In fact, other than the BMW, which by the way is actually registered to Oliver Lane, Esquire, his business name, it's like Mercy said, I can't find one thing in his name. Not even a cable bill. The guy's a ghost. Oh, and I had a phone conversation with our vic's therapist. Said he had mood swings. Thought he might be bipolar, but that Lane quit coming before he could get a good read. Where are you now?"

"Just getting on the road."

"How'd she take it?"

"She denied knowing Roberta Miles too."

"Do you believe her?"

"I don't know," I said. "I'll give you the details tomorrow. Think I need to keep my hands on the wheel. It's soup out here."

"Be safe."

"Will do."

After I hung up, I thought about Mack's question. Did I believe Diana Lane?

Starting with that first time I saw her at the beach house, I went over my encounters with Diana Lane. She was definitely a looker. I remembered her shivering while she sat on the sofa, holding that skimpy towel around her shoulders like it was a security blanket. Tears running down her face. Fear in her eyes. Was it an act?

By design, I'd been the last person to enter the church the day of her husband's funeral. The vestibule, like the Buick, and everywhere else it seemed, was hotter than hell. I found a seat in an empty pew in the back near a large industrial-type fan. Slid in, until I had an unobstructed view of her profile. That time there were no tears. She was stoic. Resigned? I remember thinking that even with her drab clothing, and her hair in that proper bun, stretched tight as silk on a loom from her hairline, she was flawless. Then I started fantasizing. I imagined pulling her toward me, undoing the knot in her hair, running my fingers through it, wrapping it around my fists, pulling her lips to mine, bruising them, shoving her against the pulpit, sliding the hem of her prim black dress up around her hips.

At the cemetery, I'd hung toward the back of the crowd. It was raining then too. The scene looked like something out of a Hitchcock movie. Black coffin. Black canopy. Black skies. Black suits and dresses. Black umbrellas. Diana Lane had added over-the-elbow gloves and a veiled pillbox hat to her ensemble. Only her lips were exposed. They never trembled. I tailed the limousine back to the church, parked on the side of the road. The storm had passed by then, yet hadn't done much to quell the heat. I watched Diana's legs swing from the car, stiletto heels step onto the pavement, head dip through the door. She looked in my direction as she stood but didn't see me. Surveillance stints in my early days had taught me the art of disappearing in plain view. She took Picasso's hand and went back into the church. I headed to her house and waited on the front porch. I remember being pleasantly surprised when she offered me tea. Maybe I shouldn't have been, I'd thought later. Whatever she might have done, she was still a Southern lady.

Or a very good actress.

That day, I chose not to see what I knew deep down: Diana Lane had not only recognized the photograph of her husband's other wife, she *knew* Julie Lane. Just like she knew Roberta Miles.

Beautiful, lucky, sorry, gun, motive, liar.

Picasso

My favorite dictionary says that a rumor is "a currently circulating story or report of uncertain or doubtful truth." That definition makes a rumor sound about as harmless as a campfire story. It's been two years since Daddy died and people are still whispering. Whereas once the rumors might've been somewhat factual, over time they've rolled around so much they've grown into a big misshapen and unrecognizable blob, which, like in that black-and-white horror movie that Daddy used to love, has sucked much of the life out of Mama and me. I'm thinking that there needs to be a new word for rumor, or at least a more fitting definition. Something that more accurately describes the ugly, vicious, and hateful stories people spread, mainly because they don't have anything better to do, and because they're ugly, vicious, and hateful themselves. In my mind there's a difference between a rumor and a lie: intent.

People tell rumors to hurt someone else. People tell lies to save themselves.

Or someone they love.

T W O

Lies

(The Events Preceding the Murder)

. . .

A lie told often enough becomes the truth.

—LENIN

The Wives

It's hard to remember when the three of us became *we*. Perhaps it was that day we first met at Rainy Cove Park. We'd chosen the setting because it was centrally located between Hollyville, Raleigh, and Boone, and because a trek through nature on a lovely autumn day seemed safe, neutral. We'd chosen the day and time, Wednesday at noon, because it accommodated our varied work and child-care schedules. It was odd how we all drove through the entrance at the same time—Diana in her silver Toyota crossover, Jewels in her bright blue Porsche Carrera, Bert in her rusty and dented Chevy Blazer—and then proceeded to park, get out of our vehicles, and walk toward one another, naturally, no huge smiles or feigned politeness, no nervous chatter, as if we'd been doing it our entire lives, as if we'd seen one another yesterday and would do so again tomorrow.

As if time was our friend.

We followed the worn dirt path deeper and deeper into the dense forest. The sound of swishing water made us pause. Peering through the trees, we saw a lone kayaker paddling in the distance. The dirt path led on, but without asking one another, we veered onto untamed ground. Twigs crinkled and snapped beneath our shoes. Tall grasses and wildflowers brushed our calves. After some time, we came upon the spot that would become our home away from home, a lovely private clearing nestled in the woodland. We marveled at the quietude. None of the noises of civilization were present: no hustle and bustle, honking horns, or squealing children. There were only the sounds of nature, the singsong wail of the cool autumn breeze, undulating drum of the cyan lake, high-pitched chirp of the graceful birds. We decided it was *our* place, a place that promised shelter and comfort. Perhaps, ultimately, that was what had glued us together in time and place: We all needed comforting.

We hurt.

Diana had brought along a plaid wool blanket and picnic basket, Jewels a brown paper grocery bag with two bottles of chardonnay in it, Bert a brightly woven tote with pink terry-cloth fabric spilling over its edge. We didn't speak as we prepared our space. Diana opened the blanket, snapped it in the air, its center billowing for a moment like a parachute then reluctantly falling to the ground. We smoothed out its edges, set the basket, bag, and tote in its center, claimed our corners, sat, crossed our legs Indian style, breathed in the musky scent of pine, spruce, and hickory.

It was Bert who broke our silence. "I brought towels. I thought we might want to swim."

We looked at one another, smiled, and as if we'd grown up together, seen one another naked a thousand times, as if Bert's swollen belly was as natural and beautiful as a bird's breast, began taking off our clothes. We ran to the water's edge laughing and screaming like children, stretched our arms toward the sky and dove, kicked our legs, went down deeper and deeper, watched each other's bodies—Diana's slim sensuous contours, Jewels's sharp athletic angles, Bert's round voluptuous curves—bending and floating and twirling: yellow, black, and brown hair streaming like mermaids. Then we straightened, thrust our arms to our sides, shot to the surface, and paddled back to shore. We wrapped ourselves in the plush pink towels, dried our skin, our hair, lowered our backs to the blanket, and slept naked under the warm autumn sun.

Perhaps we slept for only minutes, perhaps it was longer, but when we woke it felt as if hours had passed. We felt rested, refreshed, prepared to face a new dawn. We dressed, gathered ourselves into what would become our sacred circle.

Diana opened the picnic basket. "Egg salad?"

"Sounds divine," Jewels said. She uncorked one of the wine bottles.

"To us," Jewels said.

"To us," Diana and Bert said in unison. The sound of glass hitting glass rang through the air.

We sipped, assessed one another. These were the other women our husband had married? Didn't most men prefer a *type*? Our height, weight, facial features, hair color, skin tones, mannerisms, speech patterns, everything appeared dissimilar. It would be awhile before we understood that Oliver's initial interest had more to do with our mental states than physical characteristics. At the time each of us met Oliver, we were perfect prey for a man who thrived on the game, the victory, and the foil: We were broken. And Oliver preferred to keep it that way. But that day, our first rendezvous at Rainy Cove Park, we were yet to recognize the extent of our codependence. We still hid behind a veil of lies, secrets, and confusion. Rather than blame Oliver or ourselves, we blamed circumstance and one another. If asked why we'd agreed to meet, we would have said, and believed, that our decision had been based on some virtuous combination of concern and curiosity, when in fact our sole motivation was fear: fear of losing Oliver, fear of one another, fear of the unknown. Keeping one another close meant keeping control. And yet that day, though we've since wondered at the ease in which we did so, we opened our hearts and souls to one another. We talked and talked, and listened and listened, and not because we were eager to know one another's stories, on some level we already knew them, we'd lived them, but because we *needed* to know who the others were. Because, you see, we no longer knew who *we* were. We were lost. It had always been Oliver's story. While none of us had chosen to be part of the sordid tapestry we found ourselves in, we'd unwittingly become threads of its cloth. What was odd is that we didn't discuss our children or Bert's pregnancy. We didn't pull pictures from our handbags, brag of such feats as strong heartbeats, first steps and words, or academic accomplishments. Perhaps this was because, intuitively, we understood that our children were the one pure, uncomplicated part of our lives.

We felt numb as the details of Oliver's three lives unfolded. How had he pulled it off? He'd juggled three offices, three families, three wives, yet never once had he confused our names, not even in the heat of passion. There was the Oliver who golfed, grew up Episcopalian, and had no interest in the arts in Hollyville. There was the Oliver who played bridge, turned his back on Catholicism, and collected fine art in Raleigh. There was the Oliver who read literature, was a devout Lutheran, and bought coffee-table art books in Boone. Yet, although Oliver had gone to great lengths to create distinct personalities, we discovered one similarity. He told each of us that he loved us more than anyone and anything in the world, and, as if he were slicing the palm of his hand with a knife and comingling our blood, he pledged his undying love with the same, now haunting words: *I love you more than life itself.*

The first time we heard those words, we melted. It wasn't just the words that caused our unexpected reactions; it was his eyes. They were unwavering. They contained an unmistakable sincerity. Tears welled inside them. Softened by his vulnerability, tears came to our eyes as well. He reached his hand behind our necks, drew us to him, and kissed us. We had been kissed before, but this was like no other. At that moment we wanted to give ourselves to him fully, completely, without hesitation. Without fear or doubt or concern for the outcome.

And we did.

Diana was twenty-five. She'd sworn off men and attachments of any sort. Her long-term relationship with her college boyfriend had ended badly, and she was suffering from the unique pain, distrust, and loneliness that can only result from his particular transgression: He'd slept with her best friend. She met Oliver in a martini bar a few months after she became single again. It was happy hour, prophetic she later thought, because at least in the beginning, she had never been happier than she was with Oliver. Diana and her social companion (she'd also sworn off friends), Lillian, sat at the bar drinking apple martinis. The stark difference between the two women, Diana's elongated silhouette, blond hair, and white dress against Lillian's petite frame, dark hair, and black dress was, given the situation, an asset. A handsome man with dark, curly hair sat with an attractive redhead at a table nearby. He wore a dark blue tailored suit and yellow tie; his crisp white shirt glowed against his tan skin. She wore a low-cut, sleeveless emerald green dress. They were deep in conversation, now and then laughing heartily. Diana couldn't take her eyes off them, perhaps because they reminded her of what she once had, perhaps because they reminded her of what she would never have.

"He's a dream, isn't he?" Lillian asked.

"Who?" Diana asked.

"Ten o'clock," Lillian said. "Mr. Bedroom Eyes."

"I hadn't noticed," Diana said. At the time, she believed that.

"You can't be serious," Lillian said.

Diana hunched her shoulders. "He's okay, I guess, but as you can see, he's with someone."

"Her?" Lillian asked. "No future there. Besides, she's not even with him. She came from that table over there. See? The *Sex and the City* foursome? He's been checking you out for the past hour."

"No, he hasn't," Diana said.

"Trust me, he has," Lillian said.

"Let's go," Diana said. "I'm just not into this."

"Okay," Lillian said. She chugged the rest of her martini.

Diana felt a tapping on her shoulder as they passed through the door, and when she turned she found herself face-to-face with Oliver. Diana was five foot nine and wearing four-inch heels.

Oliver's smile was disarming. "I've been admiring your lipstick."

"My what?"

"Your lips, actually," he said. "But I thought that might sound too forward. If it is, I apologize."

"I'll get a cab," Lillian said. "See you tomorrow?"

Diana thought she protested, but she wasn't certain. She wasn't certain about much that happened that evening. Perhaps Oliver bought her another drink, perhaps two, before he drove her home. But there was one thing she was certain of: She remembered what happened when he walked her to the door of her apartment. He'd stood staring at her for a while, his eyes moist, and then he put his hands on her cheeks, kissed her long and hard. Like a gentleman, he stopped, stepped back.

"I need to go," he said. He must have seen the confusion (and disappointment?) in Diana's eyes, because he added, "Believe me, I don't want to. But we've both had so much to drink. I want this to be right. The moment I saw you I knew you were the only woman for me. *I knew I would love you more than life itself.*"

In six months they were married.

Everyone said that was way too fast for marriage. Generally you should wait a year, get to know the person. Diana scoffed. She knew Oliver. All of Oliver. Their minds and bodies fit perfectly. They were in sync. Soul mates. They finished each other's sentences, wanted the exact same things out of life, loved the same movies and food. Their eyes met every time they made love, and when they did, she saw true love in his. She couldn't mistake that look, could she?

"Don't be hard on yourself," Jewels said. "I thought the exact same thing. *Eyes don't lie.* One of the signs you've been in a relationship with a sociopath is that even after you know you've been burned, you still love him. And sociopaths are expert chameleons. Look at those women in Florida who were swindled out of their life savings. Police caught the guy, but none of them are pressing charges."

"Sociopath?" Diana said. "Oliver may be a lot of things, but he's not violent. He's never so much as raised his voice to me."

"Not all sociopaths are serial killers," Jewels said.

"That's true," Bert said. "I read this book that said we'd be surprised how many lead normal lives."

"Look up the characteristics, Diana," Jewels said. "It's all about winning and manipulation with Oliver."

Jewels was thirty when she and Oliver met. Their relationship began with sex. Steamy, wanton, primal sex, the likes of which she hadn't experienced before, that she'd only read about in novels or watched in X-rated movies. They had sex on the bedroom carpet, sex on the dining-room table and kitchen floor, sex in the shower and bathtub, sex on the sofa, sex on the cold, hard concrete of her townhome balcony, sex almost anywhere but in bed.

For the longest time, they saw each other only on Mondays. Their only communications outside their weekly trysts were through e-mail or at the gym. That was how they met. She'd noticed him in her building's workout space. He spent most of his time working his wrapped knee on the leg-lift machine. She found him handsome—no, more than handsome, *alluring.* Was that the right word? There was just something about him. Though they'd never spoken, or even made eye contact, she felt an odd sensation of recognition, as if she'd known him always, as if they'd been intimate, powerfully so, as if she *knew* his touch and his smile and would again, as if—dare she say—he was her destiny. Sometimes this sensation was immediate; she'd be concentrating on her run, would look up, and he was there, on his machine. When did he arrive? How long had he been there? Other times the sensation came over her slowly, like a wave flowing across her body, and within moments he'd enter the gym. When he wasn't in the room, she insisted to herself that she felt nothing, and she'd scoff at the absurdity of her girlish crush. He was just a man she'd conjured into a silly fantasy to pass the time, to take up space in her lost, hollow heart. That was her state of mind the first time he spoke to her.

"I see you like goldens." The voice came from behind her. She'd just gotten off the treadmill and gone to the drinking fountain.

She had heard it described as butterflies or nervous flutters, that warm yet dangerous feeling way down. Fear and desire combined. Up close, he was a bigger man than she had thought. More than six feet tall. Big arms. Broad shoulders.

She was taken aback. "Goldens?"

"I saw you with a golden retriever the other day." He paused. "At the dog park? It was you, wasn't it?"

She wasn't exactly a regular at the dog park, she'd been there maybe twice in the last few months, but one of those times was fairly recent. Perhaps she should have asked *When?* Or, *Where exactly did you see me?* But her brain was working overtime to make sense of what was happening, and the rest of her was flattered, so all she said was "Yes."

"Best dogs in the world," he said. "My family had them when I was growing up."

"Mine too," she said.

"What's his name?"

"Frank," she said.

"Frank?"

"After Frank Lloyd Wright."

"Commercial or residential?" He noticed her questioning glance. "You're an architect, right?"

"Residential," she said.

He bent to take a sip from the fountain. She was so close to him that she could see the freckles on his neck and smell his sweat. She marveled at the scent; like him, the man she'd spied from a distance, she was certain she recognized it. He rose, lifted his T-shirt to wipe his mouth. His hands were large, his stomach lean but not hard. *Love handles.* Her hands cupped them in her mind.

"Hey?" he asked. "Do you want to get a drink after work tonight?" He smiled, a friendly smile. Deep dimples. Warm eyes. Boyish charm. "Come on. One drink? We could talk about all our childhood goldens."

She felt immediately anxious. She knew she should say she was busy; that was what the book said to do. She'd bought it in New York after her five-year affair with her married boss ended. *Don't say yes the first time. Make him chase you. Men love the chase.* She hadn't played hard to get with Jonathan; she'd jumped whenever he called and look where that had gotten her. Would he think she was easy if she said yes? Would he see through her ruse if she asked for a rain check? Either way, he might lose interest. What would Cruel Jewels do?

Her nickname, Jewels, had been her father's idea. Her parents had been trying for several years to have a child, so when she arrived he called her his precious jewels. Her mother preferred she use her given name, Julie, at school, but, as loners often are, she was the brunt of bullying and name-calling. Ghouly Julie was born in kindergarten. Granted, the name was somewhat warranted. As the only child of older parents, Jewels spent most of her time with her mother and father, or in the interior landscape of her mind. Barbie dolls were her best friends. Her large and assorted collection led a fascinating life filled with drama, love, romance, marriage, more drama, children, and death by weird and extraordinary circumstances, such as Ken having the awful misfortune of falling asleep in an old car that was due to be crushed for scrap metal, or slipping while hiking and falling two hundred feet to his gory death. Ken died regularly and creatively. This allowed Barbie the opportunity to start all over again with drama, love, romance, marriage, more drama, children, and death by extraordinary circumstances. Sometimes, especially when she was nervous, the name Ghouly Julie and the embarrassing feelings that had gone with it popped into her head. To ward it off and keep control of situations, she'd adopted her own alter ego, Cruel Jewels. But Cruel Jewels didn't help with Oliver. She was mush.

"Sure," she said.

And so it began.

In the beginning, sex once a week with Oliver was okay with Jewels, but it wasn't long before she wanted more from the object of her desire. They were at her apartment in Raleigh, a tastefully decorated two-story townhome with a small fenced-in yard for Frank. They'd just finished making love on her faux-bearskin rug in front of a roaring fire. The scene, and the closeness she'd felt, couldn't have been more storybook. Surely Oliver felt the magic of the moment as well.

"It seems silly that we only spend one day a week together," Jewels said.

"What do you mean?" Oliver asked.

"It's just that we're so compatible," she said. "It seems only natural that we'd want to see more of each other."

"I didn't realize our relationship had gotten to this point," he said.

"What point?" she asked.

"The accountable point," he said.

"I'm not asking for accountability," she said. "I'm just asking to spend more time with you."

"You're lying to yourself," he said. "You want our relationship to change from one way of interacting to another. You want more. Wanting more leads to wanting even more and sooner or later equals accountability. I don't know if I'm ready."

"Ready for what?"

"Ready for a relationship," he said.

"I'm not asking for a relationship."

"Then what are you asking for?"

"I don't think having sex once a week is fair to me," she said. "I don't know if I want to keep doing this if it's all you want from me."

"Okay then," he said. "We won't."

Fear. She hadn't meant to give him an ultimatum. "Shit!" she said. Her raised voice startled Frank. He lumbered over, nudged her hand.

"What?" Oliver asked.

"Damn!" She rose, started pacing. "I didn't mean for this to happen."

"For what to happen?" He rubbed the top of Frank's head.

"This," she said. "Love. And I understand if you don't want to go there. It was never part of our arrangement. I fucked up."

Oliver's face softened. "Who said I didn't want to go there?" His voice was comforting. "When I said 'we won't,' what I meant was, we won't only see each other once a week. I love you too, Jewels."

She was certain, as certain as she was that she ran an eight-minute mile, that she saw love in his eyes. "You do?"

He came to her, held her, whispered in her ear, *"I love you more than life itself."*

With this, Frank barked, and Jewels took that as a sign of his approval. Jewels had been having "sex" with Oliver for five months. They made love only once before he asked her to marry him. In the beginning, to Jewels, only Barbie and Ken, at the direction of her creative mind, could have done romance better, and then only slightly. Oliver was utterly perfect. There were flowers, extravagant dinners, real jewels, and rides through the Blue Ridge Mountains in the new bright blue Porsche Carrera he'd bought her. But then daily life set in, and it wasn't long before Jewels realized there was something wrong. Cruel Jewels was no fool. Oliver's out-of-town schedule was just way too predictable.

Bert told a similar story. She and Oliver had met in the bookstore where she worked. She was twenty-four at the time. She'd just completed her PhD in English at Appalachian State. He was looking for a specific book, and she'd walked him to the mythology section. That day she'd left him there. He returned a week later, and this time asked whether she knew of any book clubs that met on Wednesday night. He loved to read, but his schedule was tight.

"My book club meets on Wednesdays," Bert said.

A relationship was the furthest thing from Bert's mind. It wasn't that she didn't find Oliver attractive, quite the contrary, but at barely five foot three and one hundred and forty-five pounds, not to mention her straggly brown hair and plain features, Bert had never considered herself pretty, especially to the opposite sex. When Oliver began showing that kind of attention toward her, she was skeptical. She'd grown up in Baltimore, the oldest and the only girl of seven children. Because both her parents worked, she'd raised her brothers. Caretaking and poverty were all that Bert ever knew. Nothing had come easy, so why would love? She got the job at the bookstore when she was in undergraduate school and worked her way up to manager. Always financially responsible, she saved enough money for a down payment on a house, took in a few stray cats, and prepared herself for a life of spinsterhood. When Oliver said the words *I love you more than life itself* to her, it was more than a total surprise. It was a gift. Though she knew she should be happy, by all accounts

Oliver was a doting and generous husband, a sense of dread had always plagued her. When Jewels showed up on her doorstep, her worst fear was realized.

Jewels summed up our experiences as evidence that Oliver was a predator. "Believe me, he did his homework." She didn't know how, but she insisted that Oliver knew Diana would be in that martini bar that night, that Jewels worked out at that gym, and that Bert's book club met on Wednesdays.

"But I'd never seen him there before," Diana said.

"That's because he didn't want you to see him," Jewels said. "He hadn't completed his homework."

It was Jewels, of course, who had discovered Oliver's ways. She followed him one day, and though she'd hoped against hope that she wouldn't find what she did, her visions of a perfect Barbie-doll life were shattered. Of all of us, Jewels had been the most romantic in her outlook on love, and thus it could be argued that her heart was the most fragile, its break the loudest, its pieces the sharpest. She thought about hiring a private investigator but decided against it, and not because she cared what people thought but because of a nagging fear she couldn't quite place. Not a fear of Oliver. What she was yet to understand was that deep inside her, the seeds of Oliver's fate had already begun to sprout. By the time she showed up on Diana's doorstep, and then Bert's, they were as insidious as kudzu.

"Oh my, look at the time," Diana said. "Oliver is expecting me home for supper. I'm making fried chicken and macaroni and cheese, his favorite—"

She stopped; she'd forgotten that two of us wouldn't be preparing dinner for our husbands that night.

"Next month?" Jewels asked.

And so we would reunite in a month's time, and then another month's time, and so on, until we were strong enough to recognize that fear, not one another, was our nemesis. Until we were honest enough to admit that we couldn't imagine a world without Oliver, that even the thought of losing him was so painful, so frightening that we would rather sacrifice ourselves than change our situation. Until we were resigned enough to accept what we considered the grim reality of our futures: losing Oliver would destroy us; loving Oliver would destroy us.

Picasso

During those months when Mama, Jewels, and Bert were swapping woe-are-we stories, I was just living my same old boring life. What with Mama's body being inhabited by an alien and Daddy's increased travel schedule, my only-child-at-home status and my generally unpopular-at-school status prompted me to pursue other, more creative and intellectual outlets. One thing I started doing was playing this game with myself where I'd close my eyes, open one of my dictionaries to any old page, zero in on a random word with my finger, and then add it to my word journal where I'd study it until I knew the ins, outs, and nuances of its meaning. Prior to this, I'd concentrated on P words, because of the substitute names Daddy was always calling me, but I figured it was time to expand my vocabulary. Getting even smarter was important. It was one of the few ways in which I could be superior to those All That Girls. As it turned out, my dictionary game was timely. There was a regional spelling bee planned for sometime in the spring, and because I'd been winning all our class contests, Mr. Dork chose me and one other kid to represent our school's fifth-grade class. Having a personal and recognizable expertise, especially one that was needed and necessary for the success of my school and fellow classmates, would surely raise the other kids' opinions of me. The fact that Ryan Anderson was the other kid was a bonus, but even though Ryan was within spitting distance of me for one hour a day, five days a week, he still barely talked to me. He didn't even seem to know my name. I decided this was due to one, not too small problem: Ashley Adams.

Ashley was Ryan's girlfriend and the prettiest, most popular girl at school. Even I liked her. She was nice. On top of that, Adams and Anderson were next to each other in our alphabetical class order, so Ryan sat behind Ashley in class, next to her in the lunchroom, beside her whenever we went on field trips, and followed her in recess lines. They both, no lie, lived on Cupid's Court. Their mothers were best friends. Their families vacationed together. And they looked alike; they were round-faced, blond-haired, blue-eyed specimens of perfection. So what else could I do but *lament* (express my grief passionately) the *futility* (unlikely to produce any useful result) of my crush? After all, it seemed the entire *universe* (all existing matter and space as a whole) was stacked against me.

Then, I found the book.

I was searching through our bookcases for the planets book Daddy had given me for my science project when I came across it. *Taking Charge of Your Life,* the spine said. I figured it was Mama's book, and for the most part I didn't much care for Mama's books, but for some reason I felt compelled to look at it. I slid it from the shelf, took it up to my room, read the entire thing in one night, and started doing everything it said I should do in the exact way it said I should do it. And, as it turned out, it was a good thing I did, because just like the book promised, my life started changing for the better. For one thing, I grew three inches (Daddy said it was just my time, whatever that meant). For another, I lost a bunch of weight. For a second another, Ryan Anderson did a whole lot more than just notice me.

How did all this happen?

Well, first of all, I quit wallowing in my own self-imposed island of grief—I mean just because Ryan and Ashley shared a few itty-bitty similarities, it didn't necessarily mean that they were meant for each other—and embraced my higher self. I took the "Journey of Transformation Through Manifestation," which basically had to do with visualizing and believing. I *saw* myself as the fantastically amazing, beautiful, and powerful Super Picasso. I *believed* I could paint the sky, rescue small children and pets from impending disaster, and rattle off the letters of a word with the speed and clarity of a master speller. I *saw* and *believed* I could make Ryan Anderson understand that *I*, not that goody-two-shoes Ashley Adams, was his destiny. I did all this by practicing three essential principles that, as it so happened, all started with the letter *P* (a sign?): patience, positivity, and perseverance.

My journey to Make Ryan Anderson Like Me began with a compliment here and there. I knew from watching Mama shower them on Daddy that boys like compliments, especially ones to do with their looks and masculinity. I told Ryan things like "I really like the color of your shirt," or "I can't believe how strong you are," or "I wish my hair were as thick and full as yours." Saying these sorts of things would help my cause in three ways. First, commenting on the color of his shirt would likely make him look at mine, and that would help him start to notice me. Second, saying he was strong would make him feel good about himself, and in turn make him feel good about being around me. Third, comparing his hair to mine in a self-deprecating manner would help him see me as modest and nice, traits he obviously liked in Ashley Adams, traits boys seemed to like in girls. Within one week of my syrupy flattery, Ryan Anderson not only called me by my given name, he didn't use a mean adjective in front of it—at spelling practice that is. During regular school hours, it was the pecking order as usual. He was with Ashley. Though no longer Plump Picasso, I was, after all, still Plain Picasso, so I had to do something else to upset our, by then, established dynamics. I had to create a situation where the kids in my class belittled and humiliated me to such an extent that Ryan, being the nice boy that he was, would have no choice but to stick up for me, thereby also bringing about another, even more important result. He would realize, at least on some level, that he cared for me. But in order to ensure my plan wouldn't backfire, leaving me even further down the rungs of the social ladder than I already was, I'd have to wait for the exact right set of circumstances.

It should come as no surprise that this took awhile. Luckily, by then I'd become an expert on patience, positivity, and perseverance. Before long it was Christmas holiday, then January, and soon February. Finally, I saw my opportunity: Valentine's Day. (Which, by the way, was also my birthday, and which, also by the way, wasn't necessarily a good day to have a birthday, since, at school at least, any special-day acknowledgment given by Mr. Dork was either forgotten or minimized by the fact that Valentine's Day was every girl's special day.)

I remembered from the previous year, and if I thought about it really hard, the year before that, that Ryan Anderson always brought Ashley Adams a heart-shaped box of chocolates for Valentine's Day. She gave him a homemade valentine, which always seemed to embarrass him. A similar type of exchange had always gone on between Mama and Daddy, and I knew, because Daddy told me, that although it was certainly sweet of Mama to give him whatever she usually did, what he really would have preferred were tickets to a Bobcats game (even though they played all the way over in Charlotte), a new golf club, or even a sleeve of golf balls, and not because those sorts of gifts were manly-type gifts but because it would mean that Mama had recognized his special likes. I was in a bind. I needed to give Ryan Anderson something that he wanted, and at the same time something that would progress my larger plan. I decided to ask Daddy for advice, because since he'd been one himself, Daddy was surely an expert on boys.

"How much cash do you have, Palomino (a horse with a golden or tan coat and a white or cream-colored mane and tail, thought to have been developed from Arabian stock)?" We were sitting on the screened-in porch in the back of our house trying out the new space heaters Daddy had installed.

"Six dollars and fifty-three cents," I said. I wasn't very good at saving my allowance, at least for very long. Our school had extra snacks you could buy, and I'd just spent a really big amount, the most I'd ever saved all at once, on the two-volume set of *The New Shorter Oxford English Dictionary,* a stellar addition to my dictionary collection.

"Hmm. That's a pretty tight budget. What sports does he like?"

"Sometimes he plays soccer."

"I don't know," Daddy said. "Playing soccer sometimes doesn't seem enough of a like to me. Is there anything else you can think of that he likes to do?"

"He likes to spell," I said.

Daddy thought for a while. "You like to spell too, don't you? Is there something you've been wanting that would help with your spelling?"

Spelling. Why hadn't I thought of that? I was awestruck. I mean I knew Daddy was smart since he always said he had a very high intelligence quotient, also called an IQ, but this time he was especially smart.

"There are these pocket-size electronic spelling games," I said. "Kind of like flash cards but more interactive."

"Sounds perfect," Daddy said.

I lowered my head.

"What's wrong, Paris (the capital and largest city of France, in the north-central part of the country on the Seine River)?"

"They cost more than I have."

"How much?"

"The one I was looking at is $16.99."

Daddy reached into his back pocket. He pulled two twenty-dollar bills out of his money clip. "How about I spot you?" he said. "Just don't tell your mama, okay?"

"Okay."

Later that day Daddy took me to Walmart, and I bought two Word Whizzes, one for Ryan and one for me.

The kids in my class always get to school early on Valentine's Day, and that Valentine's Day was no different. While Ryan was busy passing out his valentines, I put his gift on his seat. From my desk, I had a clear view of Ryan's. Probably because it was the only present, Ryan opened it first. He immediately looked my way and smiled.

Now, every year pretty much the same thing happens, and that year was no different. Jimmy Wilkes had taken a count of the number of valentines on each of our chairs, and also like every year, I had zero. He started laughing, calling me Pathetic Picasso, Porky Picasso (obviously he needed new glasses), and other embarrassing names.

Ryan Anderson stood, slammed his fist on his desk. "Stop it, Jimmy."

Then everything happened really fast. The whole class, including Mr. Dork, stopped what they were doing and stared. Jimmy Wilkes returned to his desk. Ryan walked in my direction, stopped in front of my desk, and handed me something: an envelope with my name written on it. Everyone, including Ashley Adams, watched me open it. And right then and there I think I was happier than I'd been in my entire life. Not only had Ryan Anderson stuck up for me, he'd gotten me a valentine, and on the back of it he'd written "Happy Birthday." *That* was a double bonus.

The Wives

We had been meeting for six months by the time the word *murder* crossed our lips. We were having lunch in Chapel Hill, a short distance from Jewels's home in Raleigh. By chance, Diana was attending a Junior League state chapter meeting in Research Triangle Park, and Bert was in town for a booksellers' convention. The restaurant, a chic, contemporary space with white tablecloths, wood floors, exposed brick walls, and sleek pendant lighting, was crowded. The University of North Carolina was hosting March Madness. We were enjoying a leisurely dessert and warm beverages, tea for Diana, coffee for Jewels, and hot cocoa for Bert, when Bert brought up a murder that had happened recently in Boone.

"Did you guys hear about it?"

"No," Diana said. "What happened?"

"It was all over the news," Bert said. "A woman killed her husband. Apparently he'd been abusing her for years. She got up, went about her morning routine, made his coffee, poured it in a cup, and doused it with arsenic."

"Arsenic?" Jewels said. "Wow, that's ancient. How old was she?"

"Eighty-two," Bert said.

"Seriously?" Jewels asked.

"Yep," Bert said. "When the paramedics showed up, she told

them she thought it must've been a heart attack. One minute he was eating his cereal, and the next his head was in the bowl. Later she admitted to poisoning him, said she hadn't planned it, that she'd snapped, that he'd lorded himself over her one time too many."

"Good for her," Jewels said.

"What happened to her?" Diana asked.

"Her lawyers are calling it self-defense," Bert said. "She's out on bail. Thing is she's got cancer and may not live long enough to make it to the trial."

"How sad," Diana said. "At least I guess it is. Must be hard to live with."

"Oh I don't think so," Jewels said. "The bastard had it coming to him. At least she bought herself a few months of happiness. Murder is inside all of us, you know."

"That's true," Bert said. "Psychologists say that all the time."

"How do you know what psychologists say?" Jewels asked.

"I read," Bert said.

Jewels rolled her eyes. "You don't read all the time. You just like people to believe you do. You want to sound smart. Lying about your accomplishments is a sign of insecurity, you know."

"I'm not insecure," Bert said. "And I do read all the time. You're just jealous."

"Why in God's name would I be jealous of you?"

"Because you might be street smart, but you're certainly not book smart. I have a PhD. What do you have, a high school diploma?"

"I'm an architect," Jewels said. "You know damn well that requires a college degree."

"Yeah, an undergraduate degree," Bert said. "And just because you can draw a few angles, it doesn't mean you're smart."

Diana covered her ears with her hands. "Stop it."

Two sets of eyes shot in her direction; Diana was never the least bit confrontational.

"You seem a little frazzled today, Diana," Jewels said. "Is something bothering you?"

Diana didn't respond right away. She fought back tears. "You were right, Jewels. What you said about Oliver having seen me at that martini bar before. He did."

"How do you know?" Jewels asked.

"We were just talking, reminiscing about how we met, and he said something about falling in love with me the first time he saw me sitting at that table. I almost corrected him, said I was sitting at the bar not a table when we met, but then—I don't know—I just didn't."

"Maybe he was confused," Bert said.

"That's what I thought at first," Diana said. "But then he mentioned something about some guy trying to pick us up, meaning my friend Lillian and me, and he described the guy. And it hit me: He *had* seen me before we met. Lillian and I *were* sitting at that corner table, only it was a few weeks earlier. Lillian even ended up going out with the guy. Lillian and I were talking about the guy while we were sitting at the bar that night, the night I met Oliver. In fact, that's what made me notice Oliver. He was sitting at that same corner table with some redhead."

When it came to love, although Jewels was the most romantic among us, Diana was the most trusting and thus the slowest to believe in Oliver's duplicity. While she hadn't shared it with us, she blamed herself, not Oliver, for his indiscretions. Perhaps she hadn't been attentive enough, she thought. After all, men will be men. Underneath all their bravado they were just little boys who needed nurturing, weren't they? She'd been distant of late, too involved in Junior League, too attuned to Picasso's needs. She was certain if she changed, started doing sweet things for him (he loved salted caramel ice cream and freshly pressed pillowcases), became more amorous, made herself attractive for him, wore that perfume he liked, told him more often how much she loved him, needed him, perhaps even whined—he always said he loved it when she whined, that he found it so feminine—then their relationship would change for the better. They'd get close again. He wouldn't need Jewels or Bert. They'd go on as if nothing had happened, as if his other lives had never existed. Of course she'd never mention she'd known about them; that wouldn't be wise. Oliver had to see himself as a good guy. He needed to believe in the story more than she did. And then there was his need for control; Oliver had to be the man, to feel invincible, beyond reproach. She couldn't do anything that would unsettle even one brick of their relationship, because then the entire structure might collapse.

But now, as Diana sat in a noisy, chic restaurant in Chapel Hill during the week of March Madness, at a table with a pure white tablecloth, and sipped her tea, tears stinging her eyes, rolling down her cheeks, she questioned everything she thought she ever knew. She saw empathy and understanding in the eyes of the two women she'd been secretly wishing away, emotions that came from knowledge and experience, and also sadness, like older sisters who knew they couldn't bear their younger sibling's pain. Diana would have to face the ugly truth on her own: She had married a man who not only didn't love her; he wasn't capable of love. She had married a man who didn't even love himself. She didn't love a man; she loved a mirror. And that was the harshest and most frightening realization of all, because denying Oliver was essentially denying her own reflection and the flesh and blood and heart and soul that comprised it, and if she did that, what was left? Who was she?

"It wouldn't be that hard, you know," Jewels said.

"What wouldn't be that hard?" Bert asked.

Jewels pulled a compact from her handbag, refreshed her lipstick, smacked her lips. "Murdering someone." She replaced the compact, made a point of looking at Bert. "We're *all* smart women. We could pull it off."

"Thank you for your confidence, Jewels," Bert said sarcastically.

Diana looked around to see if anyone was listening to our conversation, but nothing could possibly be heard over the loud, tinny hum of the crowd. "Jewels, what are you saying?" She wiped her eyes and cheeks with the cloth napkin.

"I'm saying, perhaps *we* shouldn't wait until we're eighty-two to be happy. I'm saying we should kill the bastard."

Diana and Bert stared at Jewels in disbelief.

"Are you serious?" Diana asked.

"Oh for God's sake," Jewels said and laughed. "Look at the two of you. Of course I'm kidding."

Diana let out a sigh of relief. "Oh, thank God."

"Enough of this," Jewels said. "What I want to know is where you got those boots, Diana. I'm thinking I should get the exact same pair."

The conversation shifted then to our latest passive-aggressive pastime: fucking with Oliver's head. Just the month before, Jewels and Bert had dyed and styled their hair to match Diana's, and the last several months we'd been charging up our credit cards with unnecessary, extravagant expenditures.

"Has Oliver said anything to either of you?" Jewels asked.

"Not me," Diana said. "He did mention my Visa being over the limit last month, but he didn't seem at all upset."

"How about you, Bert?"

"Nothing. Not that I spend as much as the two of you, but I've actually started buying our groceries at Whole Foods."

"Impressive," Jewels said. "And he hasn't noticed?"

"He did look at me a little strange the last time I used one of the recycle bags to clean out the litter boxes."

"You used a five-dollar recycle bag for dirty cat litter?" Jewels asked.

"It was only around three dollars I think, but yes," Bert said. "I thought that was the point. It isn't a pair of expensive boots, but it is honestly the best I can do. I'm trying."

"I think it's a great try, Bert," Diana said.

"And definitely a statement about Whole Paycheck," Jewels said.

"Whole Paycheck?" Bert asked.

"Never mind," Jewels said.

"What about your leather sofa, Jewels?" Diana asked.

"I got it recovered," Jewels said.

"You just bought it," Bert said.

"I told Oliver it wasn't quite the right shade of brown, that I wanted it to have a more grayish tone, as opposed to reddish. Here, I've got pictures on my phone. What do you think?"

"I can't tell the difference," Bert said.

"That's exactly what Oliver said." Jewels started laughing, and before long all three of us were.

But no matter how much petty satisfaction we got out of our little retaliation games, it didn't change the fact that we were the ones who were really fucked. We loved a man who didn't love us. We loved a man who couldn't love. We loved a man who was consciously lying to us, consciously hurting us, and yet we couldn't walk away, and though we may have had a fuzzy idea why, we didn't totally understand the depth of the power he held over us. It was as if he'd cast a spell on us.

Yes, Diana may have finally seen Oliver for what he was, but like the rest of us, she was far from over him. Her emotions would continue to fluctuate. She'd feel oozy, desirable, safe, grateful, even relieved. Relieved he hadn't left her. Relieved he still loved her. She'd feel weak, pitiful, cowardly, stupid, unattractive, utterly desolate. She'd feel loved. She'd feel betrayed. And one day soon, after she'd reached the heights of happiness and the depths of misery many times over, she'd buy a book on personality disorders, and as she read and read, and reread and reread, her heart would beat faster and faster, and her belly would gurgle, twist, then sour, the nausea increasing until she could no longer contain it, and she'd run to the bathroom, arrive just in time, and as she lay on the cold, hard tile floor she would admit to herself that Jewels had been right about everything. Oliver's stalking. Oliver's manipulative charm. Oliver's lies. Oliver's selfishness. Oliver's inability to love. Oliver's lack of empathy.

And finally, she'd stop fighting her knowing, and give herself over to truth and fate. The man she'd loved, the man she'd married, was a sociopath, and sociopaths were incurable.

Picasso

Two months after he gave me the Valentine's Day card, which was
one month after I'd seen the blue convertible in the church parking lot and three months before Daddy died, Ryan Anderson asked
if it was okay if he walked me home after spelling practice. It was
the first really nice day of the year. My initial thought was, *What
took him so long?* I'd been following my Make Ryan Anderson Like
Me plan like it was a religion. Then I got annoyed. The thing is, it
had been a really great spelling practice day. I didn't know four of
the words—nelipot, accubation, wanweird, and vigesimation—and
I couldn't wait to get home and look them up. I was in a pickle. If
I said no to Ryan's invitation, I might not get another one. If I said
yes, instead of using my walking time to mull over the four new
words in my head, I'd be sweetly, nicely, and sincerely listening to
Ryan's every word. To top it off, I figured we'd probably walk slower,
and when we finally did get to my house, it wouldn't be polite not
to offer him sweet tea, which meant we'd have to sit somewhere
and drink it, and we'd probably end up talking some, all of which
would delay my dictionary time even more. Then I had a profound
thought. Under the circumstances, saying yes to Ryan Anderson
meant I would be making a sacrifice, and making a sacrifice for a
boy would put me in a whole other girl category, practically an exclu-

sive club. I mean every girl knows that boys are high maintenance, but only girls with steady boyfriends, or husbands, like Mama, can talk or complain about boys to each other. I had this vision of myself passing notes back and forth with the All That Girls.

"I'd be delighted," I said—I'd heard Mama say that to people a lot when they asked her to do something, especially stuff she didn't want to do—and I stretched my lips into the biggest possible smile I could.

"Do you want to stop at Dairy Queen on the way?" he asked.

Drat. That would take even more time. Besides, I've never been big on runny ice cream. "Yes," I said, with a little squeal. "I *love* Dairy Queen."

Dairy Queen was filled with kids from school, including Ashley Adams, two of the All That Girls, Kelly Morgan and Gillian George, and Audu (short for Audubon) Kirkpatrick. Audu was the cutest boy in school behind Ryan, and he had the weirdest first name behind me. Apparently his mother was a big bird-watcher and a member of the Audubon Society. Their mission is to conserve and restore natural ecosystems focusing on birds, other wildlife, and their habitats for the benefit of humanity and the earth's biological diversity.

"You know Picasso, right?" Ryan asked Audu, after we got in line behind him. Audu's desk was right in front of mine at school.

"Yeah, sure," he said. "Hey, Picasso."

"Hey," I said back.

Then he and Ryan started talking about soccer.

I looked around to see if Jeannine Glick (everybody called her "Stick") was there. Jeannine was pretty much the only girl at school who ever talked to me, which should've made me happy but in all honesty didn't because Jeannine was even more unpopular than me, she had really poor hygiene, yet right then and there I would've said hey to her just so Ryan would see that even without him introducing me, people said hey to me too. Kelly Morgan and Gillian George were sitting at one of the picnic tables out front pretending they weren't talking about me because they knew better than to talk about anyone Ryan was with. Periodically, Ashley Adams, who was waiting in line right in front of Audu, glared in my direction.

"Hi, Ryan," she said, after she'd gotten her cone.

"Hey," Ryan said. "You know Picasso, right?" *Was he a broken record?*

Ashley didn't even acknowledge me. "Well, I need to get going. See you tomorrow?"

She walked off before Ryan could answer.

"Hey," Audu called after her. "Wait up. I'll walk with you." He turned to Ryan. "Later, dude."

"Yeah, later," Ryan said. He didn't seem the least bit upset that Audu was walking Ashley home.

"What do you want?" Ryan asked when we got up to the window.

"Vanilla," I said.

"Two vanilla cones," Ryan said to the girl taking orders.

"I'd rather have mine in a cup," I said to Ryan. I swear he looked at me like he couldn't believe we both liked our ice cream the exact same way.

"Make that two vanillas in cups," he said to the girl.

"What size?" the girl asked.

Like I couldn't hear or something, Ryan repeated the girl's question to me.

"Small," I said.

"Smalls," he said to the girl.

I reached into my backpack to get out my money.

"I'm paying," he said, which really surprised me.

"Hi, Ryan," Kelly said, as we passed by her picnic table. Gillian started giggling.

Ryan didn't respond, and that made me happy. All in all, the visit to Dairy Queen wasn't nearly as bad as I'd thought it might be.

Ryan and I were both done with our ice cream by the time we got to my house, so I asked him if he wanted something to drink.

"You got any Coke?" he asked.

I went and got us two Cokes and a bag of Cheetos.

"Where're your parents?" Ryan asked as we climbed the stairs to my room.

"My dad's on a business trip—he travels a lot—and Mama's at a Junior League meeting."

"My mom does Junior League too."

I knew that because Ryan's mom had been on the same committee as Mama a couple of years back, but I didn't say that because I didn't want Ryan to know I knew who his mother was. I figured he might think I'd been stalking him, which I had.

"Really?" I said.

"Wow," Ryan said when we walked into my room. "Where'd you get all the dictionary posters? They're cool." By *dictionary posters,* Ryan meant the blown-up word definitions that plastered my walls.

"My dad got them for me."

"Why are they all P words?"

"Because my name starts with P."

"Oh" was all he said.

Ryan looked around like he was trying to figure out where to sit, which I had to admit, to myself that is, was a conundrum. My room is pretty small; it's on the back corner of our house. The bed, dresser, bookshelves, and desk are pretty much crammed together on the three available walls; the closet is on the other one. There is an extra chair, in fact it's smack-dab in the middle of my room, mostly because there's nowhere else to put it, but it's always filled with dirty clothes and other stuff I can't seem to find the time to put away. Going to school and studying to be a master speller takes a lot of time and effort.

I shook off my shoes and sat on the bed. Ryan did the same thing.

We ended up talking for a long time, hours I think, all about cars and motorcycles, baseball and basketball and soccer, his bug collection, and this new video game called *Super Smash Bros. Brawl* that he was saving up for.

"I had a really good time," he said, when he was getting ready to leave.

"Me too," I said. And that was true.

I walked Ryan to the front door and watched him walk down the street; that's what a good hostess does. At the end of our street, he turned and waved. I waved back. When he was safely out of sight, I dashed back upstairs to my room, my socks slipping and sliding along the wood floors, and pulled my favorite dictionary out from its hiding place under my bed.

Maybe because I was in a state of total excitement—I mean I had officially *arrived*—I felt more like manifesting the next stage of my perfect relationship with Ryan Anderson than looking up words. But since working on my word journal had always helped me deal with stress or anxiousness, I figured I'd do that before indulging in my transformation through manifestation exercises. What was weird is that it seemed like three of the new words specifically related to my life at that very moment, and since that was the case I figured the fourth word had to be some sort of omen, and as it turned out, it was.

Nelipot: someone who walks without shoes. (That's what I had just done. I figured sock skiing counted.)

Accubation: the practice of eating and drinking while lying down. (That was what I was doing right then and there. Finishing up my Coke and Cheetos.)

Wanweird: unhappy fate. (That was what I was worried might happen between Ryan and me if I didn't continue to practice manifestation.)

Vigesimation: the act of putting to death every twentieth man.

The Wives

The next time we met, the word *murder* came up again. We'd planned to meet at Rainy Cove Park but it was closed due to mudslides caused by heavy rain, so we opted for Diana's house instead. We were sitting at Diana's dining-room table when the split pea soup she was cooking boiled over.

"I'll get it," Bert said. She hurried to the stove. "Ouch. Damn."

"Are you okay?" Diana and Jewels asked in unison.

"Of course I'm not okay," Bert said, while shaking her hand in the air. "I burned my fucking palm on the pot handle. What do you think? I just like to scream?" She turned on the faucet.

"Butter works better than cold water." Diana opened the refrigerator. "Shoot, I'm out."

"How about olive oil?" Jewels asked.

"Do you want my skin to bubble up?" Bert asked.

"Oh, stop being so dramatic," Jewels said. "For God's sake, just blow on it."

"You can be such a bitch, Jewels."

"Me, a bitch? Well at least I'm not a cheap bitch."

"What does that mean?" Bert asked.

"Stop it, Jewels," Diana said.

"It's true," Jewels said. "She never pays her portion of the bill."

"Yes, I do."

"You don't. There's tax and tip too, you know."

"That's enough," Diana said. "There's no need to take our frustrations out on one another."

"I'm not frustrated," Jewels said.

"Well I certainly am," Diana said. "What are we doing? Here we are, seven months later, and what have we accomplished? Other than a lot of complaining and spending, we're no better off than we were that day we first met at Rainy Cove Park. I thought the point of all this, the point of *us,* was to help one another."

"You guys have helped me," Bert said.

"You know what I mean," Diana said. "We're all still married to him."

"Diana's right," Jewels said. "We're nothing more than a bunch of whimpering wives."

"Worse," Bert said. "Two of us aren't legally wives. We're mistresses."

Bert's comment sobered us. We gathered in the kitchen, ladled the soup into our bowls, and ate, only the clanking of our spoons betraying our presence. During this internal interlude, we reflected on the unlikelihood of our bond.

There was lovely and sensuous Diana. She was one of those "beauty inside and out" types of women that you wanted to hate, or expose as fakes, but Diana was anything but a fake. She was kind, generous, and talented. She'd majored in fine art in college, was quite a successful local painter for a time, but gave it up when Picasso was born. Diana's father came from old Southern tobacco money. Her mother was a homemaker and, like her daughter later became, a tireless volunteer. Upon her parents' death, Diana received a large inheritance. She said that Oliver wasn't aware of her financial circumstances, but we weren't convinced. Oliver knew everything.

Jewels came from a stable, upper-middle-class background. Her father was a Wall Street stockbroker; her mother had danced for the New York City Ballet until a bad fall damaged her ankle. Jewels's architectural career began in New York, but after her affair with one of the firm's partners erupted, he suggested she either look for a new job or transfer to the Raleigh office. Attractive, but not necessarily pretty, it was Jewels's athletic physique, seeming confidence, and disarming charm that caught men's attention, but something else entirely snared them. While she strove to portray herself as disciplined and dispassionate, there was a heat forever bubbling just beneath the surface of her skin which few could escape.

Bert was opinionated, outspoken, suspicious of anyone or anything new or unknown, and in general a pain in the ass. Her father was Catholic and a fisherman, her mother Lutheran and a schoolteacher. Bert's most admirable quality was her passion for human justness and fairness. Whether she was saving whales or marching for gay rights, Bert was relentless and unwavering in her pursuit of righting wrongs. And there was something else, something somewhat frightening but at the same time intriguing about Bert. She dabbled in the occult and, although she continuously denied it, had a sixth sense. There were times we were certain she could read our minds.

Yet even with all our differences, in that place, at that time, our souls were on the same path.

Diana gathered our soup bowls, rinsed them in the sink, put them in the dishwasher, returned to the table.

"We could build an empire," Bert said.

"What?" Jewels asked.

"Our differences," Bert said. "Together we're unbeatable. After we kill Oliver, we should start a business." She paused. "Well, don't look so surprised. I know we're all thinking the same thing. Besides, it's easier to sever yourself from a dead person."

"Bert's right," Jewels said. "As long as Oliver's alive, we're doomed."

And there it was: Oliver's fate. Ineluctable.

None of us said anything for a while. Words seemed meaning-less. The future had inserted itself into our present. As if we'd just bought a new, massive piece of furniture, we'd have to shuffle things around to make room for it.

Picasso

My first important spelling competition was a big success except for two things: Ryan couldn't go because he hurt his ankle playing soccer, which meant that Ashley Adams went in his place, and Daddy didn't show even though he promised he would. Daddy had never been too good at follow-through, so I knew I should be pretty used to it by then, after all he was really important and busy and he was just who he was and he didn't mean anything by it. He had criminals to defend. I should understand that his only daughter taking first place at some regional, not even state, spelling bee just wasn't that big a deal in comparison. Besides, he called later that night to apologize and said "I love you more than life itself," which was true, that he'd "make it up" to me, which meant he would buy me something, that he was "proud" of me, which made sense since I was the reigning regional spelling champion, that obviously there would be "other spelling bees" that he "wouldn't miss," that since I was his "smart and wise Picasso" he knew I wasn't like other kids who got all "upset about little things," I could "see the big picture," and that he was confident I would "take it all in stride, Phasm (an extraordinary appearance, especially of brilliant light in the air; a phantom, an apparition)." And he was right, I would because what else could I do, and also because if a person were all those things that Daddy had said, smart and wise and didn't get upset and saw the big picture and was able to take things in stride, then that someone would be above such petty emotions as sadness, resentment, and self-ishness. In short, that person would be perfect, like an angel or something, or really, really, really "nice" like I used to think Ashley Adams was, which she obviously wasn't because she didn't even congratulate me when I won.

But the thing is, even though I knew I shouldn't be sad, all I wanted to do was cry, and the harder I tried not to, the more my chest hurt and the more I wished I could just run up to my room, lock my door, lie on my bed, and look up words.

Daddy and I talked for a pretty long time, Daddy mostly because I was afraid my voice would shake, about how hard everything was for him at work and how some other lawyer he worked with had tried to sabotage him, and I tried really hard to listen and understand because isn't that what a smart and wise and see-the-big-picture person would do? After a while, I was able to tell him I couldn't believe someone would do that to him, being that everyone knew how caring and generous he was. I think that made him feel a little better, but I could tell he was still upset, and by the time we said goodbye I felt more sorry for him than for me. And even if secretly I were still sad, which I wasn't, after what happened the next day, I totally forgot about the stupid spelling bee.

I had started listening in on Mama's phone calls the day after I saw Jewels and Bert in the blue convertible. If Mama answered it downstairs, I'd run upstairs. If Mama answered it upstairs, I'd scurry downstairs. There was an art to picking up the phone so Mama, and whoever was on the other end of the line, wouldn't hear the click of the lifted receiver, an art that I mastered. Mostly what I'd heard to that point were conversations between Mama and Junior League ladies or Mama and Daddy, but that day I hit pay dirt.

"Did you get the house?" Jewels was asking when I picked up the receiver.

"Yes," Mama said. "Luckily they had a cancellation, but it's not until July, the week of the fourth. I'm not sure how I'm going to explain the departure from our usual time to Oliver. I already mentioned I wanted to go somewhere different this year. Do you think he'll get suspicious?"

"Oliver?" Jewels said. "No way. He's too self-centered to get suspicious."

"Hopefully it won't be too crowded," Mama said.

"It's 20 Beach Drive, right?" Jewels asked.

"Yes," Mama said. "I specifically asked for it by address."

"No worries," Jewels said. "Place was desolate when I went there with Jonathan a few years ago. From the pictures, it doesn't look like it's changed much. Believe me, it's perfect for our plan."

Plan?

"What about Oliver's gun?" Mama asked. "What if he doesn't bring it?"

Gun?

"He'll bring it," Jewels said. "He brings that damn thing everywhere. He's paranoid as shit. Geez, I haven't shot a gun in years. Maybe I should go to the shooting range."

"I don't think that's a good idea," Mama said. "Someone might remember you."

"Good point," Jewels said. "It's probably like riding a bike anyway. My dad used to take me shooting all the time."

"Do you ever wonder whether we're doing the right thing?" Mama asked. "I mean obviously it's not the *right* thing. Murder isn't right. I mean do you wonder whether we should go through with it?"

Murder?

"No," Jewels said. "I don't. And you shouldn't either. We've decided to kill Oliver, and that's what we're going to do."

Kill Daddy?

I must have been in shock because I couldn't think right away, at least about anything that made any sense at all, but then I got scared and a bunch of thoughts ran through my mind. *Why,* for instance. Not only why would they want to kill Daddy but also why would they think they'd get away with it? They were obviously obtuse. I mean, Mama didn't tell me about Daddy having other wives and I figured it out. Any police officer with half a brain would too, and once they did, it wouldn't be long before they figured out who killed him. The police weren't dimwits, and Mama, Jewels, and Bert weren't career criminals. Not to mention that the three of them had kids, and with Daddy dead, what would happen to us if they got caught? I remember hoping that Mama and Jewels were just joking or bored. Maybe the whole conversation was a new type of woe-are-we story they were telling themselves or acting out, like how the All That Girls were always spinning these elaborate dramas where they liked some people some days and other people other days, and the days they didn't like certain people (like me), they made up a bunch of stuff about those people that wasn't true just to make the stories they created more dramatic. In other words, obviously they were bored.

I must've missed part of the conversation while I was thinking all these things, because I heard Mama asking Jewels something about a phone number.

"So it read out?" Jewels asked. "Damn. The package said it was untraceable."

"That doesn't mean the number won't pop up," Mama said. "And besides, if it gets to that point, the police checking the numbers on our phone bills I mean, we can just say Oliver must have made those calls."

"You're right," Jewels said. "There's no need to worry, but I suggest we stick to meeting in person as much as possible over the next few months. And I think we should get together more often.

There are a lot of details to iron out; we can figure all that out when we get together on April sixteenth."

"The *Farmer's Almanac* says it's going to be a beautiful day," Mama said.

"Thank God," Jewels said. "Those mudslides were crazy. Let's plan on meeting at Rainy Cove Park an hour early."

Rainy Cove Park?

"Sounds good," Mama said. "Do you want me to call Bert?"

"No, that's okay," Jewels said. "I will. See you at eleven."

Before they even hung up the phone, I was back in my room nursing a panic attack and frantically looking up vigesimation again. I was right; it had been a sign. There it was in plain print: "the act of putting to death," that part made sense, "every twentieth man," which was confusing, unless maybe men got killed in some universal pattern of twenty. But then I remembered that the address of the house Mama was renting was 20 Beach Drive.

Now a good sleuth only has to hear the time and location of one designated meeting to follow the bread crumbs to each of the others. For the next two months, my spying took me to Rainy Cove Park (code: RCP). During that time, I learned a lot, and not just about murder. I learned to forge Mama's signature, and smile sweetly when I gave *Mama's* notes to the school secretary. "I'm so sorry about your toothache (or your stomachache, or your dog, or your mother's car), Picasso," Mrs. Dumpling (her real name was Rumpling) would say. Or, "Remember I won't be over this Wednesday, Mrs. Jesswein (she was Mama's backup babysitter) because I have that spelling practice (or birthday party, or cheerleading tryout, or fort-building engagement, or rocket trip to Mars)." It really didn't matter what I said since Mrs. Jesswein didn't hear too well, and I swear she was forever just north of tipsy from all that port-wine sipping she did, which, by the way, she often shared with me since port was so good for my heart, or my circulation, or my hair and nails. With no other way to get to RCP, I had to take the bus. I was a little nervous since I'd never been on a city bus, but I learned that the drivers were nice to kids as long as the kids were nice back. Most of them let me sit on the seats designated for old or handicapped people right in the front of the bus, so I had a really good view out the window. Over time, I learned several routes. The only problem was that it cost money to ride the bus, so I also learned how to steal. I knew stealing was bad, but it was just a few dollars here and there from Daddy's wallet or Mama's stash drawer, and it was for a good cause: the Stop Mama from Killing Daddy cause.

I also learned a lot about lying. I was surprised how many different ways there were to lie, such as words, actions, non-actions, body language, and pretending you didn't hear or see something when you did. I learned that people lie for many different reasons, like they don't want to get in trouble, they don't want to get in an argument, and they can't admit they're weak or wrong or even right. Most of all, I learned that lies can be as sticky as spiderwebs, and once you got tangled in one, there was pretty much no way out. That was reason enough not to tell any, but what choice did I have?

When Daddy wasn't home, I started dropping Mama hints that I hoped would upset her. I checked out mystery and detective novels from the library and passed them off to her. I told her how I'd been watching *CSI* and other crime shows and how the murderers always got caught, no matter what they did to cover their tracks. I told her I learned in school that DNA, ballistics, fingerprinting, and phone-tracing technologies were advancing every second. I threw out specifics, like the number of crimes solved per year, the number of convicted murderers that were given the death penalty in North Carolina (forty since 1976), the unhealthy food they served in jail, and the number of manicures, pedicures, and massages prisoners had gotten since the beginning of time (zero). I told her that when a man was murdered, his wife was almost always the prime suspect. I did everything but come right out and tell her I knew what the three of them were planning. But as usual, Mama wasn't interested in what I had to say. Sometimes she'd nod or say "That's nice, Picasso," but mostly she'd just stare off into space.

The last time the three of them met at RCP, I got there real early because I didn't want to miss even one thing they said. At that time, I was still certain I could figure out a way to stop them. I wore a T-shirt, shorts, and sneakers, and stuffed my hoodie and an umbrella into my backpack just in case. I crouched out of sight in the same place I always did, behind a fallen tree with a trunk so big I easily could've crawled inside it. I mean there was even a hole where a knot must've broken off that I could've watched from, but like Daddy I've never been big on confined spaces.

Mama showed up first with her picnic basket and blanket. Jewels came next. On top of her regular brown paper bag with wine in it, she carried what looked like a folded-up cardboard house with a black handle. When she turned just right, I saw that it was a Barbie Dream House. I remember wondering what a grown woman was doing with a Barbie Dream House. Not that I've ever been much of a Barbie person, or dolls in general for that matter, but the three that Mama did get me—Barbie, Ken, and Skipper (she said she got them because they were "just like our family")—I'd packed up and donated to Goodwill, along with their clothes, shoes, cases, car, and house, when I was, like, eight. Or maybe nine. The point is, Jewels was old, way too old to be schlepping a Barbie Dream House. Bert was last. She was carrying the same tote bag she always did; it looked like it was made out of a rug. It was strange the way they did everything—came, went, talked—in the same exact order. First Mama, then Jewels, then Bert, the order Daddy had married them in, the order of their looks and ages and heights, Mama prettiest and oldest and tallest on down, the order of their importance in Daddy's internal pecking system, like he was one of those Mormon husbands or the huffing and puffing big bad wolf. I'd heard Jewels call it the Order of the Wives, which I thought was some sort of club at first, but later I figured out it had a double meaning.

It was a real nice day. Birds were singing. The sun made the lake look like a mirror. I thought I smelled barbecue in the distance, but then I thought it might just be my imagination. Since I'd left so early, I didn't have time for breakfast. I repositioned myself without thinking; a twig cracked. I immediately crouched, as if that would do any good, but when I finally peeked over my shoulder, I saw that they hadn't heard me. They started taking off their clothes. I closed my eyes like I always did. I mean, Mama was one thing, and Jewels was thin so probably looked fine without clothes, but the last thing I wanted to see was a naked Bert. By the time I opened my eyes again, the three of them were swimming. As usual, they stayed in the water a really long time. When they started walking back, I looked away until I was sure they'd wrapped themselves in the pink towels. They always took a nap after they swam, which I thought was stupid for two reasons: one, because it just was; and two, because there wasn't much for me to do while they were sleeping. Sometimes I worked on my word journal, but that day I'd left so fast I'd forgotten it, so I decided to take a nap too. When I woke, they were dressed. Mama was popping open little potato chip bags, Jewels was setting up the Barbie Dream House, and Bert was uncorking the wine.

"To us," they said in unison, as they clinked their wineglasses together.

They sipped.

"Okay," Jewels said. "Let's get started."

Mama and Bert reached into their handbags and pulled out little notebooks.

"No notes," Jewels said. "It's too dangerous. Today we practice remembering."

"I was just going to jot down a few key words to help me remember," Bert said. "I promise I'll burn it before—well, you know."

"No," Jewels said, firmly. "No notes."

Bert stuck the notebook back in her tote bag. Mama set hers on the blanket.

"Pretend this is the beach house," Jewels said, while pointing inside the Barbie Dream House. I saw that the inside didn't look like a Barbie Dream House at all. Jewels had covered the walls with drawings of a different house. "Oliver will be standing here. Near the fireplace."

"How do you know that?" Bert asked.

"Because he'll be watching Diana swim from the sliding glass doors, right Diana?"

"But how do you *know* he'll be watching Diana swim?" Bert asked.

"Diana?"

"He always watches me swim when we're at the beach," Mama said.

"But you need to make sure, just in case," Jewels said. "You need to seduce him, okay?"

Mama blushed. "Okay."

"Let's go over the timeline," Jewels said. "Diana, what time do you go for your morning swim?"

"Six," Mama said.

"And you don't return to the beach house until when?"

"Seven thirty."

"Are you sure you'll know what time it is?"

"Yes," Mama said. "I've been doing the same routine for years."

"Good," Jewels said. She looked at Bert. "Now this is where you come in. Tell me what happens next, Bert."

"I jog to the beach house, retrieve the gun, and shoot Oliver," Bert said. She looked proud of herself.

"Before then," Jewels said.

"Before then?" Bert asked. "You said to tell you what happens next."

Jewels rolled her eyes. "Okay, not what happens next. Tell me everything you are going to do that morning."

Bert gulped down the rest of her wine, refilled her glass, and held the bottle toward Mama and Jewels. Both shook their heads.

"I'm supposed to rent a car the night before—"

"No," Jewels interrupted. "You're not supposed to rent a car, remember? We decided they could track that. It's the Fourth of July. Cars will be coming and going; no one will pay that much attention. As long as you park far enough away, you should be fine. Oh, and remember you need to go to that restaurant in Blowing Rock the day before, and try to be memorable. It's doubtful that anyone will remember the exact day they saw you there. Just make sure you pay in cash. Got it?"

"I know that, Jewels," Bert said. "I'm not stupid. Why do you always do that?"

"Do what?" Jewels asked.

"Act like you're better than me," Bert said.

"I'm just trying to make sure we all remember what we are supposed to do," Jewels said. "That's all. It's not always about you, Bert. Don't take everything so personally."

"How can I not take it personally?"

"Fine," Jewels said. "I'm sorry if I hurt your feelings. Now, go on."

"I drive to Cooper's Island, park *my car,* and jog to the beach house."

"Did you do a trial run?" Jewels asked.

"Yes," Bert said. "Last week."

"So you know how long it will take? I imagine you're not a very fast runner."

"Dammit, Jewels," Bert said. "Of course I know."

"Okay then," Jewels said. "Good. And what about the gun?"

"Gun?" Bert asked. "You mean I'm supposed to shoot him, not stab him?"

Mama gave Bert the look I'd seen a million times. The stop-it-I-mean-it look.

"Real funny, Bert," Jewels said. "What I meant was, did you find a good place to hide the gun?"

"There's a little blue door around back," Bert said. "It leads to the crawl space under the house. Immediately to your left, there's a shelf with paint cans and such on it. I figure that's safer than hiding it somewhere outside."

"It wasn't locked?" Jewels asked.

"No. It doesn't have a lock. It's just a door."

"And what do you do with the gun after you—uh—shoot him, Bert?" Jewels asked.

"I wipe it down, put it in the garbage bag and then the fanny pack, take it with me, and once I get on the ferry, throw it in the ocean, when I'm sure no one is looking of course. Then I drive to Wildacres."

Jewels held out her glass for more wine. "Bert, I want you to know how much I appreciate you doing this for us."

By *this* Jewels obviously meant *kill Daddy*.

It felt like my heart dropped to my belly button. A vision of my future flashed before me. The police would arrest Mama. I'd be shipped off to God knows where, some foster home somewhere. I *had* to stop them. But how?

"I had no idea my boss was planning to have a hysterectomy," Jewels continued as Bert refilled her wineglass. "And that she'd tell me to go to this silly charrette in her place. Are you sure you're okay with it, Bert? I wish we could change the date, but every-thing's set. Diana rented the beach house months ago."

"I'm fine with it, Jewels," Bert said. "Don't worry. I've got it."

"Well, thank you, Bert," Jewels said. "And remember, we all are doing this thing, not just you, Bert." She paused. "Okay, let's go through it one more time from the beginning, this time ensuring we've covered every single, small detail. Diana?"

My stomach was churning. I felt faint and nauseous. I managed to get up and walk away. I didn't get very far before I vomited, but it was far enough that I didn't think they could hear or see me. By the time I got back, they were toasting again. I'd missed the "details" part, but at that point what did it matter? The future was set to fall like dominoes. I kept hoping it was all a bad dream, that something would go wrong and Bert wouldn't kill Daddy. Maybe she would run out of gas, or get in an accident and go to the hospital. Or die. I actually started wishing that Bert would die, or that Jewels's airplane would crash. Surely if one of the two of them were fatally injured, Mama would snap out of her alien-inhabited trance.

I heard Jewels talking again in her serious, bossy tone.

"We can't communicate after it's done," she was saying. "Murder investigations can take a while. We *cannot* in any way indicate that we know one another. They *will* find out about us. That's why Bert and I have to come forward first. It will look suspicious if we don't report Oliver missing. When they tell us about one another, we act the scorned but devastated wives. We say we loved our husband. We had no idea who he really was. We just act dumb. Any questions?"

That should be easy. They were being dumb.

"What about our hair?" Bert asked.

"What about it?" Jewels asked.

"Should we dye it back, change our styles? I mean, won't our looking so alike cause suspicion?"

"I think it'll look more suspicious if we dye it back now, so close to the murder," Jewels said. "And I'm thinking it might work in our favor."

"I don't understand," Bert said.

"Don't you see?" Jewels said. "It's brilliant, actually. The police will think we'd never be stupid enough to dye our hair the exact same color if we were planning to kill our husband. Besides, it'll fuck with their heads."

Mama and Bert nodded like they were those bobbing-head dolls weird people put on the dash of their cars.

"Diana," Jewels continued, "it will be hardest on you. They *will* suspect you. They *will* interrogate you, but it *will* be okay. I promise. You just need to stick to the story, got it? And put on your charm."

It would be okay? Were they mental?

"Got it," Mama said. She actually sounded scared, which was good. Maybe she'd chicken out.

"There won't be any evidence, Diana," Jewels said. "You won't have pulled the trigger."

Mama started crying. Then Bert did too; she pulled a white candle from her tote bag. I'd never seen her bring a candle before. She lit it and started chanting something. A hymn? Prayer? The three of them held hands, and Mama and Jewels started chanting too. I was stunned. They really *had* gone crazy. I mean, who does that? Certainly not the Mama I knew. The one time I did a séance with Betsy Porter, this older girl who used to live down the street, I thought Mama's head was going to pop off she got so mad. She even called Betsy's mom.

They stopped.

"Remember," Jewels said. "We'll meet right here, exactly one year from the day Oliver takes his last breath, same time, same spot."

"Noon, July third," Bert said with a nod.

"Noon, July third," Mama said.

Then they packed up their stuff and walked off, each in a different direction like they were shoots of a firework.

I waited for a while. I thought and thought, and thought more. Then I prayed (inside myself)—which I usually only did when I was sick or wanted something—for God to give me a sign. I must have sat there like that for a long time, but it seemed like only minutes. At some point I felt raindrops, and then the sun was setting. The sky had turned pale pink. Tomorrow would be a sailors' delight day for some, but not for me. My life as I knew it was about to change. I noticed that the woods were eerily quiet. The birds weren't singing. There was no buzz of people in the distance. No splash of boats on the water. No smell of barbecue. It was like the whole world had died.

I rose, shivered, brushed the twigs and dirt from the seat of my shorts, stretched my damp, scrunched-up T-shirt back over my hips, zipped up my hoodie (I had no idea when I'd put it on), re-did my ponytail, and walked to the bus stop, thinking all the while that unless I did something, one week from that day Daddy would be dead.

The Wives

We felt the emptiness the moment we walked away from our private clearing. It would be the last time the three of us saw one another for one long year. It rained on the way home. In our separate vehicles, we found ourselves lost inside the sound of the windshield wipers. Swish, swoosh, swish, swoosh. None of us remembered watching the road or even driving. We were consumed with thoughts of what was to come. We felt the inevitability of it; we'd committed and there was no going back. Somewhere along the way, time had begun running the show. Choice had been stripped from us, like patches from a soldier's jacket.

This was the way the murder was *supposed* to go.

Sometime between when they arrived at the beach house and the murder, Diana was to hide Oliver's gun behind the little blue door that led to the crawl space under the house. While seducing Oliver the second night would be a plus, she was definitely to do so the last night. That way she would ensure her scent and his lust blinded him. At exactly five o'clock the night before the murder, she was to call Jewels and verify we were still on. In the meantime, Bert was to wear a wig and a baseball hat just in case, stick a bag of rocks in her trunk, drive to Cooper's Island in the early-morning hours, park somewhere far enough away to avoid suspicion, jog to the beach house, retrieve the gun from its hiding place in the crawl space, put on her gloves, drape herself in the garbage bag she'd brought along in her fanny pack, and kill Oliver. When she was certain he was dead, she was to turn the garbage bag inside out, wrap it around the gun, put the gun, gloves, and rocks in the fanny pack, jog back to the car, dispose of the fanny pack when she was on the ferry, and then drive to her writing retreat. Diana was to return from her swim and, finding Oliver dead, call 911.

Yes, that was the way the murder was *supposed* to go.

We had discussed all the things that could go wrong over and over again. What if Oliver didn't get out of bed to watch Diana swim? What if someone saw Bert hanging around the house? Picasso was *not* an early riser, especially at the beach. Diana always woke her after she got back from her morning swim, but what if she got up uncharacteristically early? What if our research wasn't accurate, and the blood spray wasn't within the calculated distance? The garbage bag was a precaution, but what if blood did get on it or Bert and was transferred onto the steering wheel, seat, trunk? What if someone saw Bert throw the fanny pack into the ocean?

"None of this is going to happen," Jewels said more than once. "Everything is going to go smoothly as long as we *stick to the plan.*"

But, as we were to learn, no matter how detailed, how considered, how seemingly impregnable our plan had been, life has a way of making its own plans.

Picasso

Mama spent most of the next day asleep in her room. I spent most of the day looking up words and working up my nerve. I'd pretty much run the gamut on passive-aggressive approaches to the situation and none of it had even close to worked. My only hope at that point was to confront her.

At around four o'clock in the afternoon, I heard Mama get up and shuffle down the stairs. Then I heard her rooting around in the kitchen. I took a deep breath, closed my wordbook, opened the door to my room, walked into the hallway, down the stairs, through the living and dining rooms, sat at the counter, and stared at her. She was standing on the other side browsing through her catchall book, which pretty much holds Mama's entire life, like, for instance, her to-do lists, recipes, and all sorts of clippings. I sat there for at least five minutes before she realized I was there. When she finally looked up, she jumped with surprise.

"Picasso," she said. "You scared me."

"Sorry," I said.

She started taking vegetables out of the refrigerator.

"What're you making?" I asked.

"Paella and a summer salad," she said.

"Is Daddy coming home?" Daddy loved paella.

"Daddy always comes home on Thursdays. You know that."

I did know that, but how else was I going to ease into the Kill Daddy conversation. I watched her chop and prepare; watching Mama's hands while she cooks is one of my favorite things in the world to do—behind spelling and word journaling.

After a while, not knowing what else to do, since Mama was in her "zone" and I still hadn't come up with a plan to approach Kill Daddy, I stood on the rung of my stool, reached over the counter, grabbed the catchall book, opened it, and as if the inside spine had recently been smashed down, it settled on a page in the R section. And there it was. Mama must have scribbled the first part of the note when she was talking to Jewels that day, "noon, July 3rd, Rainy Cove Park, same spot," but the last part had obviously been added later because it was written in a different color pen, "one year." Even though I was still nervous about bringing up Kill Daddy, I decided my turning to that very page in the catchall book had to be a sign, and since bad things can happen if you ignore signs, because signs are messages to keep you on your right path in life, I knew I had to say something. But what? Wording was extremely important. What could I say that might trick Mama into talking? And then it came to me.

"We'll be at the beach on July third."

Either Mama hadn't heard me, which could easily have been the case since that happens a lot when she's lost in thought, and especially had been happening a lot around then, or she was ignoring me, which also could easily be the case. So I said it again, louder.

Mama looked up from her vegetable chopping, put down the knife, and wiped her hands on her pj bottoms. "What do you mean?" She attempted a look of confusion.

I turned the book toward her and pointed. "This note says you're meeting someone at Rainy Cove Park on July third, but you'll be at the beach with Daddy and me on July third."

"Not this July third," Mama said. "Next July third. A year from—"

She must've realized what she said, because she didn't finish her sentence. She bit her lip and looked at me with a combination of guilt, the kind of guilt that happens when you get caught doing something you shouldn't, and fear. It seemed like forever that the two of us stared at each other, it was like we were having a conversation without really having one, and then her eyes got watery and she looked away, and what I really wanted to do was hug her and tell her everything would be okay, but I knew I couldn't do that because it wouldn't be okay if the three of them went through with their plan. And so I think I said something about overhearing her on the phone or being clairvoyant—I can't remember what exactly—but I do remember saying in a practically begging manner, "Please Mama, don't kill Daddy. I don't want you to go to jail."

Just then, on the tail of the word *jail,* Daddy walked in the front door.

And here's the thing. Right then and there, I felt this overwhelming need to get out of there, because even if Daddy hadn't heard what I said, he could surely see that Mama had been crying, and I had no idea what might happen next, but I was pretty sure something would. So this is what I did. I quickly turned down the corner of the page so I could find it again later, which as it turned out wasn't too smart, put the catchall book back on the counter, all but ran up the stairs and into my room, shut and locked the door, found the messiest and therefore most obscure corner of my room, made myself as small as I possibly could, and prayed. Yes, prayed. Me. Picasso Lane. I prayed for God to deliver me from the evil that was about to come, the evil I couldn't stop. And I prayed for God to save Mama from his wrath, and me from his disappointment.

The Wives

Stick to the plan.

Jewels's words rang in Diana's ears as she, Oliver, and Picasso drove to the beach house, and as she swam the following day. She had every intention of doing so.

Until she heard Bert's voice message.

For weeks, Diana relived those final twenty-four hours in her mind. She remembers Oliver rubbing her neck and shoulders because they were sore from her swim. They sat on the sofa. The sliding glass doors were open, the sounds and smells of the ocean trailing inside. He'd lit candles.

"I brought some oil," he said. "Why don't you take off your shirt?"

It had been an hour since Picasso went to bed. Diana didn't necessarily expect that the massage would lead to sex. Oliver would wait for a sign from her; he was respectful. Yes, sex had been part of the plan, but she didn't intend to follow that part. She knew Oliver would watch her swim regardless.

Oliver pulled Diana's shirt over her head, carefully folded it, placed it aside. "Lie down," he said.

She rolled onto her stomach, pressed into him. It was a position they'd adopted many times before, a comfortable *couple* position. It came as natural as meeting his open hand with hers when they walked down a sidewalk, or moving with his step when he guided the small of her back to a restaurant table. She closed her eyes, heard him opening the bottle of oil. His wet palm rested on the nape of her neck for a moment, then squeezed her skin, moved toward one shoulder, squeezed again, and so on. She dozed off.

They were entwined when she woke, his cheek against hers. Their lips found each other's. The kiss was soft, sweet. He ran his fingers through her hair, searched her eyes. Tears fell from his, and then he sobbed.

She embraced him, rocked him while he cried into her chest, until he calmed.

"I love you," he said. "I'm so sorry."

"For what?" she asked.

Oliver told her *his* story, and though she didn't tell him this, it was a story Diana already knew. How he met Jewels and then Bert. The events that unfolded, the actions that led to the current situation. Two other wives. Two other lives. Wives and children he loved but knew he couldn't keep because it wasn't fair to anyone. He didn't make excuses or ask for Diana's forgiveness. He merely stated he didn't want to do it anymore. He only wanted her, Diana, and their daughter. He understood if she didn't want him any-more. Regardless, he planned to come clean with Jewels and Bert. Regardless, he planned to sever those relationships.

A tear fell from his eye, hit Diana's cheek, then another, and another. He wiped them away with his thumbs, kissed her, and she kissed him back, hard.

A woman knew the difference between making love and hav-ing sex. When making love, she entered an alternate state of con-sciousness. The place she went was wet, slippery, mystical, warm. It was a place Diana had only gone with Oliver, the man she loved. It was a place where the two of them shared the same skin, the same heart, where their feet and hands intertwined, bodies merged, a place that felt as safe as she imagined her mother's womb had. Where life and death ceased to exist.

Euphoria came later, after Diana walked on her own again, and although they had physically separated, the taste, smell, and feel of the man she loved still clung to her. And he, the object of her love, became the sole reason, sole purpose, for her existence.

The next morning, as planned, Diana went for her swim. As she paddled her way toward shore, she saw Oliver and Picasso building their sand castle. There was nothing more beautiful, more right, in the world. Oliver smiled as she walked toward them. The smile she loved. He reached for her hand, followed her into the house. They took off their swimsuits as soon as they got inside, kissed and touched their way to the bedroom, and while Picasso studiously worked on her sand castle, they made love again. Afterward, they cuddled; Oliver wiped a tear from his wife's eye. Took her into his arms. Held her.

"Why are you crying?" Oliver asked.

"I'm happy."

"Me too," he said as he wiped a tear from her cheek. "I'm going to take a shower. I won't be long."

When she heard the sound of the water, Diana walked out to the living room to gather their suits. There, sitting next to Oliver's swim trunks, was his phone. She picked it up, saw the pop-up, a voice message.

"Hi, babe." Bert's voice startled her with its loudness; she quickly turned down the phone's volume, listened for the sound of the shower. Still on. "I got your message from this morning, and all I can say is no matter what you say, whatever you feel you need to confess, of course I'll still love you. Of course I won't leave you. It *is* you and me and Isabelle against the world. Call me as soon as you get this. I love you."

This morning? Diana checked the time of the outgoing call.

Oliver had called Bert that morning while Diana was swimming, after Oliver had confessed to her the night before, after he'd so sincerely and fearfully apologized, after he'd sworn to end his relationships with Jewels and Bert, after he'd told her he wanted to spend the rest of his life with her and only her, after they'd made love, beautiful, attentive, and tender love, after he'd looked deep into her eyes and with such honesty, such humility, such vulnerability, told her that he loved her more than life itself.

Diana resaved the message so Oliver wouldn't know she'd heard it and put the phone back exactly where she'd found it. For a moment, she wondered why she didn't feel numb or devastated, why she felt clearer and more alive than she had in months, as if the lenses of her heart and mind had been polished to sharp, crystalline transparency, and then she simply accepted the inevitability of what was to come, what *had* to come, and she understood that she was the instrument of this inevitability. She returned to the bedroom, got dressed, retrieved the gun from the bureau, loaded it, and shoved it to the bottom of her purse.

Picasso

Lie: (noun) an intentionally false statement, or a situation involving deception or founded on a mistaken impression.

Lie: (verb) to get oneself into or out of a situation by providing an intentionally false statement, presenting a false impression, or being deceptive.

Lie: (ninth commandment) Thou shalt not bear false witness against thy neighbor.

Lie: (Pablo Picasso, my namesake and therefore my destiny) Art is a lie that makes us realize truth.

Lie: A lie told often enough becomes the truth.

Vladimir Lenin said that last thing. He was a mean and unpopular leader, who in 1917 led a revolution in Russia that started the form of government called Communism. We learned a little about him in fourth grade, but not what he said about lying. That came from Daddy, and whenever Daddy made a point of teaching me something I didn't already know, it meant there was a good reason I should know it. We were sitting at my desk up in my bedroom; he was helping me with my history lesson. He'd pushed all the stuff on the chair to one side and pulled it up next to me.

"What do you think he meant by that, Pinion (the wing of a bird)?" he asked.

I took my time before I answered like he'd taught me to—*You can always tell a stupid person by how fast they answer a question they don't know the answer to*—and then I said, "Sometimes it's easier for people to pretend what they said is true, because then they don't have to feel bad about themselves?"

"That's one way to look at it," Daddy said. "But another might be that when you tell a lie, you have to make sure you stick to it."

I remember being confused about that, because lying is supposed to be a sin and all, and I wanted to ask Daddy more about it, but I could tell that he was done with the subject, and when Daddy was done talking about something or doing something, he just got irritable if you kept on asking about it or doing it.

When I first started telling lies, I thought a lot about them. That's not too surprising, I guess. It's probably similar to when you buy something new, like shoes or a backpack, and you start seeing the exact same ones everywhere, on other kids, in magazine pictures, on mannequins at the mall, whereas before you bought them, you never even knew they existed. Well that's kind of how it was with me and lies. I saw and heard them everywhere. All kinds of them: intentional, unintentional, big, small, mammoth. It seemed like lies were such a part of our society that they were practically acceptable. Daddy used to say that lawyers lied all the time. Mama, Jewels, and Bert not only lied to everyone else, including the police, they obviously lied to themselves. My teacher lies about everything, not only about minor stuff like what's going to be on a math test but about his past accomplishments (like I'm betting he didn't play football for Alabama and wasn't a DEA agent). Mrs. Jesswein lies about her age; Mama says she's in her seventies, not sixties. And God lies too. Maybe not with words, but putting Adam and Eve in the garden of Eden with those apples he told them not to eat, and then acting all surprised and mad when they did, seems dishonest.

The point is, there are obviously many, many shades to lying, and I figure every living person has told at least one, which might mean Daddy wasn't such a bad person after all.

Sometimes I wish I could ask Daddy why he lied to Mama and me, and why he needed to have three families. I wouldn't get mad about his answer. I just want to know. But mostly, I guess I just miss talking to Daddy. I miss his stories. He took me to the heavens. I drank wine with Zeus, fought battles with Ares, and played the harp with Aphrodite. When Daddy was alive, I lived in the sky. I bounced from cloud to cloud. Earth was far away. I also miss Daddy's pragmatism. When I came to him with a predicament, he analyzed, reasoned, and asked me the exact right questions to enable me to solve my own problem. Just like he did with Ryan Anderson's Valentine's Day gift.

There are a lot of things I miss about Daddy, but I especially miss our secrets. I miss him always saying "Don't tell your mama," like when we got ice cream before dinner, or when he and I went to the bookstore and read mythology books together. I asked him once why he didn't just buy one of the books, and he said, "I don't need to. The stories live inside me." I miss telling him about things that bother me, like when Ryan Anderson didn't like me back or the All That Girls were bullying me. Now that he's gone, I keep secrets bottled inside me.

But I think what I miss the most is looking at Daddy. Mama always said he was handsome, and I guess he was, but I never really thought about him that way. He was just my daddy. The longer he's gone, the harder it is for me to remember what he looked like. That bothers me a lot. Mama threw out most of his pictures, but I hid a few. Sometimes I just stare at the pictures, try to memorize his face and recall its different smiles. I try to remember the way his hair moved in the breeze, what he *felt* like, or what he smelled like. I try to drown the Daddy dying memories by making movie memories. I pretend I'm watching a movie in my mind, and as if I'm holding an imaginary remote, I push the Pause button to freeze Daddy in time.

In one of my movie memories, I've gone on a picnic with Mama and Daddy to a park very much like Rainy Cove Park. We're playing hide-and-go-seek. While Daddy counts, I run from tree to tree, bush to bush, looking for the perfect hiding place. He is almost to ten when I find the perfect bush. I duck behind it and hold my breath. It seems like it's taking forever for him to find me. I hear him calling his usual variations of my name. One time, he gets very close. I fixate on the toe of his hunting boot. The dull brown leather is cracked in places; a hole has worn through. I remember thinking those boots *were* Daddy, just like the Red Sox baseball cap he wore whenever he didn't feel like taking a shower or dressing nice.

"Hey, Pip-squeak (one that is small or insignificant)," he says. "I know you're here somewhere."

His shoes disappear from my view. I hear them crunching the leaves near me. Stop. Crunching again. Moving away. I wait a little while, then another little while, just to be sure he is far enough away, and jump from the bush.

"Olly olly oxen free," I cry as I run. I'm out of breath by the time I get to the tree we designated as the safety zone, but I manage to add, "You didn't catch me, so I won."

Daddy laughs. "You sure did." He comes to me, hikes me up onto his shoulders, and holding my ankles against his chest, runs and runs.

I hit the Pause button.

My favorite dictionary says that happiness is a feeling or showing of pleasure or contentment. By this definition, happiness is *banal* (so lacking in originality as to be obvious or boring). That day, as I sat on my daddy's shoulders, felt his neck between my thighs, his hands on my ankles, and cupped his sweaty forehead in my palms, I was beyond happy. I was ecstatic.

Sometimes one of those other memories pops into my head. Like there's this one still life of a couple of old paint cans, a rusty hammer, and a beat-up kid's sand pail, green with a yellow handle that randomly appears. When it shows up, instead of being ecstatic it's there, or even happy, I feel scared and very sad. I try to get rid of it by shaking my head, but instead of finding its way out, the paint cans, hammer, and pail jump out of the still life and bang against my brain over and over, and all I can do to settle them down is turn off the lights in my room, close the curtains, crawl under my covers, curl into a ball, and lie there in the dark very, very still until the image, like Daddy, disappears. And right before I go to sleep, I lie to myself.

"I'll be just fine," I say.

THREE

Deception

(The Events Following the Murder)

. . .

Pay no attention to the man behind the curtain!

—L. FRANK BAUM

Kyle

Beautiful, lucky, sorry, gun, motive, liar, dumb ass.

Those last two words were directed solely at me. Bottom line: I had fallen for Diana Lane. Hard. What the fuck was wrong with me? Hell, no one in their right mind would go looking for love or dead bodies on Cooper's Island, and yet there I was, not even back two years and I had walked head-on into both.

Ironically, the Outer Banks used to be called "The Land of Beginnings" (prophetic?) because it was the place where England first attempted to colonize the Americas. These days, the chamber of commerce boasts of two main attractions: our lighthouses and the Wright brothers. In fact, we're so proud of these boys that even our license plates bear the slogan "First in Flight." But like most places we've chosen to forget our humbler roots. Cooper's, for instance, was once a fisherman's village, and it's still the least inhabited of the barrier islands. A majority of folks on the island at any given time are tourists, there for a week or two, but in the off-season we're left with a small, insular group of folks who rarely if ever nod to you on the street. But don't be fooled; they know your name, people, and entire sordid history. For the most part, single residents fall into three categories: men, women over sixty-five, and children under eighteen. Most women worth a second glance are either married or not interested in the opposite sex. We actually have a decent gay and lesbian population. What's left is a hodgepodge of folks, some who never left (Mack and his wife fall into this grouping), some who missed the place (Klide) even though they'd never admit it, and some who chose the place for personal reasons, misfits and outcasts looking to be left alone.

Instead, I met Diana Lane.

Although motive and opportunity, the two indicators we law enforcement types swear by, pointed in one solid direction, my cock pointed in another. Mack kept saying it was only a matter of time before we found that one fatal piece of evidence that would blow the case wide open. As it turned out, he was half right.

We were about four months into the investigation, and we weren't any closer to catching our murderer. Diana Lane hadn't tested positive for either blood splatter or gunshot residue, Julie Lane's alibi appeared rock solid, and with the exception of a few untraceable cell numbers all their phone records were clean. The three of them had steadfastly stuck to their stories: They'd never met or even heard of one another; they had no idea their husband had other wives; they didn't know anyone who'd want to hurt their husband. The only possible hole was Roberta Miles's alibi. She said she was driving to a writing retreat at the time of the murder. The folks running the retreat verified that she arrived just before noon. Both a waitress and the cashier at the Woodlands confirmed that a woman fitting Roberta Miles's description had been there for breakfast. Likewise, a waiter at the Little Switzerland Inn remembered serving her tea. She'd engaged him in a "delightful conversation about the lovely, smooth notes of our English breakfast tea, and how unfortunate it was that Americans seemed to prefer Earl Grey and its distasteful oil of bergamot." She'd left a large tip at both establishments, but when pushed to verify the exact date or time she was there, neither could be absolutely sure. Likewise, though her mother verified that she left the house around seven that morning, she later admitted to having been asleep when her daughter left the house.

Then we got a break. A witness came forward, said she'd seen the three of them together: the wives. Lindsay Middleton, a waitress and prelaw student at the University of North Carolina, had served them a late lunch at a restaurant on Franklin Street four months before the murder. She said she'd remembered Diana Lane as soon as she saw her picture on the news but didn't think much of it until she happened upon photos of Julie Lane and Roberta Miles much later. It isn't unusual for folks to come forward with so-called important information during a murder investigation, maybe they feel it's their civic duty or maybe they're just looking for their fifteen minutes of fame, but this witness appeared reliable. And here's the kicker: The reservation was made under Julie Lane's name.

Beautiful, lucky, sorry, gun, motive, liar, dumb ass, wives.

Our Sunday-morning drive to Research Triangle Park, named for the three cities that anchor it (Raleigh, Durham, and Chapel Hill), took less than three hours. Like the weather that day, downtown Raleigh had the cold, gray look associated with most capital cities. Julie Lane lived with her twin boys in a WPA industrial brick building in one of those swanky revitalized neighborhoods on the city's edges where units probably sold for more than a million dollars before the market crashed. We stood outside the security door and waited for an exiting tenant to provide us access.

A dog barked when we knocked on her door.

"Quiet, Frank," a woman's voice said. Light footsteps. A shadow across the peephole.

We flashed our badges. "Police, ma'am," Mack said.

The turn of the deadbolt.

"Julie Lane?" I asked. "I'm Detective Kennedy and this is Detective Jones, whom I believe you've already met. We'd like to ask you a few questions about your husband's murder."

The second Mrs. Lane was both surprised and irritated to see us. I'd encountered similar welcoming expressions from Diana Lane. She didn't appear to recognize Mack, which wouldn't be too surprising if she had in fact been distraught that first time they met. From a distance, one might mistake the second Mrs. Lane for the first and vice versa. There was the hair and they were both tall and slim, yet while attractive, the second Mrs. Lane was neither sultry nor damaged. This was a woman in total control of herself and her surroundings.

She invited us inside. "Place, Frank," she said to a golden retriever. He hobbled over to a dog bed in the living room. From his labored walk, white-haired face, and brittle frame, I could tell he wasn't long for this world. Poor guy.

Julie Lane didn't offer us so much as a glass of water or a seat. Obviously she wasn't from the South. I was struck by the way she moved inside her clothing. Woman and garments shared an ease characteristic of someone who is completely comfortable with her body. An athlete? She wore strappy high-heeled black sandals that exposed delicate feet and carefully painted red toenails. I guessed she wasn't planning to head outdoors anytime soon. The white turtleneck sweater she sported was neither too tight nor too loose. It casually accented the mounds of her breasts—a little too small for my taste but nonetheless worth notice. Her gray slacks hugged the curve of her ass so perfectly they appeared to have been cut from its mold. It hadn't dawned on me that Oliver Lane was an ass man. The condo itself was small but open, and tastefully decorated—chic brown leather sofa, chrome-and-glass coffee and end tables, wood floors, bearskin rug, large modern paintings. A fire burned in the gas fireplace. Frank, and a kitschy grouping of Barbie dolls that took up one entire shelf of the bookcase surrounding the fireplace, appeared to be the only blemishes in the otherwise stark, orderly environment.

"What can I do for you, detectives?" she asked.

As Mack and I had agreed, he spoke up first. "We just have a few questions, ma'am."

"Missus," she said with a bite.

"Sorry, ma'am, uh, I mean Mrs. Lane," Mack said. He reached into his coat pocket, pulled out his notebook and a folded-up computer printout of the Chapel Hill restaurant's reservation list from the day in question. He took his time unfolding it and handed it to her.

"What's this?" she asked.

"Do you recall being at this restaurant—let me see, here it is—do you recall being at 411 West Franklin?" Mack asked.

"No," she said.

He pointed about halfway down the sheet. "That sure looks like your name to me."

She squinted. "So?"

Mack didn't respond right away. My signal to chime in with a relevant comment about the surroundings I'd been diligently checking out.

"Are these your boys, *ma'am?*" I pointed to the console table behind the sofa.

"Boys?" Cool, poised, indifferent.

"The picture," I said. "Are these your sons? They look like twins. How old are they?"

Did she soften?

"Three and a half."

I scanned the room as if looking for them. It was hard to imagine two young boys romping around in the sterile environment.

"They're at play group with their nanny, *Detective.*" Said with more than a modicum of disdain.

"Handsome little guys," I said. "They look like their father, don't they?"

She glared.

"Nice family photo of the four of you," I continued. "Though

I didn't recognize you at first. You used to be a brunette?" The photo was a larger version of one Julie Lane had given the Raleigh PD when she reported her husband missing, one of the same ones I'd shown Diana Lane when I broke the news of her husband's other wife.

"I felt like a change," she said.

"Where was it taken?"

"Saint Gabriel's," she said.

"Were you and your husband churchgoers?"

"I'm not sure what business that is of yours," she said.

"Everything's our business during a murder investigation, ma'am," Mack said.

"Well, if you must know, I'm agnostic and so was Oliver. His firm made a substantial donation to the church that year; one of the partners is a member. The photo was part of the package."

Mack flipped a page in his notebook and wrote something down; Mrs. Lane's eyes drifted in his direction.

"Funny that you don't recall being at the restaurant that day," I said. "The waitress remembers you very clearly. Said she overheard the three of you talking about some woman in Boone who poisoned her husband. Thought it was an odd conversation."

"Three?" An ever so slight falter in her voice.

"Yes," Mack said. "She said you were there with Diana Lane and Roberta Miles."

"She, who?"

"Your waitress that day," Mack said. "I checked out that murder in Boone. Seems an eighty-three-year-old man named Ira Schwartz thought to have had a heart attack actually died from poison administered by his wife, Irma Schwartz. Under the circumstances, quite the interesting conversation the three of you were having, don't you think?"

"The waitress is obviously mistaken," Julie Lane said.

"The—waitress—is—obviously—mistaken," Mack said as he

wrote in his notebook. "So you know who Diana Lane and Roberta Miles are?" Mack asked.

"Of course I know who they are," she said. "The police—you—informed me about them."

"Well?" Mack asked.

"Well what, Detective?"

"Were you at the restaurant that day?"

"It's possible," she said. "I frequent that restaurant. I'm an architect. My firm has several clients in Chapel Hill. I'm sure if I *was* there—I'm not egotistic enough to believe I am the one and only Julie Lane who has eaten at 411 West Franklin—and if I *was* dining with two other women, they must have been clients. And we certainly weren't talking about some woman who killed her husband with arsenic."

Mack made a show of checking his notes. "What makes you think it was arsenic, ma'am?"

"I . . . I must have read it in the paper," she said.

"I'm afraid that's not good enough," I said.

Julie Lane's eyes shot in my direction. "What's not good enough?"

"We have an eyewitness that puts you and your husband's other two wives together *before* he was murdered. That would seem to indicate that you knew one another, and if you knew one another, then why didn't any of you say so earlier?"

"I said that the women I was with must have been clients."

"So you do recall being there," Mack said.

"That's not what I said."

"You don't happen to remember their names, do you?" I asked.

"Whose names?" The telltale stall.

"Your clients, ma'am."

"It was months ago."

"Surely a professional such as yourself keeps an appointment calendar," Mack said.

Long, introspective pause.

"Well, you're right. Normally I do, but my computer crashed a few weeks after Oliver died and I lost all my files."

"Convenient," Mack said.

I was tempted to laugh at Julie Lane's expression. She looked like an angry cartoon character. I could almost see smoke coming out of her nose and ears.

"Well, Detective," she said. "If you doubt me, then why don't you check into it? I took my laptop to the Apple store at Crabtree Valley Mall when it happened—I'm sure their records will corroborate my story." She cocked her head, smiled. "They downloaded what files they could, but weren't able to save my calendar."

"Shame, ma'am," I said.

"We'll check into it." Mack paused, looked out the window. "We should be going. Looking a little ominous out there."

"By the way," I said as we were leaving, "you ever shot a gun, Mrs. Lane?"

"What?" There was no mistaking her surprise.

"A *gun*," I repeated. "Have you ever held one in your hand and pulled the trigger?"

"No, Detective. Can't say that I have." The response was smug.

"We'll be in touch." I closed the door behind me.

On our way back to the car, Mack asked me what I thought.

"She isn't as good of a liar as she thinks she is," I said.

"Interesting that she knew about the poison being arsenic," Mack said. "Where were you going with that gun question?"

"There was a picture on the bookshelf by those Barbie dolls of a younger her and an older man in hunting clothes. Guy was holding a rifle. I'd say her father."

"Barbie dolls?" Mack said.

"You didn't see them? There had to be a dozen or more, every one of them propped on a little wire stand. Pretty weird if you ask me."

"I'll say."

"Hey, check into shooting ranges, will you?" I asked. "See if she frequents any. And while you're at it, find out more about her childhood, especially anything that proves she knows how to handle a gun. There's just something about that woman I don't like. There wasn't one bit of love in her voice when she talked to her dog."

"Kind of hard to tell from one meeting." Mack rooted for his seat belt. "About her relationship with the dog, I mean. Maybe she's just a clean freak. Pretty snazzy place she lives in. What do you think, a million? Million five? And did you get a load of the furnishings? Wife and I looked at that very leather sofa at Restoration Hardware over in Norfolk. More than six grand. And the artwork? Do you think that was an actual Julian Schnabel?"

"I didn't know you followed the art world," I said.

Mack started the car and shot me one of his shit-eating grins. "I don't have any idea who Julian Schnabel is. Just read the name on that painting with the broken plates all over it. Figured something that weird had to be done by a famous artist. Why else would anyone buy it?"

"Made a name for himself in the seventies," I said. "These days his paintings can sell for a hundred grand or more."

"Fuck, a hundred grand for a bunch of ceramic shards and paint? You've got to be kidding. Maybe I need to rethink Evan's career choice."

"Oh, I don't know. NFL quarterbacks don't do so bad."

"It's a damn shame that restaurant didn't have a surveillance camera. Think we have enough to bring them in?"

"One eyewitness? No. We've got to find some physical evidence, something that puts the second Mrs. Lane or Ms. Miles inside the beach house. By the way, did you find out anything more about Oliver Lane's financial situation?"

"Just like we thought, guy's a ghost. No bank accounts. No paper trail of any sort."

"It just doesn't add up," I said. "That guy has shady written all over him. I'm betting he had a separate bank account or stash of money somewhere. They didn't happen to find an extra key to, say, a safe-deposit box, when they were searching his homes and offices, did they? Or bank statements for a secret account."

"No, and they did a pretty thorough job."

"Did you search his car?"

"We checked it out at the beach house that day, but we didn't tear it apart or anything. There was nothing on his computers either."

I tried to settle in for our ride back to the island, but I was too agitated to relax. I kept trying to find a new word for my banner, something that summed up our visit to Raleigh, that indicated we'd made progress in the case, or that at least pointed in Julie Lane's direction, but the truth was, having a penchant for cleanliness, clean design, fine art, and Barbie dolls, and a generally uptight and bitchy attitude, didn't make her a killer.

Picasso

I think it was a Monday in December. Monday because that was Mama's Junior League volunteer day, and December because I remember it was long enough after the Thanksgiving break for Ryan Anderson to have stayed home sick for a few days, *actually* sick, not play sick like me. And just like when Mr. Dork was out of the room or we had a substitute teacher, the kids had taken advantage of Ryan's absence to spew all their pent-up insults at me. "Your mother is a murderer" was one of their favorites, along with "murderer's kid" and "your mom's going to jail," all very original and therefore not too scary or anything, but I was still pretty upset about Daddy dying, and murder or not, I was more emotional than usual and therefore at risk for victim behavior, which the *Taking Charge of Your Life* book says is about as damaging to self-actualization and the development of personal power as one drop of alcohol is to an alcoholic, so I'd decided that staying home for a while, at least until Ryan returned to school, was the smartest course of action. I resorted to my usual trick. I covered my face with a really hot rag for several minutes, immediately thereafter made a point of finding Mama and telling her I didn't feel well, and when she felt my forehead, she got all concerned and said, "You're burning up Picasso," to which I responded with the most sickly and pitiful "My belly hurts" possible, and she went off to look for the thermometer, which was safely hidden under my pillow, and finally after not finding it, she pronounced me too sick for school and told me she'd check in with me throughout the day. Somewhere during the whole Daddy dying mess, Mama had completely forgotten her worry over me staying home alone.

I would've played sick that day regardless, but the fact that Mama had Junior League was a bonus. That way I didn't have to act pitiful all day long. I could watch TV and chow down on Cheetos and Coke, read my dictionaries, build on my word journal, or just stare out the window and manifest snow (we hardly ever get snow in North Carolina). The possibilities were endless.

About ten minutes into my channel surfing, I thought I saw Detective Kennedy's car drive by. But since he didn't drive into our driveway, I figured it was just somebody with a similar car. After a while, I saw Detective Kennedy knock on Mrs. Jesswein's door, which she opened, and then he went inside. He came back out. Then he walked on over and knocked on Mr. Buttons's door, and then Mr. Purdy's door, and then the door of that new couple that had just moved into the house right across from the Presbyterian Church where Mrs. Cutshaw, bless her soul, used to live. The *Price Is Right* came on sometime during all this, but I turned it off; I hate that show. I mean who can guess all those prices right, what with the economy fluctuating so often, and, seriously, how could every store in their viewing area sell stuff for the exact same price, so for those reasons, and because I've personally checked them out, I know for a fact that some of those "right" prices are just plain wrong. One time I even wrote to the show at their recommended address and told them they'd quoted incorrect prices for certain products, which of course I detailed, but they didn't respond, which is no big surprise I guess. Nobody likes to be wrong.

Since I hadn't seen Detective Kennedy for a while, I figured he'd left, so I decided to do some random-closing-my-eyes-and-pointing-my-finger-at-any-old-page word searches.

The first word I zeroed in on was *hypogynous* (having floral parts, such as sepals, petals, and stamens, borne on the receptacle beneath the ovary). After I'd slowly printed it and its definition out in my word journal, I tried using it a few times in sentences, which turned out to be a great success, so I decided I especially liked that word because I could use it in everyday speech.

The next word my finger landed on was *mojo* (a magic charm or spell, sometimes an amulet worn on a necklace or kept in a small flannel bag by adherents of hoodoo or magic). I remember thinking that was one of the coolest words ever and I was definitely getting myself one of those amulets since even better than being able to say the word, I could wear the amulet every single day. As far as I knew there wasn't any dress code about necklaces at my school, and if by chance there was some small print somewhere disallowing mojo amulets, I could just button up my shirt all the way to hide it, and, this is the best part, then I could cast unlimited spells on the All That Girls.

I heard the side door to the garage door open and close, which was weird because Mama usually locked it. I put down my dictionary, slid my feet into my slippers (I was still wearing my pj's like all sick kids do), put on my coat, went out the front door, down the side steps, and looked around the corner at the garage. I didn't see anyone. Then I heard the trunk of Daddy's car shutting. I walked over to the door and peeked inside. It was Detective Kennedy. He saw me too and made his crooked smile.

I opened the door. "What are you doing?"

"Just a routine search," he said. "Why aren't you in school today?"

"I'm sick," I said.

"That's too bad." He was looking in the glove compartment. "Flu?"

"Yes," I said.

"You getting lots of rest?" Checking behind the visors, inside the ashtrays, under the seat.

"Some," I said. "I've been watching TV."

"I used to do that when I was sick, still do sometimes. The first time I saw *Casablanca* I was home sick."

"Casablanca?"

"Humphrey Bogart and Ingrid Bergman? Do you know it?" Now he was searching the backseat.

"No."

"We'll have to watch it sometime."

"What are you looking for?" I asked.

He stopped, looked at me. "A key."

"What kind of key?"

"I'm not sure. It might have numbers on it. And it would be in a safe place."

"You mean like a secret hiding place?" A feeling of excitement washed all over me.

"Maybe," he said.

"Want me to help you look?"

"I'm almost done." He closed the car doors. "You should get back inside. It's cold out here. See those clouds? It's looking like school just might get canceled for snow." He winked. "I'm betting it's been kind of hard with the kids talking about your dad's murder. I'd stay home too."

"Do you want to come in for a while?"

"Can't," he said. "But thanks for the invitation." He unfolded a piece of paper that looked pretty official. "Will you let your mama know I had a warrant? In case she asks about me searching the car? She's at some sort of Junior League thing, right?"

I wondered how he knew that. Detective Kennedy seemed to know everything. "It's okay. I won't tell her you were here."

Detective Kennedy cocked his head and studied me. I knew he

was trying to decide whether me not telling Mama would get him in trouble with her down the road if she did find out.

"I promise," I said. "It'll be our secret." It was the first time I'd shared a secret with anyone since Daddy, and I remember it made me feel good inside, like in that moment everything was right again.

Detective Kennedy walked me to the door of the house and made sure I locked it from the inside before he left, which I did. Then he walked off down the street toward the church. I never did see where he parked his car.

I spent a while searching for the key in all Daddy's usual hiding spots, his sock drawer, penny basket, and the empty (of shoes) shoe box he used to keep way back in the corner of his closet under all his full shoe boxes, but which was now safely hidden in my closet. I'd discovered it a few weeks after Jewels showed up. There were all kinds of things in it, like pictures of his other families, two old people (a woman and a man), and a few of someone named Peter—him as a baby, him in a football uniform at about my age, and him with a girl at some dance. There were also some old coins, postcards (to the same Peter guy), and a ring that looked like one of those ones high school kids get when they graduate, but no key, so I shoved the box to the back of my closet, covered it with dirty clothes, returned to the sofa and my dictionaries, and decided to do something I don't usually do. Instead of zeroing in on any old word, I specifically looked one up.

Secret has a bunch of meanings, eight for when it's used as an adjective, and four for when it's used as a noun, which is what I concentrated on: 1. Something kept hidden from others or known only to oneself or to a few. 2. Something that remains beyond understanding or explanation; a mystery. 3. A method or formula on which success is based: *The secret of this dish is in the sauce.* 4. A variable prayer said after the Offertory and before the Preface in the Mass.

Now, of course I'd known the general meaning of the word *secret* before I looked it up that day, but as I've come to understand, none of us really knows the entire meaning of a word because of the very fact that so many words are overused and misused. Like for instance, I had no idea that *secret* had anything to do with church, which shouldn't have surprised me I guess, because just about everything seems to somehow connect back to religion. I also hadn't really thought about a relationship between secrets and mystery, though that seemed perfectly obvious once I'd read it. But the meaning variation I found most intriguing was the third one: a method or formula on which success is based. I found that particular definition profound on many levels.

I was still making a list of potential interpretations of that meaning variation when Mama came home. The second thing she said after she walked in the door was "Why is the side door to the garage open?" (The first was "How are you feeling?")

I acted like I didn't hear her so I could run a bunch of answer scenarios through my mind first. One: I could tell the truth. (I threw that option out pretty quickly.) Two: I could tell a partial truth. For instance, I could say I didn't know, which was sort of true given that I didn't remember leaving the door open when Detective Kennedy and I left the garage and it was possible that the wind blew it back open or the lock didn't catch or any number of other things that I wouldn't know had happened. But if I said that, Mama might get worried and call the police, and then it might lead to me breaking my secret with Detective Kennedy. Three: I could lie.

"Picasso?" Mama said.

"I went in there," I said.

"Why?" Mama asked.

"I was looking for a book in Daddy's car," I said. "The Sue Grafton book I took to the beach."

"Did you find it?"

"No, I think it got left at the beach house." That last part was true. I had to buy another copy just so I could finish the last eighteen pages.

"That's too bad," Mama said. "I thought I'd make homemade chicken soup for dinner. How does that sound?"

"Good," I said, and coughed a couple of times.

Kyle

The following Wednesday, Mack and I headed to Boone. We'd called Roberta Miles in advance to ensure she'd be home. The closer we got to the mountains, the browner the clouds in the sky, indicating the onslaught of a major snowstorm. I was taken aback when she opened her door; Roberta Miles looked as if she'd lost twenty pounds or more. The transformation was amazing. She was wearing designer jeans, a lavender cashmere sweater—the color looked amazing on her—and the mole on her cheek was gone, only a faint scar belying its prior existence. Like before, she was gracious, invited us to follow her to the "tree house."

"Unfortunately, you just missed Isabelle. You always seem to stop by just after she's gone down for her nap." Said casually, as if we were old friends. "Hot cocoa and tea, wasn't it?" She left without waiting for our responses.

"We've had a break in the case, ma'am," Mack said, after she'd returned with our cups.

"Really," she said. "What sort of break?"

Mack proceeded to tell her about Lindsay Middleton spotting her with two other women in the Chapel Hill restaurant. She didn't flinch.

"Of course, she could be wrong," Mack said. "But being that she's a prelaw student and all . . ." He stared directly at her.

"Was there a question in there somewhere, Detective?" Her smile was radiant.

Mack laughed, nervously. Roberta Miles's sly sense of humor had caught both of us off guard. What happened to the *soft,* in more ways than one, woman we first met?

"We were wondering why the three of you were there," Mack said.

"I've never met my husband's other wives, and I have no intention of ever doing so."

Mack looked at me questioningly. "I don't recall saying anything about other wives, do you?"

I made a show of checking my notes. "Nope."

"Well, what other 'three of you' would you be referring to, detectives?" she asked. "Perhaps Isabelle, me, and one of her playmates?"

Mack cleared his throat. "She—um, the waitress—said she overheard the three of you talking about a murder here in Boone. A Mrs. Schwartz?"

"Irma," she said.

"So you know about it?"

"Of course, Detective. Everyone does. It's a small town."

"Refresh my memory," Mack said. "What happened exactly?"

"The police thought her husband had some kind of attack at first, but she later confessed to poisoning him—oh my, now I can't remember his name. Anyway, she used arsenic. Can you believe it? She was eighty-two. Pretty spunky."

"You find that spunky?" I asked.

"Why yes, Detective, I do. Don't you? She said he'd been abusing her for years, and she'd finally had enough."

"Is that the way you felt about your husband, Ms. Miles?" I asked.

"Oliver never raised a hand to me, Detective Kennedy. And back to your earlier question, no, the three of us weren't talking about Irma Schwartz or anyone else. The three of us weren't together at that restaurant. The three of us have not met."

"So you're saying the waitress lied?"

"I'm saying she was mistaken," she said.

Mack flipped through his notebook. "Just as I thought. Julie Lane used almost those exact same words. Don't you find that odd?"

"Not really, Detective. If someone is mistaken, they're mistaken. It would be rude to state otherwise."

Mack showed her the computer printout. "As you can see, the reservation was in Julie Lane's name. So obviously the waitress wasn't mistaken about one of you being there. We're still waiting on the restaurant to give us the feed from their surveillance equipment. When they do, I'm sure it will corroborate the waitress's story."

Without even the slightest show of concern, she said, "Oh, I'm sure it won't, Detective. I've never been to that restaurant."

It hadn't crossed my mind that Roberta Miles would be a good liar. The more I knew about the woman, the more I understood why Oliver Lane had found her attractive.

"You've lost a lot of weight," I said to her. "In a short amount of time."

"Stress," she said.

"It appears to agree with you," I said. "You look great."

A coy smile? "Why, thank you, Detective. More tea or cocoa?"

"No, ma'am," I said. "We better get on home. That snow's coming down pretty hard. Thank you for your time."

"We'll be in touch," Mack said as we rose.

"Let me walk you to the door," she said.

The phone rang as we passed by one of the over-packed bookshelves in her living room.

"Will you excuse me for a second?" she asked. "One of my cats has been gone longer than usual. I have the entire neighborhood looking for him." She hurried into a room off the hallway.

I could make out more bookcases and part of an antique wood desk. For a moment, as if I were Sam Spade or Philip Marlowe, I considered having Mack distract Roberta Miles while I rifled through its drawers. But what did I expect to uncover that qualified search teams hadn't? We'd scoured Oliver Lane's homes and offices months earlier. I focused my attention on the bookcase. There was an entire shelf on mythology and another with coffee-table-size art books. One caught my attention. I pulled it out, paged through it.

"False alarm." Roberta Miles startled me.

"Julian Schnabel," I said, indicating the book. "Are you a fan?"

"My husband was. Oliver always wanted to buy one of his paintings, but we just couldn't afford it."

"So you weren't aware that your husband had purchased one?"

"What do you mean?"

"Oh that's right. You said you never met Julie Lane, so of course you wouldn't know that there's a large Julian Schnabel painting hanging on her wall. I imagine it cost a pretty penny. We'll be on our way then." I handed her the book.

"You keep it, Detective." Her look was a combination of knowing and spite. "You're more of an art connoisseur than I. You can study it over your scotch tonight."

I was dismayed, but put on my blank face. I had never mentioned anything about liking art or scotch to Roberta Miles.

"I hope you find him," Mack said.

"Find whom?" she asked.

"Your cat," Mack said.

"Oh, me too. It's cold out there."

There was a table next to the front door with a lamp and some pictures on it; I picked one up. "Interesting," I said. "Where was this taken?"

"At our church. Trinity Lutheran. Why?"

"Diana Lane and Julie Lane have very similar ones in their homes. All of them seem to have been taken around the same time. A coincidence, don't you think?"

Roberta Miles's smile was condescending. "Really, Detective. You're obviously more astute than that. There's nothing coincidental about it, now is there? We all had the same husband, remember?"

I replaced the picture. "Oh, just one more thing."

"What's that, Detective?"

"Did you ever see your husband with an unidentifiable key?"

"A key?" she said. "Oh, thank God. You found out about him. He told me to stay out of that room, but I just couldn't control myself. It's full of all his previous wives. Hanging from the rafters, chopped up, you name it. If he hadn't died, I could've been next."

"Funny," I said. "I'm guessing that's a no."

Like she had on our first visit, she stood by the door as we walked to our car.

"What was that about?" Mack asked as he pulled away from the curb.

"Bluebeard," I said. "It's a fairy tale. Guy kills all his wives, leaves their bodies in a secret room, and sets up subsequent wives to find them before he kills them too."

"That's a fairy tale? Don't think I'll be reading it to Evan."

"Good idea," I said.

"Speaking of fairy tales," Mack said. "What do you think? Wolf in sheep's clothing?"

"Definitely more to her than I first thought," I said.

"What do you make of her saying they couldn't afford one of those paintings? And she looked pretty surprised when you mentioned the one in Julie Lane's house."

"Yeah," I said. "Bit of friction there. But I think it's more to do with him being a liar. She's probably seeing that more and more, and each discovery stings. Roberta Miles isn't the flashy type;

she's careful with her money. She wouldn't have been interested in a man who squandered money on fine art. He probably told her some story about growing up dirt poor and working his way up that he thought would impress her."

"Interesting that she said the surveillance tapes wouldn't incriminate her," Mack said. "Do you think they checked the place for cameras before they decided to eat there?"

"No," I said. "She knew we were playing her."

What I didn't say was that I thought Roberta Miles had some kind of psychic ability. Nor did I say that of the three of them, I was pretty certain she'd be the hardest to crack—though I'd thought the exact opposite at first.

That night, like I'd been doing since my mother died, I walked into a house so empty it echoed. Maybe it wasn't dank and filthy like my apartment in Detroit, but it was just as spare, just as depressing: cold wood floors, empty fridge, bare cupboards, blank walls, fireplace that hadn't seen a piece of wood in nearly a year. My rickety table and chairs had moved with me. I took off my suit coat, hung it over a chair, went to my liquor shelf, grabbed my trusty bottle of Redbreast and a shot glass, and drank one after another while I paged through the book Roberta Miles gave me, my flash cards waiting patiently for that magical moment when just the right amount of scotch rendered me brilliant. But I didn't find the sweet spot that night; I never even got to the cards. At some point I must've dozed off, or entered some sort of dark fairy-land, because one of Julian Schnabel's paintings was fucking with my mind. The plates were crashing against my skull, shattering, piercing my brain, while the damn words just curled their way through them, undaunted, unharmed.

Beautiful, lucky, sorry, gun, motive, liar, dumb ass, wives, guilty as sin.

Picasso

Destiny: the hidden power believed to control what will happen in the future; fate.

Smart: having or showing intelligence; capable of independent and intelligent action.

Ever since I was a little girl, people said I was smart. Daddy started it. He told me that a lot of parents think their kids are smart when they do stuff for the first time, like roll over, sit up, talk, walk, or read those stupid flash cards, especially if they do it before all the other kids their age.

"Did I do all those things before other kids?" I'd asked.

"No," he said. "And that's how I knew you were smart."

"I don't understand," I said.

"You might not have done things first, but you did them all at once. You never crawled. You never took a few steps and fell. One day you just up and walked across the room, smiling and laughing the whole time, like your mama and I were idiots to have worried. Don't you see? You waited. For just the right moment."

I wasn't surprised when Detective Kennedy showed up with Detective Jones not even a week after he'd been rifling through Daddy's car, but I was worried. Detective Kennedy had been coming around with "one more question" for a while by then, but I could tell there was going to be a lot more than one question this time. I remember thinking that since I'm so smart shouldn't I be able to figure out some way to stop Mama from getting arrested, and consequently me from going to foster care? Then I started thinking about destiny and how sometimes even when you try to make something not happen, it still happens. Just like Daddy dying.

Mama sent me to my room, which was no surprise, but if she were paying any attention at all, she would've noticed that the wood floor was a bit more worn around the corner from the top stair. By then I was an expert eavesdropper. Mama wasn't paying much attention to anything. I could swear in front of her, which I sometimes did just to see, and she wouldn't even notice. Life with Mama had become a string of "That's nice, Picasso"s or "What did you say, Picasso"s. I could've been planning to jump off a roof, rob a bank, or even run away from home to live with wild monkeys and she wouldn't have known, or cared.

While Detective Jones asked Mama a million questions about some restaurant near some church, I was thinking about how upset Mama surely was that they had stopped by unannounced. Mama hated when people didn't call first; it wasn't polite. Losing your privacy was obviously one of the side effects of someone dying. There were a bunch more. Like sometimes I actually forgot that Daddy was dead. I expected to hear him showering in the morning. I swore I heard him calling my name, or I'd hear the mailman's heavy boots on the front-porch steps and get that excited feeling that starts in your chest and washes over your entire body. Sometimes I even ran to the door. What was really weird was that I saw him everywhere, like at the grocery or drugstore. He'd disappear around a corner, and sometimes I'd drop whatever I was in the middle of doing and scurry after him, but it wasn't him. It was some other kid's dad. Then there was all the practical stuff. Like for the longest time, Mama and I lived in the dark. I don't mean dark in the metaphorical sense. I mean burned-out lightbulbs didn't get replaced. We also lived in *squalor* (a state of being extremely dirty). The trash just sat there in the kitchen until it spilled over the wastebasket, and same thing with the garbage can outside. The yard didn't get mowed. The bushes grew long, wiry tentacles. Ivy about choked the life out of the tree in our front yard. A bunch of dry sticks with crispy leaves stuck out of flower beds and flowerpots. The point is, before Daddy died, I didn't understand about maintenance; I didn't even know it was happening. It was just always done. Someone's dying was bad enough, but when you stack all those other unexpected things on top of it, it pretty much sucked. That's what Ryan Anderson said anyway. Well, what he actually said was "Life sucks"—he was upset about losing a soccer game—but I told him I figured death sucked more.

"You were in Research Triangle Park for some sort of meeting that day, weren't you, ma'am?" Detective Jones was asking. Detective Kennedy hadn't said one thing, at least that I heard. I figured that was because he liked Mama.

"A Junior League state chapter meeting," Mama said. "But I don't remember going to that particular restaurant."

"The waitress will testify that she saw the three of you together that day," Detective Jones said. "And she's a pretty credible witness. Prelaw student at UNC."

"She's mistaken," Mama said. "I've never met my husband's other wives."

"Where have I heard those words before?" Detective Jones asked. "Oh yeah, Roberta Miles, or was it Julie Lane, or both? Well, we'll know soon enough who was or wasn't there. We're waiting on the restaurant's surveillance tapes."

Surveillance tapes? Like from a camera?

That was it. Foster care was my destiny. Although I didn't know too much about foster care back then, I did know from watching

TV that I would most likely go live in some big old drafty house with a bunch of other parentless kids, many of whom took drugs that numbed their brains, and a so-called mom and dad who really didn't care about me or the other kids, only the money they got for taking us in. I remember thinking that I would probably end up living at a house like that forever, or until they threw me out, because nobody wants to adopt older children, and there was a good chance I'd end up using drugs too, or even worse I could end up a prostitute, and Ryan Anderson would definitely not like me if I were a prostitute.

"I'm certain the tapes will show that I wasn't there," Mama said.

"Really?" Detective Jones asked. "Why is that?"

"Because I wasn't," Mama said.

I didn't know for sure, but I figured that was a big fat lie.

After Detective Kennedy and Detective Jones left, I wandered downstairs. Mama was sitting at the dining-room table with her head down and her hands rubbing her forehead.

"Are you okay, Mama?" I asked. She didn't say anything, so I added, "What was Detective Kennedy doing here?" I'd learned it was good to pretend I didn't know what I knew, partially because it didn't do much good (Mama had never even once brought up the Don't Kill Daddy conversation we sort of had) and partially because there was the outside chance she might actually answer me truthfully.

"He just wanted to update me on the case," Mama said, which wasn't the whole truth but surprised me anyway. I mean at least she was present.

"Do they know who killed Daddy?" I asked.

Mama straightened, looked at me. "No."

"That's good," I said.

She cocked her head, furrowed the skin above her eyebrows. "Why do you think that's good?"

The question put me in a pickle, so I had to think for a while about a response that would get me out of it. "Because once they find who killed him, we won't see Detective Kennedy anymore."

"There is that," Mama said, and she actually smiled.

"Have you called anyone since they left?" I asked.

More wrinkling. "Why would I call someone?" Another unexpected question. Had Mama finally woken up from her alien-inhabited state?

Again, I had to make something up. "I thought you said something earlier about having to call someone about Junior League stuff."

"Did I?" she asked, her eyes staring off into space again. And then she said something that scared the bejesus out of me. "You'll be okay if anything ever happens to me, won't you Picasso? You're a very smart girl, and very strong."

I remember I was just getting ready to say something like "No, I won't be okay, Mama," or "I'm not as smart or strong as you think I am, Mama," or, what I wanted to say most of all, "Please don't leave me, Mama," when she just got up from her chair, walked toward the living room, and without even looking back at me, turned and headed upstairs.

Kyle

I admit I was relieved when the restaurant sighting turned out to be a dead end. Lindsay Middleton, poor thing, called several times to follow up on our progress.

"I know it was them," she kept saying.

"We believe you," I'd say. "But unfortunately it's your word against theirs."

She ended her last call by saying, "I'm very disappointed in our country's judicial system." The click sounded louder than I'm sure it was. I wondered whether she'd stick with prelaw.

With no additional leads, there was every indication that Diana Lane, Julie Lane, and Roberta Miles would get away with murder. This boiled Mack. I understood. In all honesty, I was feeling righteous too, but not because of the wives. Because of Oliver Lane. Here was this guy who had successfully conned three women, and most likely would've continued had he not been murdered. I would've loved to put the asshole in jail, but where was the crime? Sure, he'd led them on. Sure, he'd lied. He might have lived the role of husband with all of them, but legally he'd only married one. The marriage certificates for the others were bogus, the ceremonies shams. Diana Lane was the only one who could openly grieve. Julie Lane and Roberta Miles were little more than concubines. Whether or not the three of them did it, and whether or not we'd ultimately catch them, I was happy they'd spend at least one more Christmas with their children.

That year, like every year, Cooper's Island did Christmas up right. There was an annual Christmas dance held at Cooper's Alleys. Our chamber of commerce did a nice job with the Christmas decorations. All the trees and storefronts were wrapped with little white lights. The local hardware store ran Christmas music on a loop on its outside speakers. A huge tree stood in the town's center. Our one nondenominational church held a yearly Christmas Eve service. The mayor, like most politicians, hadn't wanted to risk losing voters by bowing to any one religious group, so he had declared the church open to all worshippers and their various gods. I had always loved Christmas on Cooper's Island. In my heart, even with our cheesy plastic Santa and reindeers flying in place above Main Street, the ancient mechanical window displays sporting elves with broken ears and chipped paint, and Jimmy O'Neill's drinking problem (our Santa had spent more than one Christmas Eve in jail overnight), there was no place I'd rather be for the holidays.

On Christmas night, Lisa, Mack's wife, invited me to their house to celebrate a combination Christmas and birthday party. Mack turned twenty-eight on the thirtieth; twenty-eight was a distant memory for me. Mack and Lisa had bought a fixer-upper on the west side of the island, the denser side, one street off the beach in the midst of rental land. It was the first time I'd been over since they'd completed the renovations. The permanent fixtures were decidedly male—dark cabinets, dark wood floors, stone fireplace. The decor was all Lisa—red canvas slipcover on the sofa, brightly patterned easy chairs, useless pillows, white pine dining set. After dinner, while Lisa cleaned up and put Evan to bed, Mack and I smoked a cigar on the front porch. Because the house was on a hill and rested on stilts, we could see the ocean through neighboring properties. The night air was crisp but pleasant, the temperature in the high fifties, the smell of the ocean still overpowering, the sound of the waves as robust as a Rachmaninoff symphony.

Mack sucked on the end of his cigar, tore off the tip with his teeth. "Damn, I forgot, want a drink?"

"Nah," I said. "Taking a break from the juice."

"What's up with that?"

"Trying to lose a few pounds."

"Really?"

"No," I said. "Not really."

"Oh," Mack said.

I didn't want to belabor this line of questioning, so I switched the subject to one that made me even more uncomfortable, domestic bliss. "Lisa seems, well, happy. Being a mother and all."

Mack laughed. "She is. She keeps telling me she's found her true calling. Who would've guessed it? Tomboy Lisa loving motherhood. When we were kids, she was always beating the shit out of me."

It was my turn to laugh. "Her cooking has definitely improved."

"You liked the cioppino?" he asked. "Fresh catch."

"Cioppino?" I said. "When did you learn that soup came in flavors?"

"Don't tell her I told you, but she's been taking cooking classes over in the church basement. You wouldn't believe all the new cooking terms I've learned. Did you know there was a difference between basil and oregano?"

"Wow, really?" I smiled. "Well, tell her it was great. Fine dining to me."

"You should tell her yourself. It'll make her night."

We were making small talk, trying to avoid talking about work, but some conversations are unavoidable.

"Did you find out anything more about our vic's background?" I asked.

"Nothing," Mack said.

"Not even a parking ticket?" I asked.

"Nope. How is that possible?"

"It isn't," I said. "Trust me, he made a mistake at some point."

"Any luck on that safe-deposit box key?"

"No, you?"

"Maybe there isn't a key," Mack said.

"Or maybe the killer has it," I said, and smiled. "Could be what he was looking for at the beach house that day."

"You still doubting that the wives did it?"

"I'm not doubting anything. Only . . ."

"Only what?" Mack asked.

"Even if the three of them did get together before the murder, there's no indication they've communicated since. Don't you find that strange? Seems if they did do the crime together, they'd have a hard time staying away from one another."

"Maybe they don't want to be reminded of what they did," Mack said.

"Maybe. But I will say this: Whoever did pull that trigger probably did the world some good. Guy was an asshole and a sleaze."

"Yeah, but no matter what he was, it's still a crime," Mack said.

Although I didn't say this to Mack, in my opinion the law isn't a one size fits all. It's fallible. Innocent people go to jail more than we like to believe. Guilty people go free. Mobsters, goddamn financial crooks, and dope-running kingpins don't do time because they have resources, or serve shortened sentences at facilities that are more or less spas. And here were these three decent women, three loving and caring mothers, who were just living their lives, when some narcissistic asshole blindsided them, changed their whole world outlook, sucked them into a dark vortex where the code of civilization—honor, integrity, compassion, hope, strength, and love—was meaningless, where sin was the only way out. Sure they'd crossed the line, but at some point hadn't we all?

By the time I'd made the decision to return to Cooper's Island, my mother's Alzheimer's had advanced to the point that she didn't know me. My sister had moved down from Wilmington several months earlier; the kids stayed with Brian, their dad. Kelly was happy to have me there; she'd had it rough. The house was exactly as I remembered it, a midcentury modern up on a hill, the only one like it on the island. My dad had it designed. I remember him saying that the house style was all the rage in the big-city suburbs, all the architects were designing them, all the jet-setters lived in them, and obviously the islanders were backward with their colonials, cottages, and stilted ramshackles. From our living-room window, you could just get a peek of the ocean. Growing up, the kids at Saint Anne's school on Bodie Island had judged your status, and thus popularity, by whether or not your house had an ocean view. Mine just squeaked by and, as it turned out, so did I. I was almost popular, almost handsome, almost smart, but I thought then, and still do, that being "almost" gave me character. We weren't lifers, my family. I'd spent the first five years of my life in Detroit, and though I hardly remembered it, and probably because I knew I'd have an in, I chose to start my law enforcement career there. My dad had worked for Detroit PD as a beat cop, and while he was well respected by his peers and superiors, his lack of a college diploma meant no chance for advancement. So when a position opened up on this little island in North Carolina that we'd never heard of, even though it wasn't a promotion per se and was located in the "backward, mandolin-playing South," he had romantic visions of small-town life, of the sound of seagulls instead of car horns, the smell of the sea instead of our neighbor's bacon, a backyard instead of a fire escape, of slow nights, clear skies, and warm ocean water, the stuff of a leisurely and stress-free existence. The stuff that would cure his taste for alcohol. The stuff that would make him a better man, a better father. Unfortunately, life on Cooper's Island didn't turn out the way he planned.

He was too gruff, too determined, too busy in his mind to live the island life. With no friends, and no social outlets, he took to the bottle even more. He slept through entire mornings, blew off dispatch calls, got in barroom brawls, pissed off half the island and scared the rest, and then one day the employment termination notice came and he lost his pension and his pride. I was nine then, old enough to understand that something really bad had happened but too young to worry much about it. Maybe if I had known how to empathize, how to console him, he wouldn't have beat me. Maybe if I had loved him more, he would've loved me more. Maybe if I hadn't gone crying to my mother, he wouldn't have beaten her too.

My dad died when I was fifteen years old, six years after he lost his job. In the last months of his life, he was a changed man. Cancer had eaten away his meanness and left him a sniveling, shriveled-up invalid, and my mother, after all that man had done to her, after years of surviving his abuse, years of working herself to the bone to pay the bills he should've been paying, years of spending what little free time she had helping those less fortunate, my dear sweet mother dutifully changed my father's bedpans and wiped his fucking ass until the very end. Until the day, unbeknownst to her, I saw my mother remove my father's oxygen mask, wait patiently through his choking coughs, and after she was certain he was dead, replace it over his mouth.

I never told my mother what I saw, but for years I could barely look at her, and the day after I graduated from high school, I headed to Detroit. I wrote off my hatred and my leaving as a normal reaction to what I'd seen; my mother had done the unthinkable. Then she got sick. I told myself that obligation brought me back to Cooper's Island. My sister shouldn't have to care for my mother alone. Those last few months as I watched my mother fade away, I had a lot of time to think about why I'd mentally and physically left home. It's hard to admit to yourself that you're capable of murder, so much easier to deflect a weakness in oneself onto another. When I understood my anger had been misdirected, that it was me I hated, it was as if the dark clouds that enshrouded me had lifted. When I saw what my mother did that day, I'd not only felt a perverse satisfaction; I'd realized my father's murderer could've been me.

After Lisa put Evan to bed, she came out holding two guitars and the rusty harmonica I'd left at their place several months earlier. "How about we do some caroling?" she said.

The three of us strummed and hummed our way into the night. And, as I always do on magical nights like that one, I thanked the angels for putting me in that place at that time. And even though I'd been asking a lot of questions and having a lot of doubts about *my* religion, I thanked the god of cops for choosing me to be one of his sacred messengers.

Picasso

Mama's funk reached an all-time low after the holidays. She slept all the time; quit shopping for anything, including groceries; ignored basic beauty essentials like getting her nails done or waxing her eyebrows; and the only baths she took were these really long, weird ones late at night where instead of using bubble bath, she'd put a bunch of rose petals in the water. More than once I thought I heard her talking to someone in there even though I knew she was alone. I remember worrying she might be going crazy. The sleeping and bad-hygiene thing got so bad that sometimes I'd shake her awake and make her take a shower. Other times, especially at night, I felt so sorry for her that I'd just lie down next to her. That's how I found out about her nightmares. She'd talk or scream or thrash or cry, and sometimes she'd say Daddy's name. I always woke her when the dreams got bad, mainly so I could get some sleep myself. I'd started nodding off in class, which got me sent to the principal's office.

One morning, after I got dressed for school and found the Pop-Tart and cereal boxes completely empty, not to mention the milk sour, I decided I'd had enough. If Mama was going to sleep her life away, then I was going to take money from her stash drawer and do the grocery shopping myself. I knew where at least one grocery store within walking distance was, but I had a hankering for fresh jelly-filled doughnuts and I knew for a fact that that grocery only carried the boxed kind. Now, it's not that I'm entirely opposed to preservatives, it's just that the fresh doughnuts Mama always got from either Krispy Kreme or Whole Foods (which carried Krispy Kreme), both of which were at least a twenty-minute car ride away on a good traffic day, tasted so much better. They practically melted in your mouth they were so tasty. I decided to do an Internet search for grocery stores or bakeries that carried Krispy Kreme or something comparable, but couldn't find any. I even called the bakeries, thinking maybe they just didn't list everything, but everybody acted like I was from some other planet. Three bakeries in my town, and not a one of them had doughnuts? In my opinion, the world is carrying this healthy-food-item thing way too far. Then I remembered how Mr. Dork was always eating doughnuts, and that his came out of a white paper bag, not a box, so it stood to reason they'd be fresh, so even though I didn't find the prospect of asking Mr. Dork for anything, given that he'd obviously interpret my question as me thinking he was smart, what choice did I have?

Mr. Dork was staring out the window when I walked into the classroom. Mr. Dork is okay-looking I guess. He shaves his head, which is kind of cool, and he isn't fat or anything, but he wears the same cowboy boots every single day. He says they're made from an alligator that he killed himself. He also says he has climbed Mount Kilimanjaro, run the Boston Marathon, played college football, was a narc, which I mentioned earlier, and dated Nicole Kidman (he keeps a framed picture of her on his desk) when he was in high school. No way Mr. Dork went to an all-girl high school in Sydney, Australia. Mr. Dork is one of the stupidest liars I know, the kind that thinks people believe stuff just because he says it. I mean it's the information age. Ryan Anderson smiled at me as I walked to my seat. I smiled back. I hoped the entire class saw.

Especially Ashley Adams, who I had decided wasn't that nice after all. Since Ryan and I had showed up together at Dairy Queen, she'd started doing things to get his attention, like bringing him candy, flipping her ponytail, or *accidentally* brushing his shoulder as she walked by him. She gave me the stink eye whenever she thought Ryan wasn't looking. She'd also glued herself to the All That Girls.

When the bell rang, the kids who weren't there already, which was a bunch of them, scrambled to their desks.

"Quiet down," Mr. Dork said. He wrote the word *phlegmatic* on the chalkboard. "Who knows what this means?"

Nearly half the class raised their hands. I mean, seriously? He wrote that same word on the board every day. If it weren't for Ryan Anderson, who, thankfully, hadn't raised his hand, I probably would've gone to the principal's office three grades ago and begged to switch into the regular (read "dumb") kids class, which probably would've been an even bigger waste of my time, but at least I would've had Mrs. Fun (her real name was Bunn) all these years. At my school, you're stuck with the same teacher, same classroom, and same kids from kindergarten through eighth grade.

"Ashley," Mr. Dork said.

"Having a calm and unemotional disposition." I rolled my eyes. Ashley was also a kiss up, not to mention ever since she'd taken Ryan's place in the regional spelling bee, she'd been trying to worm her way into Ryan's and my afternoon spelling practices.

"That's right," Mr. Dork said. "So let's all put on our calm and unemotional dispositions, shall we?"

The day proceeded like any other. Math first, followed by English, recess, science, lunch, spelling, history, and, finally, social studies. After the last bell, I waited for the other kids to shuffle out of the room and went up to Mr. Dork's desk.

"Mr. York, do you mind if I ask you where you get your doughnuts?" He looked at me questioningly, so I added, "Mama asked me to stop and get fresh doughnuts on my way home. And since I've noticed that you eat doughnuts sometimes, I figured you might know of a grocery that carried them. Or a bakery."

"How is your mama?" he asked.

"Fine, sir," I said.

"That's good." He started stacking papers on his desk. "My wife generally gets them directly from Krispy Kreme"—*Mr. Dork has a wife?* I couldn't imagine any woman, especially a smart woman, marrying Mr. Dork—"but there is this one place. What street do you live on, Picasso?"

"Magnolia," I said.

"Ah yes, the flower streets." He'd said *flower streets* as if there were a bunch of them when in fact there were only four, that I knew of anyway: Magnolia, Honeysuckle, Sunflower, and Daffodil. And they were *Lanes* not *Streets*. Before I figured out that being an only child was a good thing, and before I knew I actually had two half brothers and a half sister, which wasn't a good thing, I used to ask Daddy if I could have a little sister, and he always said why did I need another sister when I had four of them already—Magnolia Lane, Honeysuckle Lane, Sunflower Lane, and Daffodil Lane. "We're practically neighbors," Mr. Dork continued. "My wife and I live on Bonnie Blue." Bonnie Blue is a street; it's one over from Cupid's Court where Ryan and Ashley live, and six streets over from Magnolia. In my opinion that isn't "practically neighbors."

"Really?" I said, even though I, and everyone else in my class, especially Jimmy Wilkes and Hayden Matthews, knew exactly where Mr. Dork lived. Who did he think toilet-papered his house last Halloween?

"There is a small mom-and-pop grocery store just a few blocks past your street called Ken's Market. I'll draw you a map." He went to the art cabinet and grabbed a sheet of red construction paper and a black marker—how old did he think I was?—and proceeded to draw.

"Thank you," I said, when he handed it to me.

"You bet," he said. "Just be careful, okay. You'll have to cross Sixth Avenue, but there are pedestrian signals."

I started walking away.

"Oh, and Picasso."

"Yes, sir?" I said.

"Keep up the good work. The school is grateful to you and Ryan. The two of you have put us in the regional spelling bee the second year in a row now. Principal Harper is even considering sending you two to the state competition if you finish well, which I'm confident you will." He winked.

Ryan was waiting in the hallway. He walked with me to Ken's Market, which, as it turned out, was in the little strip mall where Mama had taken Daddy's shirts to be cleaned, and where Pizza Palace and Ming Lounge were located, my two favorite takeout and delivery places.

"You want to go upstairs and play a video game?" I asked him, when we finished unpacking the groceries. "I just got *Civilization*."

"Cool," he said. "Where's your mom?"

"Sleeping. She's not feeling well." That was kind of true. I grabbed the doughnuts and some Cokes and we went to my room.

Ryan stayed until dinnertime. Mama still wasn't out of bed when he left, so I made one of the Marie Callender's chicken pies that I'd gotten from the grocery. I figured Mama wouldn't be too happy, if she knew that is (I planned to stuff the empty box deep into the outside garbage can), since she prides herself on her chicken pies and says the frozen ones taste awful, but I must admit I really liked it. In fact, I think I might've liked it even better than Mama's pies because, in all honesty, I'm not too big on broccoli.

The Wives

Murder, like lies, comes in many colors. Early on we'd decided that ours was pink.

Every time we met at Rainy Cove Park, we'd perform the same ritual. After our trek through the dense woods, we'd lay out our blanket and sit in silence for a while, then we'd take off our clothes, fold them neatly, stand side by side, hold hands, walk into the lake, and as if we were engaging in a baptismal ceremony, submerge ourselves in the water's warmth, invite its spirits to cleanse us of our impending act. For we each believed in our own almighties and thus knew on the most cellular of levels that what we planned was indeed one of the gravest of sins. When we returned to our sacred circle, we'd close our eyes, raise our faces to the sun, and imagine we sat inside a field of pink flowers, their velvety corollas tickling the skin of our necks, chins, cheeks, brushing across our naked breasts, bellies, thighs, toes, capturing us, folding us inside their stigmas, styles, ovaries, and only then, when we were fully buried within their ovules, fully soaked in their sweet redolence, only then were we at peace.

It was Bert who taught us the power of the pink petals. She recommended we continue this ritual: that we perform it in our hearts and minds while we killed Oliver and during the year we were apart.

We designated twelve "pink days." At exactly one minute past midnight on the third day of each month, the monthly anniversaries of Oliver's murder, we'd light candles, steep ourselves in baths of floating petals, and imagine ourselves communicating with one another. We'd share our pain, the difficulty we were having maneuvering our way through the empty hours, our moments of newfound joy. The only territory completely off-limits was the events of that fateful day. That information would only cross our minds and lips once, the day of our reunion. Not because we lamented or feared our crime; because we honored it. We held the act itself in the highest regard. We were part of an exclusive club. And we *knew,* because the winds and the water and the bark of the trees had whispered our destiny:

We would kill only once.

We would not get caught.

Yes, in the beginning, there would be chaos. Our lives would be shapeless and empty. Darkness would hover above us. But one day, long after Oliver's flesh had drooled from his bones and dried to ash, long after we'd suffered pinnacle upon pinnacle of the greatest anguish we'd ever known, long after the gods had called light back into our lives, we would reach our fullest potential.

The first several times we took our pink-petaled baths, we tried to sort through our emotions about Oliver. How had we been so wrong about him? How had we missed the signs? Prior to making the pact to kill him, we'd read as much as we could find on the topic of sociopaths, and we learned more than we ever wanted to know about such a man. We learned the truth, and because each of us was a mirror for the others, we could no longer live in denial. We could no longer go back to the way it had been, to the life we'd known. We could no longer be the women we once were.

We remembered the day we finally faced ourselves. For Diana it was that moment when she realized Oliver had seen her in the martini bar before. But there had been other clues, clues she now understood she'd chosen to miss. There was the time right after Picasso was born. She remembered being so tired, her body spent from natural childbirth, her breasts swollen with milk. She'd been half asleep when the phone rang, thought it was a wrong number because the woman on the end of the line had asked for someone named Peter.

"There's no one here by that name," she'd said. Oliver yanked the phone from her hand and rushed out of the room.

"I told you not to call here," Diana heard him say; she hardly recognized her husband's voice. It was cold, angry.

"I don't care if he's sick," he continued. "Fuck, I don't care if he's dead. Got it? Do not call here again."

It startled her when he threw the phone across the room.

Moments later he came back into the bedroom, sat down next to her, rubbed her shoulder. "Can I get you anything?" he'd asked. Kind. Soothing. The Oliver she knew.

"Who was that?" she asked.

"What do you mean?"

"On the phone."

"It was a wrong number, sweetie," he said. His eyes were clear, honest. "Lie back and get some rest."

For Jewels there was no specific clarifying event, but there was a moment of acknowledgment. For her, knowing had seeped into her in the way that dog urine soaks through an area rug. Things Oliver said didn't ring true. At times his actions didn't feel genuine. More and more there were his lies, his need to control, his skillful ability to manipulate even her, his lack of conscience. Most of all, there were those chilling eyes and that smile, the eyes and smile that weren't those of the man she'd married, the eyes and smile that brought to her mind one word: evil. She'd never considered herself the jealous type, and yet following him had seemed as natural as making love to him. She wasn't surprised by what she found, but she was afraid. Deep down she knew she couldn't confront him. There was nothing to gain by doing so, and a lot to lose. Approaching Diana and Bert was the only possible course of action. She *had* to know them. She *had* to understand how and why. She *had* to make sense of her role in this story. A story she could never have written. For Jewels, love departed as quickly as it had arrived. Diana and Bert had spoken of *feelings,* like pain, humiliation, betrayal, but she never felt any of those emotions. Fear was her only nemesis, and she'd realized quite soon after she discovered Oliver's ways that she could control the fear. She just had to keep one step ahead of it.

For Bert, realization came before she married Oliver. It came on a warm, sunny day when they were driving back from having dinner in town and their car hit a dog, a yellow Lab. The dog was still breathing when she'd gone to him, and she'd begged Oliver to put him in the car and take him to the vet, but he'd refused.

"He'll get blood all over the car," he said. "And look at him. He's almost dead anyway."

Bert had stayed behind after Oliver drove off. She knocked on nearby doors, found the dog's owner, accompanied her to the vet, paid the bill, consoled the woman when the dog died. Oliver was gone when she finally got home; not gone forever. Her days were merely up for that week. When she saw him again, she brought up the dog, but he insisted there'd been no such accident. His insistence was so pure, so steadfast, that she doubted herself rather than him. That day she realized it had always been that way. Oliver changed his story; she doubted her memories. And yet she'd married him.

The books we read painted a picture with which we were all familiar, but we'd ignored what we saw. We'd chosen only to see the Oliver we met. The handsome, charming, perfect man. The man who was so like us it was uncanny. Who knew our thoughts before we said them. Who walked in step with us. Whose eyes met ours with such keen, abiding interest. Whose touch could send shivers throughout our bodies. Whose declarations of love had changed our worlds.

The man who was too good to be true.

Picasso

Like: to find agreeable, enjoyable, or satisfactory.

Love: an intense feeling of deep affection; a deep romantic or sexual attachment to someone.

With the exception of the word *sexual,* which definitely didn't apply, although I must admit to being curious about, that definition very, very, very closely described the way I felt about Ryan Anderson. But since it wasn't one hundred percent accurate, strictly speaking I couldn't say I *loved* Ryan Anderson, but saying I *liked* Ryan Anderson wasn't right either. I spent several days searching for a word that was smack-dab in the middle of love and like but didn't find one, so I was left with having to say that I *really, really, really liked* Ryan Anderson.

At first, I blamed my dictionaries. I mean how was it possible that there wasn't a word out there somewhere that applied to me and my particular situation? Surely I wasn't the only eleven-year-old girl in the world who didn't use words carelessly or misuse them altogether. Then I remembered what the jacket of my newest dictionary said: "We Define Your World." It also said it was a new edition that included sixty-one thousand entries, which would indicate that its previous editions had fewer words. This raised two questions. Who were "we"? And how did new words get into dictionaries?

To find the answers, I abandoned my dictionaries (for the time being) and began searching the Internet. This was what I learned.

"We" were an undefined number of editors that spent hours scouring books, magazines, and periodicals for new words, new meanings of existing words, and different spellings of the same words. New words got into dictionaries based on usage, which raised another question. Who made up those new words? Answer: a neologist. More information: Neologism wasn't an official job; anyone could be a neologist. All you had to do was make up a word and get enough people to start using it so it made its way into books, magazines, and periodicals for dictionary editors to discover.

Right then and there, I decided to be a neologist. My new smack-dab in the middle of love and like word was *slike,* which I got by combining the word *super* with the word *like.* I mean how easy was that? Other than the fact that it sounded weird, which didn't worry me too much (since I figured all new words had probably sounded weird at first), it seemed like a pretty appropriate, even obvious choice. I remember wondering why nobody else had thought of it. I also remember thinking that since I had, I was obviously a natural at this neologism stuff. I rolled my new word over and over my tongue, said it out loud, and made it into sentences. I slike Ryan Anderson. I slike walking home with Ryan Anderson. I slike spelling. I slike my dictionaries. The possibilities were endless.

Now, obviously I was a big fan of dictionaries. In what other book could you read something and know with certainty that it was one hundred percent accurate? Even the Bible fictionalized stuff, mainly because it made for better reading. Dictionaries were not only stuffed with cool words but included descriptions of the nature, scope, and meaning of those words, also known as definitions. But even with all their positive features, I had to admit to myself that there were some not so small problems with dictionaries. They didn't include any practical instruction or advice on how to apply either the words or the definitions in real-life situations, and they didn't provide links or references to places that might offer further information. The words *boyfriend* and *girlfriend* were good examples. They both had pretty lame definitions that didn't include any information on how to get or keep one or the other. I mean at the very least the definition of *girlfriend* should have referenced the words *self-sacrifice, modesty,* and *pretense.* If it had, then maybe I would've been able to avoid the series of events that led to the ultimate demise of my first boyfriend-girlfriend relationship.

It started with Mr. Dork. One day, he told us about this hunting trip he took to Canada and how he saved a bunch of his friends from certain death by shooting an arrow straight into a bear's heart. Most of the kids listened intently, even nodded now and then. As usual, I got annoyed. I couldn't figure why the kids in my class were always acting all interested in Mr. Dork's lies, laughing at his jokes, and raising their hands to answer his ridiculous questions, even though they said they hated him. I asked Ryan Anderson about this phenomenon on the way home from school.

"They think he'll give them a better grade if they do," he said.

"That's moronic," I said. "All they have to do to get a better grade is study."

"Easy for you to say." He sounded irritated.

"What does that mean?"

"Not everybody is as smart as you, Picasso Lane."

I must admit that at the time I thought that was a compliment, I even thanked him, but he got kind of weird after that, and when we got to my house, he said he couldn't stay. The next day at school, he was back to normal Ryan again.

Then, a week later, something else happened. It was the regional spelling bee, and Ryan and I were the last kids still standing, which I thought was a good thing but, as it turned out, wasn't. It was Ryan's turn.

"Mr. Anderson, are you ready?" the pronouncer asked.

"Yes, sir," Ryan said.

"The word is chrysalis," the pronouncer said.

"May I have the definition?" Ryan asked. I figured he was just asking that because he could. Who didn't know the definition of chrysalis?

"A quiescent insect pupa especially of a butterfly or moth," the pronouncer said.

Ryan thought for a while. The room was so quiet you could've heard a bug crawling.

"You have thirty seconds, Mr. Anderson," the pronouncer said.

Ryan cleared his throat. "Chrysalis, C—R—Y—S—A—L—I—S, chrysalis."

I was stunned.

"I'm sorry," the pronouncer said. "That is incorrect."

All at once, the people in the room let out a moan of disappointment.

Ryan sat back down. I felt really bad for him, but at the same time I felt really good for me.

"Miss Lane," the pronouncer said.

I stood. A really weird feeling came into my belly, kind of like I was afraid, but I knew there wasn't any reason for me to worry because I knew how to spell *chrysalis,* and I was pretty certain I'd be able to spell the next word right too. If I didn't, Ryan would get another word. It wasn't until later that I realized that somewhere in the back of my brain I probably knew that Ryan coming in second place to my first place would be a problem, but like I said, I didn't know that then. I rattled off the correct spelling of *chrysalis.* The crowd clapped and cheered. I looked at Ryan and smiled. He not only didn't smile back, he didn't even look at me.

"Miss Lane," the pronouncer said, after the noise from the crowd had died down, "the word is supercilious."

Ryan was all nice to me after I won, he even congratulated me, but he didn't walk me home the next day, or the next, and before I knew it a whole week had gone by, and I was strongly considering making a big show of breaking up with him so everyone would think that us not speaking to each other was all my idea, but the truth was, I didn't want to. I still sliked him.

Now, I had hated the All That Girls since before I could remember. I had vowed never ever to talk to any of them, but I was desperate. The next day at lunch, I filled my tray with only healthy food items, because that's how they ate, walked boldly toward the table where they were sitting, and asked if I could join them.

They stopped talking and stared at me. Kelly Morgan, the self-appointed group leader, was the first to say something.

"Where's Ryan?" It was hard to believe that someone could sound snotty when they said only two words.

I shrugged and tried to act as if I didn't care one bit where Ryan Anderson was. "I don't feel like eating with him today. I'm mad at him."

Ashley Adams, who had been part of the All That Girls for more than a year by then, flipped her ponytail and said, "Isn't that just too bad."

They all laughed.

"What? The two of you ran out of words to spell together?" Ugly Cindy asked. Unlike me, Cindy Schneider had never grown out of her fat and, really and metaphorically, had a big mouth. How she ever got in with the All That Girls was a mystery to me.

More laughter.

"Yeah, cut the shit, Picasso," Kelly said. "We all know that Ryan was the one who stopped talking to you, not the other way around."

I was busted. But it didn't upset me all that much because I was still reveling in the fact that Kelly Morgan had referred to me by my real name, and that she hadn't placed an unflattering descriptive adjective in front of it.

"Look," I said, "I need some advice, and you guys are the only ones that can give it to me."

Nobody said anything, which was awkward. I thought about all the things I wanted to do right then and there, like stick my nose in the air and walk away, tell Gillian George she had some salad dressing on her chin, which she did, drop my tray *accidentally* on Kelly's head, and there were a bunch of others. I mean of all the things I wanted to do, not a one of them was resort to groveling. But what choice did I have?

So I said, "There seems to be general agreement that the four of you are very savvy, about boys that is, so I figured I may as well test that assumption."

"Savvy?" Gillian George asked.

"Knowledgeable on the realities of life," I said.

They all looked at Kelly Morgan, as if they'd run out of insults and expected her to figure one out.

"*Why* do you know this stuff?" Kelly asked.

"I know a lot," I said. "Like I know how you can pass the social studies test tomorrow." I was pretty sure this statement would pique Kelly's interest since her grades were so bad she was close to getting kicked off the cheerleading squad.

"How?"

"I know exactly what's on the test." And I did, because I was late to school the previous day and had to stay after. Mr. Dork said that since I was there, I could help him do some filing, and then he fell asleep at his desk, which wasn't unusual, so I figured, well, why not take a peek at the social studies test. And guess what? He'd already made a bunch of copies, probably the ones he intended to pass out, so I folded one up and stuck it in my underwear. "How about we consider this a trade. You tell me how to get Ryan back, and I'll share the test answers with you."

Four sets of eyes widened. They all started talking at once. It was pretty hard to decipher their exact words, but the gist of it was they were considering it. Then they stopped talking, again all at once. It was like they'd rehearsed. There was a long pause.

"We accept," Kelly said. "We'll tell you how to solve your problem."

"That's not enough," I said.

"What else?" Kelly asked.

"It has to work."

"Believe me," Kelly said, "it'll work. Unfortunately the idiot still likes you."

"He does?" I waited for one of them to call me Pitiful Picasso.

"You are so inept," Kelly said.

Wow. A big word for Kelly. "All right. Tell me."

"First, you have to apologize," Kelly said.

"For what?"

"It doesn't matter. Just say you're sorry and you miss him."

"That's it?" I asked.

"That's it," she said.

She'd said *first,* which implied there was a second. "Then what?"

"Do you have any idea why he's mad at you?"

"No," I said.

Kelly rolled her eyes. "Maybe you're the idiot. He's upset because you won the stupid spelling bee."

"Why would he be mad about that?"

"Because he didn't win."

"But that's not my fault."

"Do you want him to be your boyfriend or not?"

"I guess," I said.

"Then you need to act like a girlfriend," Kelly said.

"I don't understand."

"Girlfriends let their boyfriends win. Girlfriends are never ever smarter than their boyfriends."

"That doesn't make sense," I said. "I can't help it if I'm smarter."

"You're lame," Kelly said. The other All That Girls nodded. "Don't you get it? It is a widely known fact that girls are really the ones in charge of relationships, but since boys have fragile egos, we need to let them think they are. All we have to do to keep them happy is pretend. Pretend we aren't as smart. Pretend we can't lift things or open doors. Pretend *you,* Picasso Lane, don't know how to spell every single word."

I'm certain I must have looked as stunned as I felt. I mean, that was the most illogical thing I'd ever heard. Why would I pretend I didn't know how to spell?

"Trust me on this," Kelly said. "If you do what I said, you'll get him back, but if you lose him again because you're not willing to pretend, that's not on me."

Kelly Morgan was the last person I'd ever trust, but I knew she wanted that social studies test bad, and what did I really have to lose, other than my pride that is, so I did exactly what she said. I apologized to Ryan and told him that I missed him. At least that last part was true. He immediately got nice to me again and resumed the practice of walking me home. I gave Kelly Morgan and the other All That Girls copies of the test. They all got A's. I got four new friends.

This was what I learned. One: I needed to find out how to get a job as one of those dictionary editors. Two: Or better yet, I could write a new, holistic dictionary. Three: Having a boyfriend was a lot more difficult than I thought. Four: In order to keep a boyfriend, on top of being nice, sweet, and a good listener, you had to practice self-sacrifice, modesty, and pretense; in other words, you had to be an expert liar. Five: Self-sacrifice just wasn't a strong enough word. Losing an entire spelling bee? That was *martyrdom.* Six: The All That Girls, especially Kelly Morgan, weren't that stupid after all, at least about some things.

Kyle

They say timing is everything. That's certainly the case with a murder investigation. It's also the case with lovemaking. Usually the two don't go together.

I'll start with the murder investigation.

Remember Julie Lane's solid alibi? She was at a design charrette in Philadelphia the day of the murder. We'd done our job. We'd verified that she had checked in and boarded both of her flights. We'd verified that she was at the charrette. In the event that she'd been able to sneak away, commit the murder, and return undetected, we'd verified that no cars had been rented and no flights had been reserved in her name. End of story, right? Wrong.

It was like my mentor back in Detroit had said, a cop should always be looking for the world he doesn't know exists. It was all there right in front of us, and yet we didn't even think to look for it.

Mack and I were at the office filing our monthly reports. "It's impossible to keep these names straight," he said. "I know I keep saying that, but it's not getting any easier. There's the first Mrs. Lane, the second Mrs. Lane, and the third Mrs. Lane, better known as Ms. Miles. I get all that, but I keep mixing Diana and Julie up on these reports. I say Diana did or said something when

it was actually Julie and vice versa. I even get the women themselves mixed up, Diana and Julie especially. There's the hair thing,
they both have blue eyes, and they're about the same height."

"I don't think they look that much alike," I said. "Diana's a little
taller, and . . ." I paused.

"More attractive?" Mack said.

"Well, yeah."

"To you maybe," Mack said. "I'm betting the average Mary or
Joe wouldn't notice that big of a difference. Geez, they could probably take each other's places. You know, like those twins in that
movie."

"*The Parent Trap?*" I stopped writing and looked at Mack.
"Wait a minute. What did you say?"

"I said it's like they're twins."

"No, I mean before that."

"They could take each other's places?"

"Yeah, that," I said.

"Wow," Mack said.

"Didn't you say something about not finding Diana Lane's
driver's license at the beach house that day?" I asked.

"Yeah," Mack said. "She said she'd misplaced it. Shit. Why
didn't we think about this earlier? I'll get Bonnie to search all the
airline databases."

"No, have Klide do it," I said.

It didn't take long for Klide to find a reservation in Diana
Lane's name for a one-way flight from Norfolk, Virginia, to Philadelphia, Pennsylvania, on the morning of Oliver Lane's murder.
She also found a reservation for a rental car in Diana Lane's name
that was picked up in downtown Philly at 11:03 the night of
July 2nd and dropped off at Norfolk International Airport at
9:28 the next morning. Assuming we were right about Julie Lane
orchestrating this entire thing, which I would've bet my meager
life savings on, that left plenty of time for her to drive to Cooper's

Island during the night, do the murder, drive to Norfolk, drop off the car, hop on a 10:15 a.m. flight back to Philly and make her scheduled 11:50 a.m. flight home to Raleigh.

The next morning, Mack and I headed back to the mainland. It wasn't a Sunday, but we didn't need to worry about catching anyone at home. We'd decided to make this an official visit, and Captain Mercy had been more than willing to loan us one of his interrogation rooms.

Julie Lane didn't look as in control in the small, spare room as she had at her condo. She wore a gray silk blouse under a charcoal suit that looked like it had been tailored specifically for her, which meant it was, and looked, expensive. Mack asked her to sit across the table from him. I was leaning up against the wall behind her chair with my arms crossed. She looked at me briefly as she sat, but then focused her eyes on Mack. She didn't wait for any formalities.

"Why am I here?" she asked.

Mack set the airline and rental car reservations down in front of her. "Take a look at these, Mrs. Lane," he said, "and tell me what you see."

She looked, but didn't touch them. "Some sort of list from US Airways."

"What else?"

"A Hertz Rent-a-Car statement."

"What name is on them?"

Without checking the paperwork again, she looked straight into Mack's eyes and said, "Diana Lane."

Mack stared back at her and didn't say anything.

"What does this have to do with me?" she asked. "I don't even know Diana Lane. Why would I know anything about her future travel plans?"

"Past travel plans," Mack said.

"Whatever," she said.

"Did you note the date?" Mack asked. "Why don't you take a better look?"

She looked at Mack defiantly. "I don't need to take a better look, Detective. I saw the date just fine."

"Don't you find it interesting that Diana Lane was in two places that day? At the beach house and on a plane?"

"That's the wonder of air travel, I suppose," she said. "If you're resourceful, which I'm assuming this woman is—Oliver wouldn't have been attracted to a neophyte—you can get places pretty quickly these days."

"In this case, resourcefulness wouldn't cut it, ma'am. Detective Kennedy and I, along with ten other people, can attest to the fact that Diana Lane was in a beach house on Cooper's Island when that plane took off. Are you implying she's a magician?"

"I'm not *implying* anything, Detective. I don't care what that woman is. Nor do I care whether or not she was on some airplane."

"Mrs. Lane," I said. She seemed startled by my voice but didn't look at me. "Detective Jones is being polite. What he's trying to say is that we know it was *you*."

She twirled a lock of hair. "What do you mean, me?"

I walked around the table and faced her. "You used Diana Lane's name and identification. You rented that car. You were on that plane."

"I told you I was at a design charrette. A lot more than ten people can verify that. And besides, these days, with such tight airport security measures, it would be impossible for someone to impersonate someone else."

"Tight security also means plenty of surveillance," I said.

"It wasn't me," she said. Her voice sounded hollow. "And even if it was, what does that prove?"

"Motive and opportunity," Mack said.

"And how about evidence, detectives?" A thin, satisfying smile crossed her lips. "I'm not answering any more questions without a lawyer. So if you think you have something on me, then arrest me. Otherwise, I've got to pick up my boys from preschool." She rose, and without looking back, she walked out the door.

"She's right about evidence," I said to Mack. "Even if we can prove she rented a car and got on a plane, we've got to put her at the scene."

"What about Diana Lane?"

"What about her?"

"We going to talk to her?"

"I'll handle that," I said. "You follow up with the airport cameras and the crime scene. And show her picture around. See if she got gas somewhere along the way. The guys on the ferry may not have recognized Roberta Miles, but they may remember a slim, leggy blonde."

Diana Lane looked thin and tired when she opened the door, but I wasn't any less drawn to her. In fact, she looked even lovelier, even more vulnerable. As always, I couldn't take my eyes off her. And as always, I wondered what it was about her that could so easily unsettle me, make me lose my mind and my cool. It was like I was fifteen all over again, and Harriet Tanner had smiled at me as I passed her locker.

"You sound under the weather," I said, when she placed the tea pitcher on the coffee table.

"I can't seem to get rid of this bug," she said.

"Have you been to a doctor?"

"It's nothing, Detective. It'll pass eventually."

"Is Picasso at school?"

"Yes," she said. "What can I help you with?"

I told her about the airline ticket and rental car agreement.

"My name? But that's impossible." She seemed genuinely confused. In the past when she'd answered uncomfortable questions, I could always tell she wasn't providing the entire truth. This time I would've sworn she was. She seemed surprised yet hurt, as if something that she hadn't understood, something that had been bothering her, had become clear, but not in the way she'd hoped.

"Do you have any idea how Julie Lane might have gotten your driver's license?"

"No," she said.

"You misplaced it, right?"

"What do you mean?"

"You mentioned it at the beach house that day, the . . . um . . . day your husband died."

"Did I?" she said. She began wringing her hands. "Oh, that's right. It was a false alarm. I found it a few days later, under the sofa. It must've fallen out of my bag. I have this habit of putting it in there loose— Oh my. I never poured our tea." She reached for the pitcher, but her hand was shaking too badly to grasp the handle.

I took her hand in mine to steady it. I meant to say "Let me do that," but instead I pulled her to me and kissed her. And then I couldn't stop kissing her.

Somehow we got to her bedroom; *that* I remember. The rest was a wash of skin: her lips, her thighs, her neck, her breasts, her sweet, sweet ass. Then I was inside her, lost and found simultaneously. Like murder, there's a smell to sex, a heady combination of sweat and pheromones. Sometimes the stench two people make is stale, sour, and you can't wait to wash it away with a shower. Other times the smell is fragrant, seductive, better than anything your body can produce on its own, and, like a kid who gets the best attributes of his parents, any resemblance to you alone is lost. That's how it was with Diana Lane.

I didn't drive back to Cooper's Island that afternoon; I got a hotel room. I took a shower and camped there until I was sure my showing back up at the house wouldn't tip Picasso off to what I'd been doing with her mother. On the way over, I stopped off at the grocery store to pick up dinner and wine. I tried not to think about the case. I tried not to think about the fact that even though it might look as if Julie Lane killed her husband, the entire thing could just be a red herring. I tried not to think about the fact that even if Julie Lane was the shooter, Diana was still complicit.

Picasso answered the door when I returned, two grocery bags in my arms. "Mama said you were coming to dinner. Are you cooking?"

"What gave it away?" I asked, and smiled.

Picasso

Smad: to be very, very, very angry with someone.

Hate: to feel intense or passionate dislike for someone.

Everything changed for the better when Detective Kennedy started coming around the house in an "unofficial" capacity. It was January, which was about halfway through Mama's, Jewels's, and Bert's year apart, also known as Purgatory Year or just plain *purgatory* (a place or state of suffering inhabited by the souls of sinners who are expiating their sins before going to heaven). I'd randomly zeroed in on that word a few days after Daddy died, and even though Mama and I aren't religious, and especially aren't Roman Catholic, I remember thinking it was a positive sign. After all, spending a little time expiating was far more desirable than the alternative. For the most part, Mama and Detective Kennedy did about the same stuff Ryan Anderson and I did. They sat on the porch swing, if it wasn't too cold out, or the sofa, or at the dining-room table, and talked. They watched movies. They even played board games like Scrabble, Monopoly, and Clue. They didn't seem to mind if I hung out with them. It was hard for me to stay away from a game of Scrabble. I really liked it when Detective Kennedy visited, and I think Mama did too. She quit sleeping so much, and she started wearing makeup again. But, more important, everybody seemed to have forgotten about Daddy's murderer. There was no sign of Mama or anyone else going to jail. Detective Jones hadn't been to our house in forever. Detective Kennedy had stopped asking official questions. And the rumors had died down.

What was weird was that sometimes it seemed like none of it ever happened. Jewels didn't show up at our door that day. I didn't spy on her and Bert when they were parked in the church parking lot. The three of them didn't meet at Rainy Cove Park and plot to kill Daddy. Daddy wasn't murdered. In fact, sometimes it felt like Daddy never lived at all, or if he had, it was a long, long time ago, in a place that wasn't real, like maybe another dimension. Nobody ever talked about him, and since Mama had finally gotten around to taking his clothes and other stuff to Goodwill, it was easier to pretend I never had a daddy. That way I could imagine that Mama had found me on one of her ocean swims. What a pleasant surprise I'd been—a fully grown and pretty eleven-year-old standing on a big white shell, hair all flowing like Aphrodite's. She loved me from the instant she saw me and decided to raise me on her own. Detective Kennedy was a bonus.

One day, when I was feeling pretty bad about liking Detective Kennedy so much, Kelly Morgan, who for some reason was being really nice to me, grabbed my arm as I was walking by her. She was eating lunch with Ashley Adams, Gillian George, and Ugly Cindy two tables over from where Ryan sat with Audu, which I already said was short for Audubon. What is interesting is that Audu is really good at biology, like I'm good at lying. When I have kids, I'm going to be really careful what I name them.

"Here sit." Kelly patted the bench. The other All That Girls shifted around to make room for me. "How's it going with Ryan?"

"Fine," I said. "Everything's pretty much back to normal." For the most part it was, but I had to admit, at least to myself, that Ryan wasn't quite as attentive as he was before the incident that I ended up apologizing for, even though I was being self-sacrificing and modest, and was letting him win all the spelling bees.

"Pretty much?" Kelly asked. If there's one thing Kelly is, it's astute. "Are you sure? You didn't look too happy when you were walking by just now. If I hadn't stopped you, you probably would've run into a wall, you were so distracted."

"No, really," I said. "It's good. I was just thinking about something else." No way I was going to say anything about Mama and Detective Kennedy to Kelly Morgan. It'd be all over the school by the time lunch ended.

"Hmm," Kelly said. "Well, just so you know, one boyfriend is as good as another. They might look different and smell different, but when it comes right down to it, they're all the same. So if stuff doesn't work out, just know you can replace him."

"Ryan Anderson isn't replaceable," I said.

"Oh yeah?" Kelly said. "What do you think, Ashley?" Ashley had finally stopped flipping her hair at Ryan. Her new boyfriend was Audu.

"Kelly's right," Ashley said. "I don't miss Ryan one bit."

"That's because Audu is so hot," Gillian said.

Ashley's back was to the table where Ryan and Audu sat, so she had to turn all the way around to look at him. "He is, isn't he?"

"See," Kelly said to me. "Not just replaceable, better."

Audu caught Ashley staring at him. He smiled wide, motioned her to come sit with him. She balanced her tray as she carefully rose and stepped one foot at a time out of the bench. "Want to come?" she asked me.

Awkward. "I'm good here," I said.

All four of us—the three remaining All That Girls and me—stared at her with open mouths as she trotted over and inched her way between Ryan and Audu. Then Ryan motioned for me to come over.

"Don't," Kelly said. "You need to play hard to get. That way you keep the upper hand."

I pretended I didn't understand he was inviting me over and just waved.

"Laugh," Kelly said.

"What?" I asked.

"Act like I told you something really funny. You know, like you're having a really good time without him."

Now, I wasn't one to show excitement of any kind, but because Kelly told me to, and by that time I was doing pretty much anything Kelly told me to do because I totally trusted her insight into boyfriend-girlfriend relationships, I laughed bigger and harder than I ever had. Within a few minutes, Ryan was standing over me asking if he could walk me to class.

The thing is, I liked Detective Kennedy from the very first, and when he started coming around to see Mama and me, I liked him even more. But did I like him as much as or better than Daddy? I will say this: I was happy when he started sleeping over. They didn't think I knew what they did in Mama's bedroom. What is it with adults? Do they think we can't see or hear? For example, one time when Detective Kennedy came over for dinner, he started rubbing Mama's leg under the table. I could tell because his arm was moving back and forth. I dropped my fork on purpose so I could see for sure. I figured they'd at least stop rubbing at each other when I went to pick it up, but they didn't. They didn't even notice. I mean the fork had made a pretty loud ping, ping sound, and the chair leg squeaked so loud when I pushed it back that it hurt my teeth, not to mention that I disappeared under the table and watched them for I don't know how long, but even if it were only a few seconds, you'd think they would've wondered where I went. Obviously adults are the ones that don't see and hear stuff.

At least right then and there, I did like Detective Kennedy better than Daddy. Thinking about Daddy made me feel sad and guilty, and being around Detective Kennedy made me feel happy and light, and the truth was, everything had gotten so much better since Daddy died. My horizontality seemed to have morphed into verticality. Not only was I tall and surprisingly okay-looking (though I worried since if that had changed once, it could again), I was clearly and officially Super Picasso. The kids at school seemed to like me. Mama and Detective Kennedy were so busy being in love that I could pretty much do whatever I wanted at home. Thanks to Kelly Morgan's advice, Ryan Anderson seemed to have completely gotten over losing the spelling bee. But destiny, or maybe it was karma (a Kelly word), was determined to ruin my first boyfriend-girlfriend relationship.

A new girl moved to town; her name was Lucy Baxter. And guess what? It was bad enough that she was in my grade and that Mr. Dork shuffled the whole class around to fit her into alphabeti-cal seating order, which meant right behind Ryan Anderson, but on top of that, her parents had bought the house right next to Ryan Anderson's, which was also down the street from Ashley Adams's. Not that I was worried about Ashley anymore, but liv-ing on Ryan's street had worked for her, so it stood to reason it might for Lucy Baxter. The first time I saw her, my jaw *literally* (that means not really, but used for emphasis or to express strong feeling) dropped. I had never seen a prettier girl, even prettier than Mama, definitely prettier than Ashley Adams or Kelly Mor-gan. Her eyes were as blue as one of those Blue Raspberry Arctic Rush slushy drinks at Dairy Queen, so blue they looked fake, like she was wearing colored contact lenses, and her long straight hair was almost white it was so blond. We were all getting breasts by then, but hers were as big as a teenager's, and she wasn't even fat. *Svelte* was the word Ryan Anderson used to describe her. We'd just gotten it in spelling practice, but still it was a kind of big word for him. I mean, don't get me wrong. Ryan Anderson was really smart, but he was also a true boy, so he had an image to uphold. Our class was in the gym playing tennis when he said it. It was a special track with a professional teacher. We did four that year: gymnastics, volleyball, golf, and tennis. Ryan and I were sitting out the rotation. His eyes followed Lucy's every movement.

"What do you mean, svelte?" I'd asked.

"Slender and elegant," he said. Since losing that spelling bee, Ryan had become a walking dictionary. He'd even copied me and started a word journal, which I have to admit bothered me. Mama always says when people copy you it's a form of flattery, but I think she's wrong. I think when somebody copies you it's the same thing as stealing from you. That's why they invented patents.

"I know the definition of svelte," I said. "I was wondering if you meant it as a compliment." I was fishing, of course. How could it not be a compliment?

He didn't answer right away. "She's not my type." He was lying. If anybody could tell a liar, I could.

"Am I your type?" I asked. I sounded so pathetic.

"For someone so small, she's a pretty good athlete. Did you see her last serve? Watch. She's up again. Wow, did you see that?" He stood and clapped.

Ryan Anderson clapped? He never even raised his hand, or did much of anything spontaneous. Actually, I was kind of embarrassed for him. I looked around to make sure no one had noticed his brief departure from coolness. Then, to my utter horror, he put his thumb and forefinger in his mouth and whistled.

Everyone looked, including Lucy Baxter. All the way from where she stood on the tennis court, she smiled.

Bitch.

"Who's a bitch?" Ryan asked.

I hadn't realized I'd said it out loud. "I said *rich*."

"Oh," he said. "That would make sense."

"Why?"

He hunched his shoulders.

"Why?" I asked again.

"She just seems so confident."

And I'm not? I decided that was a good time to use the power of suggestion, something else I'd learned form Kelly Morgan. "Really? She seems a little too whiny to be rich."

"Whiny?" Ryan hated whiny girls.

"Oh that's right," I said. "How would you know? She was whining to Kelly and me about the snow when we were all in the bathroom together this morning. Apparently she hates snow because it gets her hair wet. And she hates all winter sports. She practically hibernates all winter. Oh, and she doesn't like to read either."

"Huh," Ryan said.

That got his attention. No way Ryan could like a girl who didn't read.

The bell rang then and we dispersed to the locker rooms to change back into our school uniforms.

One week later, I saw Ryan and Lucy leaving school together.

Now, I'd tried to convince myself that Ryan wasn't actually walking Lucy home; they'd just happened to leave school at the exact same time. And even if they did walk together all the way home, it didn't necessarily mean anything. After all, they lived right next door to each other, and since they probably walked at the exact same speed, it made perfect sense that they'd end up walking side by side all the way home. I never did actually hear Ryan offer to walk Lucy home, like he'd always done with me before we became boyfriend and girlfriend. Obviously I had just imagined that Ryan seemed preoccupied the previous week. I must not have heard him right when he told me he couldn't walk me home that day because his dad needed his help with something, because if that was true then I couldn't have seen Lucy and him at Dairy Queen. The same Dairy Queen where he had taken me the first time he walked me home after school. The same Dairy Queen where at least half my class had decided to show up. I mean, did I miss an intercom announcement that said, "Be at Dairy Queen right after school today so you can witness the total and utter embarrassment of Picasso Lane"?

So there were the three of us trying to act like nothing was weird about just happening to all be at Dairy Queen at the very same time, even though at least I knew that I hated runny ice cream, especially in the winter, and we all knew that Dairy Queen was not even close to being on any of our ways home.

"Hi, Picasso," Lucy said. She was all teeth.

"Oh yeah, hi, Picasso," Ryan said. "What are you doing here?"

What am I doing here? "I came to get ice cream," I said, wanting badly to add, *Do you have a problem with that?*

"Wow, me too," Lucy, bless her heart, said with high-pitched excitement. "I'm so happy you're here. I've been so wanting to get to know you and your friends." *Friends?* She looked over at the table where Kelly, Gillian, Cindy, and Ashley were sitting, so I did too. Kelly saw me and waved me over, which made sense because I'd gone to Dairy Queen to meet them in the first place, since Ryan had plans, but right then and there no way could I act all fun and cool, prerequisites for All That Girl meetings. "I can't believe how smart you are," Lucy was saying. "Oh, do you think you might be able to help me out with spelling? I suck at spelling."

"Why don't you ask Ryan," I said. "He's the best speller at our school."

Lucy looked confused.

"Didn't he tell you?" I asked.

She looked at Ryan. "You said spelling was for geeks."

Ryan didn't say anything.

"So now I'm a geek?" I asked Ryan.

He looked down at his shoes as if he'd just noticed something on them that he'd never seen before.

"Oh, sorry," Lucy said. "Of course you're not a geek. I sure wish I was better at spelling."

"Right," I said, and stomped out the door and down the street. I'd gone pretty far when I heard someone calling my name.

"Picasso, wait up."

I turned to see Lucy only steps behind me. "I'm sorry, Picasso." She sounded out of breath from running. "I didn't mean to say that about spelling. I don't know why I said it. It was insensitive."

Insensitive? I was surprised she'd used the correct word. "I really want to be friends with you and Kelly and the other girls. The five of you sure seem tight." *Five* of us? "I'm really sorry. Please forgive me?"

"Are you sorry for stealing my boyfriend?" I said, and walked off.

The farther away I got from Dairy Queen, the lighter my footsteps got. I realized I was smiling. I knew I should still be smad at Ryan Anderson, and that I should hate Lucy Baxter, which I obviously was and did, but right then and there I felt even happier than the day Ryan Anderson gave me the valentine because Lucy Baxter thought that I, Picasso Lane, was an All That Girl.

The Wives

It was the seventh month of our year apart when we first allowed ourselves to summon positive memories of Oliver. Prior to that point, we'd concentrated on the pain he'd caused us, perhaps because that was how we'd always been able to justify our crime, but that night as we lay inside our pink-petaled baths, each of us welcomed joyous thoughts.

Diana recalled the day she taught Oliver to paint. It was before they'd married, before he'd built her the studio above the garage, when she still kept one in town. She'd invited him over. She remembered him walking by each painting, slowly, stopping to admire a figure, a still life, a brushstroke; telling her his bones didn't contain an inch of creativity. She pulled out a large, newly primed canvas, several jars of paint, cans of brushes, palette knives, turpentine, and wipe cloths.

"The first rule is not to think," she said. "The second is to use your entire body, not just your hand or your wrist. The third is to paint for you, no one else. Finally, paint a world you'd like to live in, not one you'd like to see."

"Will you pose for me?" he asked.

Nude modeling was something Diana had done in college for extra money before her parents died, before she'd received the proceeds of her father's estate and insurance policies. It wasn't necessarily that she was an exhibitionist, but she'd never been shy. Shyness was for the modest, and modesty was for those who aspired to perfection not for those who'd been born with its gift. Diana, though raised a gracious Southern lady and far from vain, had always known that her physical form was lovely, her curves elegant, and with the same understated confidence as a cat, she knew what light, what color, what fabric would add regality to her odalisque poses.

That day Diana chose to lie on an antique settee covered in deep blue velvet. Under the diffused lighting, her olive-toned skin appeared milky white. Strands of blond hair wound around her neck, obscured one nipple. A long floral silk scarf wrapped around her hips, wandered between her thighs, loosely bound her ankles. Her eyes, nearly the color of the sofa, challenged her captor. Oliver was a quick study. He mixed and swirled and brushed and scraped. He used broad gestures, thick lines, bright colors. Periodically, he'd make mud of what he'd done, dip the cloth in the turpentine and wash it all away. Hours passed. Diana fell asleep. It was dark out when she woke. Oliver still painted. She rose, rubbed her stiff joints, and walked to him.

"May I see?" she asked.

He turned the canvas toward her. She saw a never-ending field of lilies. In places, the flowers were so dense the colors bled together. Where this happened, the paint was rich, thick, lush. She laughed. "It's beautiful, but it looks nothing like me."

"You said to paint a world I'd like to live in," he said. "This is the inside of you."

Jewels recalled the time she and Oliver drove to the Hamptons to meet her parents. It was the weekend after they'd confessed their love to each other. She remembered him being nervous. While this hadn't surprised her, after all she was very close to her parents, especially her father, she had paused. Oliver had always been so in control, more so than even Cruel Jewels, and watching him fidget, get lost twice on the way, fumble and drop his keys in the driveway when they finally arrived, endeared him to her.

"My father will love you," she said. "Really. There's nothing to worry about."

Oliver had smiled, and said, "Worried? Who's worried?"

Just as she thought, her father had liked Oliver immediately. They discussed the law, stocks, and current events. Her father told the story of how he met her mother.

"I was a student at NYU and had taken another girl to the ballet, but when I saw Genevieve dance, I was mesmerized. I sent my date home in a cab and waited outside the theater door. I was amazed she agreed to have coffee with a lowly finance major."

"An extremely handsome finance major," Jewels's mother interrupted.

Jewels's father touched his wife's cheek, kissed her. "We were inseparable after that night. Our precious Jewels was born fifteen years later. Like me, she grew up in this very house. It's been in the family for three generations."

Jewels's mother brought out the album of clippings from her dancing career. Oliver watched patiently as she paged through them, commented on a costume, a plié, a review.

"I see where Jewels gets her athleticism and grace," he said.

Her mother blushed. "Our Julie is quite the runner," she said. "She placed in the Junior Olympics, you know."

Oliver looked at Jewels with such admiration. It was as if before that moment, he hadn't really *seen* her. "I had no idea. Do you have pictures?"

"No, Mother, please," Jewels said, but her mother wasn't to be deterred.

While a fire popped and cracked in the stone fireplace of the small cottage, her mother shared album after album of her daughter's life and childhood. Later they played bridge, watched the news, had nightcaps. After her parents retired, Jewels took Oliver into the attic and showed him her Barbie collection. He helped her set up the Dream House, gave movement and voice to Ken. That night, two unusual things occurred: Ken didn't die, and Oliver and Jewels didn't have sex. Instead, they fell asleep in each other's arms.

Bert recalled hiking the Appalachian Trail with Oliver. They walked eight to ten hours every day. At night, they met up with other brave souls, shared campfires, and slept under the shade of trees or in the pup tent Oliver carried in his backpack. Oliver had surprised her with his knowledge of wildflower species and his seemingly innate survival skills. He could make a fire by rubbing sticks together, walk miles without tiring, and his temperament never changed. He seemed happier, more at peace than she'd ever seen him.

One night they came upon a river. Just as she had that first time the three of us met at Rainy Cove Park, Bert suggested they take off their clothes and go for a swim. The moon reflected on the water. A dog howled in the distance. When they left the water, Oliver built a fire. That night, Bert was certain she saw their futures in the flames. Ever since she was a child, she'd had visions, and sometimes she knew what people were thinking. It wasn't like she heard voices, nothing as frightening as that, it was more like she saw thoughts in a person's eyes or felt their auras. Over the years, she'd read about others who shared her gift, and she'd attended classes and seminars to sharpen it. Oliver would have many children, and not only ones spawned by his sperm in her womb. She saw the shadows of two other women, and while perhaps that should have bothered her, it didn't. The women were her sisters; in the not too distant future, they would comfort her. She saw herself birthing a daughter, and many years later with grandchildren by her side, and though Oliver wasn't there, she saw love, happiness, and fulfillment. She lied to Oliver about what she saw. She told him the two of them would grow old together, surrounded by many children and grandchildren, and because she created that story for him, she decided to believe it too.

What she didn't see was Oliver's murder. She didn't see herself firing a gun. She didn't see the bullets piercing his chest and stomach. She didn't see him dying.

Picasso

Deception: the act or practice of deceiving someone by concealing or misrepresenting the truth; to trick or fool.

Kill: to cause the death of a person, animal, or other living thing.

There was this boy at school who accidentally shot his twin brother. I was seven years old then. They weren't in my grade—they were older than me by a year—but I still knew them. Their names were Jason and Jeremy Green. Unlike Daddy, Jeremy's dying did make the front page of the *Hollyville Herald,* so even though people talked about it for a while, they couldn't spread rumors. The facts were all there. After cleaning his gun, Jason and Jeremy's dad put it away, but he forgot to lock the cabinet in the garage where he kept it. The boys found it while searching for their basketball. The Green family moved soon after the incident occurred.

For a long time I thought what happened to Jeremy Green was the only form of killing that wasn't murder, but a couple of months before Daddy died, I walked in on him staring at the barrel of a gun. He was sitting on his bed.

"Is everything okay, Daddy?" It wasn't that I was surprised he had a gun; I'd heard Mama and Jewels talking about it on the phone that time. It was the way he was holding it. I mean, everyone knew it wasn't very smart to point a gun at someone, especially yourself.

When he saw me, he quickly pulled the gun away from his face. "Hey, Pimpernel (any of various plants of the genus *Anagallis,* especially the scarlet pimpernel, with creeping stems and flat, five-petaled flowers)." He spun the chamber; bullets dropped on the off-white comforter making little dents in its puffiness. "Do you want to hold it?"

"Won't Mama get upset?"

"I don't think there's any reason to tell her, do you?"

"I guess not." I took the gun from him, held it. It was small but heavy. "Why do you have it?"

"So I can protect you and Mama if a bad guy comes into our house."

"Why would a bad guy come in our house?"

"He won't," Daddy said. "It's just in case."

Daddy was big into just-in-cases. Like he'd say "Let's pick up some milk just in case we're out" or "Let's record *CSI* just in case we don't get home on time." The thing is, when we'd get home there wouldn't be any milk and *CSI* would be over, so when he said that about bad guys coming into our house, I didn't sleep for a week.

"But won't you go to jail if you shoot someone?" I asked.

"Not if it's self-defense, Paramount (more important than anything else; supreme)."

Later, I looked up self-defense. It meant defending your interests, especially through the use of physical force, which was permitted in certain cases as an answer to a charge of violent crime. "Defending your interests" was pretty broad, and what exactly was considered a "charge" of violent crime? Could it refer to your insides as well as your outsides? I mean if someone deceived you, like Daddy deceived Mama and Ryan Anderson deceived me, it felt like a million arrows were piercing your heart. Defending yourself against them was practically a reflex, but while the Ryan-Lucy thing had helped me understand how Mama felt when she found out about Daddy's other families, there were two big differences between Mama and me: One, even though I was really mad at Ryan, not once did I consider murdering him, and two, I had no intention of befriending Lucy Baxter; in fact, I had put together a long list of mean get-backs.

It started with unflattering nicknames. Because I'd been the brunt of them from the same girls who were now my friends, I figured they'd be happy to help me come up with some for Lucy. Loose Lucy. Lippy Lucy. Lame Lucy. Loco Lucy. Just to name a few. Lucy didn't take it too well, definitely not as well as I had. She cried right in front of us. At least I'd had the good sense to wait until I got home. Also unlike me, she kept trying to kiss up to us, which made picking on her even more satisfying. Since we weren't little kids anymore, this form of revenge got tiring pretty fast. It was Kelly who finally came up with something really devious. What I didn't know about Lucy Baxter right away was that she actually had naturally curly hair (like me). Apparently she spent hours blowing it straight every morning (unlike me) with a hair dryer and that's why it always looked so perfect. Kelly decided that we should fill a balloon with water, wait for Lucy to come into the girls' bathroom like she did every morning before class started, and throw the balloon at her. As planned, it popped, completely soaking her hair in the process. She cried of course, but not like the other times. This time she looked completely demoralized. I actually felt sorry for her, but not for long because when her hair dried, it looked really good, curly and full, not frizzy and disheveled. As planned, Lucy did get a nickname, but not the kind I'd had in mind. The boys started calling her Sexy Lucy, which I thought was really ignorant. I mean sexy doesn't even start with L. After a couple more weeks of Get Back at Lucy Baxter pranks, such as hiding her bra while she was in gym class and putting hot sauce on her spaghetti at lunch when she wasn't looking, she showed up at my house, which in retrospect was very courageous but at the time annoyed me.

"What do *you* want?" I asked, when I answered the door.

She handed me a wrapped box with a card taped to it. "Happy birthday," she said, and walked off, leaving me gawking. Now, it's not that I'm overly paranoid, but I was a bit concerned about the box's contents. I held it up to my ear. No ticking. I shook it. Something heavy moved back and forth. I stared at it for a while, and thought things like *How did she know it was my birthday* and *Is she kissing up, trying to trick me?* I figured I'd start with the card, which I considered burning in the fireplace but then decided I could just as easily burn it after I read it. This is what it said:

Dear Picasso,

Happy Birthday! ☺ (The smiley face was definitely overkill.)
   I turned twelve two days ago. Isn't that weird that our birthdays are so close together? That means we are both Aquarians. That's an astrological sign. (Seriously? Did she think I didn't know what an astrological sign was?) *Aquarians are supposed to be innovators, which I don't know about me, but that certainly fits you. In fact, in Greek mythology it is said that the Aquarians through their planet Uranus invented the earth. Isn't that cool? I love Greek mythology, don't you?* (I mean, call me suspicious, but that was just too weird. Did she know I loved mythology too, because of Daddy?) *I especially like all the stories about Aphrodite, who you remind me of.* (Maybe she's a little insightful.) *Aquarians also have amazing eyes, which you definitely do, and are imaginative, resourceful, quirky, inventive, ingenious, and original, all traits that you have.*

Anyway, I just wanted to say that I think you are one of the truest Aquarians I have ever met, and that Kelly, Ashley, Gillian, and Cindy are really lucky to have such a smart and pretty friend. I also wanted you to know that when Ryan asked if he could walk me home I didn't know that the two of you were boyfriend and girlfriend. After the Dairy Queen that day, I even asked him about you, and he said you were just friends. When I found out that he lied to me about that, I got really mad, and I told him he was shortsighted to quit being your boyfriend (my thought exactly!), *and that he didn't deserve you, or me.*

I hope you enjoy your presents.

Someone who wishes to be your friend,

Lucy Baxter

P.S. Let me know if you want to team up and get back at Ryan.

I decided to unwrap the present.

There were two books inside the box, a dictionary and a book on Greek mythology. Both were bound in leather and had gold-trimmed pages. They looked really expensive.

After I got Lucy Baxter's letter, I figured out why Mama got mad at Daddy instead of Jewels and Bert. What I hadn't understood before then was that Ryan had deceived Lucy too. The thing about deception is that it's a lot like a chameleon. Even though both are pretty-sounding words, the things they're the names of are actually pretty ugly, only it can take a long time to discover that, sometimes forever, because they have this amazing ability to hide in plain view.

Kyle

Gravity's a bitch.

When I was in Hollyville, my head was back on Cooper's Island, and when I was on Cooper's Island, my head (and cock) was back in Hollyville. It was like I was stuck in some in-between world. Even my words were stuck, like an LP skipping on an old turntable, the same words kept repeating: *Beautiful, lucky, sorry, gun, motive, liar, dumb ass, wives, guilty as sin.* No matter how much Redbreast I drank or how many cards I shuffled, no new words were joining the ticker tape parade in my head, and none of my characteristic epiphanies were emerging out of my drunken stupors.

The case itself was as stuck as me. We weren't getting any breaks anywhere. We couldn't verify portions of Roberta Miles's alibi, yet we couldn't find anything to dispute what she said. We had cracked Julie Lane's once solid alibi, yet we could only track her whereabouts so far. We couldn't find a gas station attendant who recognized her. We couldn't prove without a doubt that she was on that plane. Even though at least two people, one TSA agent and the rental car clerk, both male, remembered an attractive blonde fitting Julie Lane's description, both fingered Diana's not Julie's picture. We'd dusted the beach house for fingerprints again. We'd combed the carpet for hair follicles, blood, and shoe impressions. What it always came down to was this: The only wife in that house the day of the murder was Diana Lane.

"What if Diana really was the one who rented the car and bought the airline ticket?" Mack asked. We'd just left the scene of a domestic dispute. Wife hit her husband over the head with a cast-iron pan. Lucky for her (or maybe not so lucky, depending how you look at it), he would live.

"What do you mean?" I asked. "We know she couldn't have."

"We know she couldn't have been on that 10:15 a.m. flight, but what about the night before? Do we know for sure she was there the previous night?"

"So you're saying she somehow got to Philly, rented the car, and drove back down to Cooper's Island all in one night. Why would she do that?"

"I don't know. Maybe to throw us off? Did you ask the kid where her mom was the night before?"

"There wasn't any reason to," I said. "Besides, wouldn't she have told me if her mother was gone all night?"

Mack shrugged. "Maybe she didn't know her mother was gone, or maybe she did and just isn't telling us."

I thought about that look on Picasso's face the morning of the murder. Picasso obviously loved her mother, and there was no question she was fiercely loyal to her, but I just couldn't see her lying like that, because that's what it would be. Omission was a lie no matter which way you cut it. But Diana aside, Mack was right. As much as I wanted Julie Lane for the murder, I had to admit to myself that maybe I wanted her for the wrong reasons. If Julie Lane had pulled the trigger, that would mean Diana hadn't.

"It just doesn't make any sense," I said. "Why would she go to all that trouble when all she had to do was go for a swim?"

Mack pulled up to the office. "She probably didn't. It's just that these wives have got us running in circles. You still heading out tonight?"

The island had been overrun with spring breakers since the end of March, and the noisy keg parties, cars backing into neighboring mailboxes, disregard of water safety, and late-night road racing had finally come to an end—until next year. I'd decided to take Mack up on his offer to cover for me for a few days and head to Hollyville. By now I was pretty sure he'd figured out I was seeing someone, but luckily he wasn't one to pry.

Diana and Picasso seemed as excited to see me as I was to see them.

The first night was all about Picasso. She'd cooked spaghetti, and then we had plans for a marathon Scrabble game. I commented during dinner on how good the Bolognese sauce was.

"We can teach you how to make it," Picasso said.

"Maybe Detective Kennedy already knows how to make it," Diana said. She still called me Detective Kennedy in front of Picasso. She said she wasn't ready for Picasso to know about our relationship yet, but of course Picasso already knew. Picasso didn't miss much.

"I'd like that," I said.

"Okay," Picasso said. "Tomorrow we'll make pizza. Pizza uses the same red sauce, just without the meat."

The next night, the counters completely cleared for my cooking class, Picasso handed me an obviously well used chef's apron, and we set to work. Diana was taking on the dough, Picasso was doing the chopping, and my job was the sauce.

"The recipe is in Mama's catchall book," Picasso said.

"Where's that?" I asked.

Diana pointed to something that looked more like an art project gone bad than a book. It was so stuffed with pages cut out from magazines and newspapers that the binding was split and frayed. There were recipes, pictures of flower arrangements and furnishings, paint chips and material samples, some glued down, some not.

"It's under R," Diana said.

"It's alphabetized?" I asked.

"Sort of," Diana said.

"Why R and not S?"

"Red sauce," she said, and laughed. "White sauce is under W."

I flipped to the pages that had R written on their top-right corner; it was one of the longer sections of the book so I started turning one page at a time, until I came to one that was dog-eared. A small note in the margin read "Noon, July 3rd, Rainy Cove Park, same spot." It was written with blue ink. As if they'd been added later, the words "one year" were written in black ink at the end. I nearly dismissed it, but then the date hit me: July 3rd. It could be any July 3rd, I reasoned. Maybe the note had been there for years. Maybe it was just a coincidence. *Since when do you believe in coincidences?* I remembered Mack saying.

Picasso was staring at me when I looked up from the book. She quickly looked away, but there'd been no mistaking the fear in her eyes. Had my face betrayed my discovery?

The pizza was a success and so was I. I'd spent the entire evening trying to act as if I hadn't seen what I did. It was still dark when I got in my car the next morning. I flipped on the interior light and typed Rainy Cove Park into my smartphone browser. The place was the perfect setting for a reunion. "Quiet and remote with small clearings for picnicking, hiking trails, and a small lake perfect for kayaking," the description read. Remote was an understatement. From the road, all anyone could see was a long dirt driveway, which appeared to open up to a parking lot, a parking lot totally obscured by tall evergreens.

I sat in the car and processed for a while. Usually I think pretty good when I drive, but that time it wasn't about thinking, it was about feeling. I knew that unless you were some kind of psychopath, without conscience, killing another human being wasn't something you walked away from clean. I'd taken more than one life in Detroit, and they'd all fucked with my head in one way or another. The act itself is a sick sort of intimate; the look in that person's eyes when he realizes you are his grim reaper turns your stomach and pumps your adrenaline simultaneously. And then there's the aftermath. You see his face in your mirror and dreams, hear his final wheeze or choking cough in an elevator, mistake the smell of your own blood or shit for his. And yeah, there comes a day when you just learn to live with it, but that day doesn't come for a long while. In the meantime, you find yourself searching the eyes of random people in crowds, behind checkout counters, at urinals, searching for a kindred spirit, someone who understands, can relate, someone you might be able to unload on. So you can breathe fresh, clean air again. So you can feel that sense of lightness that you know you once felt but now can barely even describe.

The wives hadn't needed to go searching, they had one another, and yet they hadn't talked or met since the murder. Hell, they hadn't even e-mailed or texted. Why not? What was I missing? I slowly repeated the words I'd seen in the catchall book: "Noon, July 3rd, Rainy Cove Park, same spot, one year."

One year.

I'd underestimated the three of them. Not their brains; I'd always been impressed by their intelligence. I'd underestimated their bravery, their determination, their patience. They'd been biding their time, waiting until it was safer, until it was far enough in the future for the police to have lost interest in their crime. And damn, it would've worked. The police, shit even I, would've lost interest in the three of them, no matter how attractive they were or how compelling the case was. The irony was that my interest in Diana had kept me interested in the case. Working to prove her innocence had in fact sealed her guilt.

Like I said, gravity's a bitch. Nothing and no one can stay stuck forever.

A new word floated down from the sky of my mind. It tumbled across each of the other words on its way to the end of the line, and as if it had been the key they needed to wind them back up, they all began dancing.

Beautiful, lucky, sorry, gun, motive, liar, dumb ass, wives, guilty as sin, rendezvous.

I turned on the ignition, backed out of Diana Lane's driveway and onto the road. As I drove away, I stole a brief look at the front porch, and there, watching me through the window, was Picasso.

The Wives

At exactly midnight on the final pink day before our rendezvous, we lit candles and submerged ourselves in our baths of floating petals. The water was warm, the cloak of secrecy we'd carried since we'd murdered Oliver still so heavy, but we had faith that our chests would soon empty, our hearts lighten.

We imagined the morning of our reunion. We would feel anticipation when we rose. The expectancy would build to hopefulness as we made our drives to Rainy Cove Park, Diana in her silver Toyota crossover, Jewels in her bright blue Porsche Carrera, and Bert in her rusty and dented Chevy Blazer. We'd wait inside our cars until each of us had parked, and then we'd come together, hold hands, and walk. The familiar sounds of crunching twigs and singing birds would accompany us through the dense wood. Together we'd veer off the trail. Up ahead, we'd get a peek of the lake. Our footsteps would quicken then, so excited we would be to reunite with our little bit of earth, the place where we had come together and grown together. The place where the wind had heard our collective thoughts and swirled them through the air and the trees and the wildflowers, through the crest of the water's ripples and the dew that dripped from the leaves, until finally returning them to us, larger and more defined. Once there, we'd perform our ritual. We'd lay our blanket on the ground, take off our clothes, and cleanse ourselves in the warm water. When we returned to our sacred circle, we'd hold hands. We would take a few moments to absorb the sights and the scents and the sounds of the magical place that had been our home away from home, and once at peace with our surroundings, we'd uncork a bottle of wine and toast.

Toast to murder. Toast to life. Toast to victory.

We would talk, well into the afternoon, of course, about our current lives and loves. As before, we wouldn't discuss our children, not because they were sacred territory as we'd convinced ourselves in the past, but because murder had touched something deep inside us, a knowledge, a chord of honesty, and so we'd admit what we always knew, that we'd selfishly wanted the time for ourselves. After all, weren't we the real victims? A quiet would come over us. Perhaps a cloud would float past the sun or a bird would whistle a single note. In that moment, without so much as uttering a word, all the questions we'd pondered regarding the events of that fateful yet glorious day would be answered. Light would enter our hearts and minds. Love would ooze from our pores. Satisfaction would rise from deep inside us and, like a snake, would curl itself through our bodies and out of our mouths. We would speak. We would gloat. We would rejoice.

We'd say goodbye to the man we'd shared, the man we'd loved, the man whose memories we'd feared, whose dreams we'd denied. For we knew our reunion was our crescendo. Oliver's death had been a prelude, the year in between an interlude. And so we'd light a candle, close our eyes, imagine every inch of him, and feel him, all of him, his breath on our necks, hands on our breasts, his maleness inside us. We'd taste the morning, or the day, or the night on his lips. We'd smell soap, or aftershave, or sweat on his neck. We'd hear him say our names, softly, lovingly, just before he climaxed. Physically and spiritually we'd orgasm. Inside this *petite mort,* every second, every minute, every hour of our lives with Oliver would pass before us. We'd experience every emo-tion each had brought forth. Finally, exhausted, as if he were an unsightly speck of dust, we'd flick the memory of the man who had scorned us into the air. We'd blow him a kiss as the mouths of darkness consumed him. And we'd pray, not for Oliver but for ourselves, because though the worst had passed, we weren't cer-tain we'd recognize the good that was yet to come.

As we rose from our baths, fully cleansed, petals sticking to our wet flesh, fingers and toes wrinkled and rubbery, we imagined how we would feel after our reunion. We imagined the heaviness lifting. For one split second we believed we felt a supreme light-ness, an omniscience, omnipotence, omnipresence. For one split second we felt angelic. After the sensation passed, we blew out our candles, dried our bodies, wrapped ourselves in fluffy pink robes, glided to our bedrooms, crawled beneath our blankets, and for the first time in many months, welcomed our dreams.

FOUR

Truth

(The Murder)

. . .

Art is a lie that makes us realize truth.

—PABLO PICASSO

Oliver

You *see* things when you're dead, and you *know* all there is to know. Everything—your memories, your senses, especially your vision—is sharpened. For some, the hereafter is nirvana, a state of transcendence where there is no suffering or sense of self, where beauty and happiness abide. For others, like me, death is an acid trip. Faces, furnishings, objects, trees are clear one moment and then stretching from their bones and frames the next, elongating, melting like Salvador Dalí's clocks. I prefer my death to that other one. I prefer surprise to status quo, sordid to vanilla, bizarre to boring. I prefer to have my cunning and acumen tested. When I refer to faces and such, obviously I don't mean me. I no longer have a face or a body. I am a shape-shifting mass of shimmering molecules, white and silver and gray and black. My home is the air. Though some hover near their grave sites, there is no designated place for the dead, no good place or bad place. We are merely energy fields, wafting, watching, reading minds and emotions. Me? I do more than simply watch and read, I fuck with the living. They may feel a breeze, a change of temperature—some say it gets cold when we are near—but they can't see me.

I can't help but wonder if everyone's transition is similar. In those last moments before I died, knowing it was inevitable, I felt many emotions, surprise, confusion, anger, but none of those accompanied me to death. Here I feel placid. It's not that I'm apathetic, quite the opposite in fact, but I am distracted. How could I not be? I'm forever drifting through the vast feast of the living, forever surrounded by lust and evil and crime, forever devouring and gorging and delighting in all I see. There will come a time when I leave this air, when my molecules will find their way into the womb of another woman, but the details of that journey are not yet known to me. So for now, I wander and wait.

At this moment, I float near Diana. I see the detective, the one who is investigating my murder, touching *my* wife's skin, traveling inside her. In my death, they become clay on a wheel. I feel nothing as they spin into one, as their skin moistens, compresses, rises, and falls, nothing but curiosity. As everything did, and everything always will, it all began with me. Diana's story is my story. It's hard for me to remember what life felt like, but even now I remember that sensation of having my breath stolen the first time I saw her. I remember wishing I could crush my entire being into hers. Wishing I could own her, that I could dig my fingernails into her flesh until it bled, hear her screams, watch her face contort in pain. That was how much I admired her beauty. I remember holding back every time we made love, being proud of my ability to command her body, cause it to quiver beneath mine, without destroying her. In that, I always knew I was different. I always knew that my lack of empathy, my unquenchable desire to control, to hurt was unique, and thus so was I. That I could manage these overwhelming urges, that I could bend them to fit my needs, that I could so skillfully hide them from the world was testament to the fact that I was special.

After I died and before the detective shared her bed, I'd watch Diana masturbate, her fingers touching those magical places, her body stiffening and releasing. Sometimes I'd wind myself around her neck, whisper into her ear, tell her I'd known what the three of them were planning all along, praise her for outwitting me.

I hadn't considered the beach house. I hadn't seen you. But I see you now.

I know she is thinking of me, not this detective. He is no match for me, no match for her. He is soft, gentle with her body and emotions, honest with his own.

Can you hear me? He is weak.

"Touch me," she says to my air. *Haunt me.*

It is obvious to me now why so many murderers go free. The detective allows his heart to rule his head. Why did it take him so long to believe what he knew? And why is he searching for a key? Yes, he was right about me hiding money, money I'd rather see go to waste than fall into the hands of my ungrateful wives, and, yes, he was even right about me having a safe-deposit box, but my box doesn't require a key. It can only be accessed by a six-digit code. Mine is the numeric equivalent of Ares, god of war and my given surname. If this detective had any wits about him, wouldn't he have discovered that by now? Wouldn't he have discovered the box itself, the bank that contains it? Wouldn't he have discovered my real name? Sometimes I surprise even myself. Clearly I was a skilled illusionist. Getting away with stealing someone's identity while alive is one thing, but how many have maintained the ploy after death?

Oliver Lane was born in the same hospital and on the same day as I. He died eight minutes after he entered the world. We shared the same space for three of those. Though we never met, when I decided to change my identity he was my choice. His mother was fifteen years old. Her well-to-do socialite parents felt blessed when he passed because they could continue telling their lie: that their daughter had merely been staying with her grandmother for a few months. Even someone who lives eight minutes needs a birth certificate, but no one filed for a social security number or death certificate, and he was never buried. Along with used bedpans, bloody gauze, and wasted syringes, the hospital disposed of him in the same way his mother disposed of his memory. I felt an affinity with Oliver Lane. My mother was older than fifteen, but like his, she didn't care two shits about me. I never knew who my father was. My mother created some story about him going off to war and dying a hero; she never said which war. I had a slew of uncles. The one that lasted the longest, Ray, beat me when he got drunk. He had a penchant for the belt. I'm not complaining, I'm just saying my childhood was fucked up. The trouble started when I was nine years old. I was small for my age, got bullied. One day I fought back, beat a kid, got expelled. That kind of behavior continued until I found my calling: women.

I was fourteen when I had my first woman. She was a friend of my mother's. I was delivering her paper when she called to me from her porch, asked me to come in and change one of her lightbulbs. I climbed onto a chair, started unscrewing. She undid my fly, stuck her hand through the opening in my underwear, and I was done. A woman's hand was a beautiful thing. For the next few months, I wandered over to her house to fix this or that, and she taught me the art of seduction. At fifteen I decided to practice what I knew on a girl my own age, and before long another, and another. I took pride in the fact that I could make them feel good. I could save them from themselves, free them from the confines of their virginity. It wasn't long before I realized that I had a gift for duplicity. With women *and* crime. By the time I was sixteen I had an admirable rap sheet, petty stuff mostly, robbery, assault, and voyeurism. I liked watching women through the filmy, fluttering curtains of their windows at night. I liked watching them perform the mysterious practices of their sex: shaving their legs, rubbing their bodies with lotion, applying makeup and perfume for a night on the town, emerging from a bath wet and glistening, their hair fastened into a makeshift bun. I loved everything about a woman's body, that lovely curve where her neck meets her shoulder, those few strands of unconfined hair at the nape of her neck, her delicate wrists and ankles, but mostly I loved her helplessness, her vulnerability. Her shape and size, even her age, never mattered. I found and still find, even in death, all women beautiful.

There was one woman I watched for a long time. She lived in the rich part of town in a big house, probably much like the house where Oliver Lane's mother lived while she incubated him in her belly, while the muscles of his heart grew, each beat pumping blood through his developing lungs and forming body, sprouting arms and legs and toes and fingers, the capacity to see and hear and feel pain. The woman's husband went to work in a suit and tie every day. There was just something about her, the way she moved, as if the ground were a cloud, so sensuous, so inviting, so choreographed that I was certain she knew I was watching. Her grace and delicacy were in stark contrast to her husband's large awkwardness, his fat hands, hairy back, paunchy belly, selfish lovemaking. Yet even when he sloppily rolled from her, his body disgusting and sweaty, she didn't voice dissatisfaction. She smiled and kissed him, rubbed his chest and shoulders as he mentally reentered the world. I remember thinking that one day I wanted a woman like her, that she deserved a more attentive lover, a man who appreciated her fine gifts, but I knew that the boy I was would never be attractive to the woman she was. I would need to be a man, a powerful and wealthy man.

It was then that I decided to become Oliver Lane. With my computer skills and a little help, I created an entire person. Oliver Lane had gone to the best prep school in Boston. Oliver Lane had gotten straight A's and extremely high marks on his college entrance exams. Oliver Lane had won several awards for academic achievement and intellectual talent. Not surprisingly, my creation won a scholarship to Syracuse. Not surprisingly, my creation excelled. Not surprisingly, my creation went on to Harvard Law. And over time, my identity became so fused with that of my creation that I hardly remember that other boy, the boy who grew up in the wrong part of town, the boy who stole and beat and watched, the boy who kept no less than three women happy at a time.

I'd been practicing law for nearly four years when I first saw Diana. My Boston law firm had just opened a satellite office in Raleigh, North Carolina; we were working on a large money laundering case there and needed someone on-site full time. At first I'd resisted the offer, but then a partnership was dangled in front of me. I was having drinks at a ritzy martini bar with some clients down in Fayetteville, near Diana's hometown of Hollyville. She and another woman were sitting at a corner table; some guy had zeroed in on them. She was exquisite: light and lovely with the golden hair and physical attributes of the goddess Aphrodite. I decided to watch her before I moved in for the kill like any good warrior would do, study her habits, what she liked and disliked. A man can smell an experienced woman, one who loves the act of lovemaking for its pure pleasure. That wasn't the only thing that drew me to her. She wasn't easy prey; she was damaged. She'd lost her parents and brother in an auto accident while in college, and had just ended a relationship with an unappreciative asshole. I liked that she'd chosen to make her home in the small town where she grew up. I liked that I could disappear there. I was determined to disarm her, conquer her, make her love me like she'd never loved any man. I knew that first time I talked to her that it wouldn't be easy to gain her trust. I also knew that she wasn't the type of woman who had affairs; she was the kind of woman you married. I had never intended to get married, but Diana was worth it, and for a long while I didn't stray.

Things changed when we had Picasso. Don't get me wrong. Although I'd never much taken to kids, Picasso was different. She was funny, whip smart; her brain could decipher any puzzle I threw at her—she took after me in that respect—and she cherished those dictionaries I bought for her. It wasn't Picasso herself that changed things, it was the way Diana loved Picasso, with a kind of protective fury, an unwavering focus: the way Diana used to love me. I'd become second, something I couldn't be.

Jewels was an experiment. Intuitively I knew that having a mistress would bring Diana back to me. She would sense my withdrawal. I was having lunch at a sidewalk café near my office in Raleigh when I saw her. She was running toward me, her ponytail flipping back and forth, her body so lean that from a distance you could mistake her for a kid, her legs wiry and sculpted. She passed me, stopped at the curve, waited for the light to turn, held her side, bent forward at the waist, her running shorts creeping up, exposing a fine ass, small, round, firm. She straightened, walked across the street, and entered an office building on the opposite corner of the intersection. I threw money on the table and ran after her. After a maddening maneuver through rotating glass doors, I caught a glimpse of her getting into an elevator alone. According to the digital readout above the door, it stopped on the second floor. There was a shiny metal directory on the wall near the elevator doors. Three things were located on the building's second floor: a coffee shop, a cafeteria, and a gym. I bought a one-month membership.

In the beginning it was only sex, but then she fell in love. I can't say for certain why I asked her to marry me. I didn't love her, at least not in the way that most men love, the way that the detective loves. In all honesty, I didn't love Diana either; I didn't even know what people meant when they said they loved someone or something. I didn't experience those other sensations either—sadness, fear, compassion. I'd done a lot of reading on emotion, so I was certain no one knew I was acting, but there were times that I'd forget. I wouldn't respond on time, register the correct sentiment, or the true me would show himself, but I noticed that even if I did get a questioning or confused look, that as long as I got it right a large percentage of the time, and as long as I went over and above in the kindness, romance, and gift-giving categories, I could get away with pretty much anything. It's true that like Diana, Jewels pleased me. I told myself I married her because I wasn't ready to lose that, but it was probably more likely that I didn't want to lose the adrenaline rush, the excitement of the balancing act.

When the twins were born, it felt more like an inconvenience than a wonder. Several guys in the Boston office had boys. They were always bragging about their athletic accomplishments, or their coaching positions on their sons' baseball, basketball, or soccer teams. I'd expected to feel at least some of their fervor, some pride, but all I felt was tired. Tired of hiding. Tired of pleasing. Tired of losing.

Bert was perhaps the biggest surprise of my life. I didn't find her remotely attractive when I met her, but nonetheless I was drawn to her. I wanted to penetrate her defensive posture toward men. I'd gone on a camping trip in the Blue Ridge Mountains outside of Boone to reconnect with nature. My blood pressure had registered high at my last annual appointment; the doctor said I had too much on my plate (if he only knew), and the anxiety and depression I'd battled since childhood was looming. I went into town for supplies, stopped in the local bookstore. The mousy, overweight clerk walked me to the mythology section. Like I had with Diana, I imagined my hands cupping her breasts, squeezing her flesh until she begged me to stop. Until she whined. I imagined returning that night, following her after she left work, putting my hand over her mouth, holding her against me. After the camping trip, I thought about her day and night. I dreamed about her.

Bert and I married three months later.

Soon after, Jewels started asking questions. She wondered why I'd been working so much, where I went when I wasn't in Raleigh with her. My answers never appeased her. She began following me, which was fun at first, like a little cat-and-mouse game, only, contrary to what she thought, I was the cat. It wasn't long before she discovered Diana and Bert, and then everything took a turn for the worse. The three of them began meeting. Within a few months they'd dyed their hair the same color and were dressing alike. A month or so later, they were making extravagant expenditures and maxing out their credit cards. And then, one day, when I was taking out Jewels's and my garbage, I found an empty burner phone package. I carried it back inside.

"What is this?" I asked Jewels while holding it up.

"I have no idea," she said. "What does it say it is?"

"A disposable phone."

"How odd," she said. "Maybe one of our neighbors put it in there."

"It was in our wastebasket, not the Dumpster."

"You're sure? Like I said, I have no idea. I haven't purchased a disposable phone if that's what you're wondering. Why on earth would I? I have a brand-new cell phone, and we have a landline."

The following afternoon back in Hollyville, I walked in on a teary Diana and very upset Picasso. Picasso was smart, but she'd never been able to disguise her emotions. In that way, she was like Diana. The look on her face was a combination of pleading and fear. When she saw me, she ran upstairs to her room without even saying hello. Diana was shaking. I asked her what was wrong, tried to hold her, but she shuddered at my touch.

"Nothing," she said. "We were just talking about school."

"School?" I asked. "Seemed pretty serious for a discussion on school."

I didn't tell Diana what I'd heard Picasso say right before I opened the front door: "Please Mama, don't kill Daddy. I don't want you to go to jail." I didn't tell Diana that with those words all the puzzle pieces had fallen into place. I found it comical at first. Not one of my three wives was intelligent or brave enough to perform the act of murder. Then I got curious. How did they propose to do it? Diana and Bert were humanitarians, and Jewels was fastidious. Guns were messy. Knives required strength. Poison pointed directly at them.

The sense of malaise that had been lingering for some time got worse. It's difficult to describe how and why suicidal thoughts enter a man's mind. For me, they came on quickly. One day I was fine and the next day I felt something I couldn't quite identify, and since I had no experience with feelings, I panicked. My blood coursed with uncontrollable anger as I held the gun. My wives were supposed to love me whether or not I loved them. They were supposed to be grateful. I'd provided for them, given my children everything they wanted. I hadn't stolen their truths from them: I let Diana keep her inheritance a secret, allowed Jewels to believe she was a great architect, told Bert she was beautiful on a daily basis. I'd mirrored my wives, molded myself into each of their ideas of the perfect husband. It was one thing to meet behind my back, but to plot my murder? Although I was certain they wouldn't go through with it, couldn't go through with it, I found the fact that they'd even considered it unacceptable.

I imagined my lips wrapped around the gun's barrel, the bullet entering my mouth, blowing my brain into pieces. I imagined the fireworks I'd see, sparks of red and green and yellow and blue, and somehow that alone seemed worth the challenge. I brought the gun to my face—

"Is everything okay, Daddy?" Picasso said. She stood in the bedroom doorway.

I pushed the gun away from my face, wiped the sweat from my brow with a sleeve, asked her if she wanted to hold the gun.

"Won't Mama get upset?" she asked.

While I taught my eleven-year-old daughter how to handle a gun, I came alive. I realized that they were the problem, not me. Their petty dissatisfaction was their childhood baggage, their unacknowledged hatred for their fathers. Sure some men were assholes, but that didn't even slightly apply to me. "Oliver Lane" was utterly perfect; *I'd* created him. My head began spinning with schemes and tactics, and then I knew what I had to do: play them against one another.

I gave myself a timeline. By the time Diana, Picasso, and I got home from our annual trip to the beach, my plan would be in motion. All I'd have to do was sit back and watch the three of them battle it out.

As I stood drinking my coffee and watching Diana swim that final morning, I was struck by a feeling I can only describe as euphoria. At that moment, I did feel something for Diana: The pride an owner feels for his finest thoroughbred. The one he's groomed, poured every ounce of his sweat into. The one he's loved as much as he could love anyone. I'd felt the same for Jewels that last time we'd made love, and the same for Bert when I called her from the beach house. But none of that mattered. I would take their children, their money, their homes, anything and everything they ever cared about. I would destroy them.

The two of them are sleeping now, Diana and the detective. She's buried inside his arms. I allow him to breathe me in. I travel through his mouth, his nostrils. I swirl through his mind, join the words dancing inside it, consider adding the name of my killer, but see the situation for what it was. If I hadn't underestimated my wives, I'd still be alive. It's true that I'm not angry and that I no longer care about life, but one cannot escape one's nature. The game isn't over yet.

I float by them one last time, curl around them, and then pull myself away. Spread. I am a mass of shimmering molecules, white and silver and gray and black. I don't know how long I'll be here. How long death will grace me. I do know the air is always changing, and we who inhabit it are forever reborn. And so I wait. One day a body will take me prisoner again, and though I will fight life, will kick and scream my way into it, I will overcome it. I will be the brightest, most cunning, most powerful. I will win all games. Manipulate all circumstances. Fell all adversaries.

That is who I am.

Thank you, Oliver Lane, for lending me your name, for allowing me to build those eight fragile moments into a larger life. If you are still here somewhere, still wander, or you've left and returned, look for me hovering near my grave site, the one with the stone that bears your name. I'm there for several moments every night visiting the body beneath it, a man who hides in death as he did in life. A man named Peter Ares. A man his wives and children never knew.

Kyle

Beautiful, lucky, sorry, gun, motive, liar, dumb ass, wives, guilty as sin, rendezvous, Picasso.

I'd waited a week before I told Mack about the note I found in Diana's catchall book, mainly because telling him about the note meant I'd have to tell him why I'd been making pizza with Diana and Picasso in the first place. I tried to play it down, but I'm pretty certain Mack was putting two and two together. It wasn't that I was worried about Mack ratting me out to the brass—I knew he wouldn't—I was worried about his opinion of me. He'd always looked up to me, and I didn't want that to change. Not then. Not when it already felt like my life was falling apart.

"Wow," he said. "We got them then, right?" We were at Cooper's Alleys having a beer. It was packed, the tourist season was back in full swing, so finding two seats together had taken some maneuvering.

"Maybe," I said. "The note didn't say who she was meeting."

"So what do we do now? Bring them all in?"

"If you wouldn't mind, I'd rather ease into this. Verify I'm absolutely right before we do anything."

"What're you thinking?"

"Asking the kid. It's obvious she knows something. I'm just not sure how much."

"How do you know she'll tell you?"

"She trusts me." Saying those words made my stomach hurt.

I'd decided to stay away from Hollyville for a while. I needed some distance to get my thoughts in order. I even quit calling Diana; thinking about her sitting there waiting for my call somehow made me feel less like a cop who broke protocol and more like a man who was in control. But after several days, I was not only itching to call, I realized Diana hadn't called me, and any notions I'd had of taking control of myself and my relationship with Diana slipped away.

"Mama's been sick all week," Picasso said when she answered the phone.

"Did she go to the doctor?" I asked.

"He said the flu is going around. He told her to get plenty of rest and drink a lot of water. I said she should call again, but she won't. I don't know what to do. I'm really worried."

I immediately got in the car and drove.

I used the spare key Diana had given me to let myself in. She looked like shit. She hadn't showered in days. Her skin was gray, hair matted. She was burning up. I carried her to my car and drove to the emergency room. I thought I'd known that I loved Diana Lane, but that day as I waited for the doctor to come out and give me the prognosis, I realized I'd break if something ever happened to her. When I was finally allowed to see her, she was sleeping and hooked to an IV.

"She'll rally," the doctor said. "But it's a good thing you brought her in when you did. Pneumonia isn't anything to play around with."

I cashed in on some unused vacation time, stayed with her those nights in the hospital, took care of her when she got released. Other than my daily trips to the grocery or drugstore, and walking Picasso to and from school, I was by Diana's side.

One night, I decided to head out to the back porch and have

a drink; I hadn't touched the juice since some time during my stuck phase. One became several. At some point, I closed my eyes. My parade of words got longer and longer, and then it went crazy. Instead of streaming, it spun through my mind, creating layers and layers of concentric rings, each new one closing in on me, until I was inside a swirling mathematical vortex, the words adding and subtracting—guilty/not guilty, prison/acquittal, murderer/innocent—until only two remained.

Rendezvous, Picasso.

Picasso

It was about a month before Mama's, Jewels's, and Bert's reunion, and a few months after the Ryan Anderson walking Lucy Baxter home incident. Long enough for Lucy and me to have become best friends (as it turned out we were the only two Aquarians in our grade and we smart innovators needed to stick together so we could cause world change); for the two of us to have done some major Get Back at Ryan Anderson pranks, like puncture the tires on his bike and glue the pages of his math book together; for Ryan to have gotten a new girlfriend, Kelly Morgan of all people; and for Detective Kennedy to have temporarily moved into our house.

Mama had gotten sick with pneumonia and Detective Kennedy came to take care of her. I'd forgotten how much I missed having a daddy; it was like being part of a family again, an even better family. Detective Kennedy walked me to and from school every day, did things he said he would, seemed really interested in everything I had to say, and knew as much or more than Daddy about pretty much everything, including Pablo Picasso. He took me to a traveling retrospective exhibit at the Mint Museum of Art in Charlotte and, so I could remember what I'd seen, bought me an expensive book about the artist. Now, we'd studied Pablo Picasso in school, so I didn't need the book or the exhibit to tell me that he and another artist named Georges Braque created cubism, but seeing so many of his paintings, especially the cubist ones, in person did help me to understand what Pablo Picasso had meant by that quote: *Art is a lie that makes us realize truth.* There were all those angles put together in the shape of a woman (for instance), and although anyone could see it wasn't a woman, the paint and the brushstrokes and the colors and the composition made it something even better. The lie made the truth prettier. As I've come to learn through this whole Daddy dying experience, sometimes people prefer a lie to the truth. But the thing is, if you aren't careful, that can get you in trouble.

Detective Kennedy is a good example of this. He knew all along that Mama, Jewels, and Bert knew one another before Daddy died, and he suspected them of killing Daddy, and yet because he liked Mama so much, from the very beginning when he first walked into the beach house that day, he chose not to see the truth. But the biggest irony of the whole Kill Daddy mess was when I realized *I* had actually become a victim of my own name. Because Detective Kennedy had been being so nice to Mama and me, I chose not to see that he was a detective.

It happened on the way home from school one day. Detective Kennedy suggested we stop off at Dairy Queen. He ordered for us: a chocolate cone for him and a vanilla for me. I'm not too big on cones, but at least he'd remembered the vanilla part. He suggested we eat at one of the picnic tables outside, which was fine by me. The table was right out front between the Dairy Queen and the road, so everyone in the world could see us. I felt proud and safe.

As usual, I was wearing my school uniform. Detective Kennedy almost always wore a suit when he was being in his official capacity, but since he'd been staying at our house he was dressing more casually. That day, he wore jeans, a *pink* polo shirt (which looked pretty nice on him, but still surprised me), and running shoes. He didn't look anything like a detective, but people were staring and whispering anyway. Ever since Mama and he began holding hands in public, the rumors had started up all over again. I guess that goes to show that there's no such thing as a dead rumor; at best rumors hibernate. None of this penetrated my Super Picasso armor. Lucy Baxter and I just ignored them. That was the difference between her and Kelly Morgan; Lucy was loyal.

Detective Kennedy licked a drip of chocolate ice cream off his hand. "Sure gets hot here early, don't you think? It's not even officially summer yet." He didn't seem to want me to answer his question. Detective Kennedy was big into rhetorical questions. We both licked for a while and then he dropped the first bomb.

"Bet your mama is excited about her reunion with Jewels and Bert."

The safe feeling scurried away as fast as a cockroach. I stopped licking and practically dropped my cone. All I said was "Reunion?"

"Yeah, you know," he said. "When people get back together again after a long time apart." Did he think I was two years old? I knew what *reunion* meant.

So there I was, cornered, like a bug by a cat. Should I act dumb? Should I ask who Jewels and Bert were? Should I tell him they weren't planning a reunion, at least that I knew about? But if I did that, it would be like admitting that Mama knew Jewels and Bert. I decided not to say anything, which I guess was kind of like acting dumb. That worked for about five seconds.

"Rainy Cove Park, right?" he asked.

And right then and there it was like the road and the ground shook and the Dairy Queen and the picnic tables and the utility poles and the cars driving by started crashing and breaking and collapsing into a big black hole while I just stood there watching. And I remembered the sad expression on Detective Kennedy's face when he was looking at Mama's catchall book, and the fear I'd felt then, and how I'd pushed it away because lying to myself was easier than believing what I knew to be true, that Detective

Kennedy *had* seen that note about Rainy Cove Park that Mama wrote in the margin, just like I'd seen it that day when I tried to tell Mama I knew what the three of them were planning.

As if the first bomb hadn't caused enough chaos, he dropped a second.

"Did your mama tell you we found the gun?"

Found the gun?

I started sweating, and not because it was hot out. My heart was obviously pumping so much blood to the rest of my body that it was boiling my skin. Detective Kennedy was staring at me. I wondered if he'd watched Mama's face when he told her about finding the gun like he was watching mine.

I shook my head no.

"That makes sense," he said. "She's probably protecting you."

"From what?" I asked.

"Well, you know, uncomfortable information. Some kid, about your age in fact, found it washed up on the sand about a mile from the beach house. We didn't connect it to your daddy's murder right away, but when we ran the ballistics—" He stopped. "You probably don't know what ballistics means, do you?"

Seriously? Of course I knew what ballistics meant, and not from one of my dictionaries. I watched TV, didn't I?

"No," I said.

"Well, it means we had the gun studied to see if its bullets matched any recent shootings on Cooper's Island. Took us a while because we only went back a few months at first, and then Mack, Detective Jones I mean, thought we should check back further, so we were able to match them to the ones that killed your daddy. But that still didn't necessarily mean it was the same gun. Lots of guns use the same bullets. Then we ran the serial number. Did you know your daddy had a gun, Picasso?"

"No, sir." I could feel my face getting red, and then my eyes got so wet I couldn't see through them.

"I'm sorry, sweetie," Detective Kennedy said, but I barely heard him because I'd started crying.

I couldn't believe it. I'm not even sure what started it. And when I say crying, I mean tears were running out of my eyes so fast they were falling off my chin before I even had a chance to wipe them away with my sleeve. I was really embarrassed, but as it turned out it was a good thing because Detective Kennedy got all concerned.

"I didn't mean to upset you," he said in a very soft and soothing voice. "You're so smart that I keep forgetting you're only a kid."

He came around to my side of the picnic table like he was going to put his arms around me or something, but there was no way I was getting hugged. Besides, my ice-cream cone, not to mention my hand and part of my arm, was a gloppy mess by then. I stepped over the bench, walked to the trash can, and threw what was left of my cone away. Luckily I remembered there was one of those napkin holders on the metal shelf by the Dairy Queen's outside window, so I grabbed a bunch and started wiping the sticky cream off me. I remember I rubbed for a long time. I think I was trying to figure out what to do or say next. I didn't understand why Detective Kennedy was telling me all that stuff. I guess it could've all been innocent, like maybe he was just filling me in, which would be pretty cool, because that would mean he really did think I was smart and that he wasn't just saying so, but then I started thinking that maybe none of it had been true, that he'd just been pretending to be Mama's boyfriend, and maybe just like Ryan Anderson and Daddy, he had done it all for selfish reasons, in this case so he could catch Daddy's killer, which under different circumstances would be a good thing, but in this circumstance definitely wasn't, and so maybe I should just raise my head high and stomp, stomp, stomp away from Detective Kennedy and keep stomping until I got home, and then never ever talk to him again. I was so confused I couldn't tell the difference between whether

I just *wanted to believe* that Detective Kennedy had good intentions, or whether deep down I knew that what I felt was true: that Detective Kennedy *was* different, that he really did love Mama and me, and that he would never intentionally hurt us.

Then I realized none of my thoughts even mattered. What had happened, happened. Daddy was dead, and the police had the gun that shot him. Which meant if this whole story were a painting, the painting would suck. I hadn't lived up to my name. Instead of making things prettier, everything, all the rumors, all the lies, all the deception, was its ugly self. And maybe because at that moment I felt like my heart was breaking into a million pieces and that it would never ever grow back together again, and my stomach was churning so bad I thought I might throw up, I asked Detective Kennedy the question I most wanted an answer to, but had always been afraid to ask, at least out loud.

"Is Mama going to—?"

Before I could get the last word out, I started to sob.

Kyle

There are cases you take to the grave; I had a pretty good idea that this would be one of them, but not for the usual reasons. Usually it's a case you can't solve, that you keep picking at over and over in your head. Something you missed that bugs you. Something you can't find, like that key. Something that plays with your mind. Maybe there never was a key, you think. Maybe there wasn't a safe-deposit box. Maybe there wasn't any money. The maybes can drive you crazy if you let them, but this case hadn't been about maybes; it was about denial. The key, the interviews, the mix-ups with the wives, the time of death, the hair, Lindsay Middleton, all of it was just details. We always had motive. We always had opportunity. We always had our eyewitness: Picasso. I saw it on her face that first day when she was sitting on the sofa holding her mother's hand so tight her knuckles were red. I saw it on my way down the beach-house stairs when she was working on her sand castle. I saw it when I looked up to see her staring at me right after I found the note in the catchall book. I saw it as she watched me from the window when I drove away from the house that next morning. Fierce protectiveness. Just like that dog in Michigan. And knowledge.

I lied to Picasso at the Dairy Queen that day in the way that

any good interrogator does; I provided enough truthful information to make her believe that the crap I threw at her was true. As
part of our routine investigation, we did run the serial number of
Oliver Lane's missing .38-caliber handgun, but we had nothing to
match it against. There was no kid about Picasso's age who found
it washed up on the shore. There was no gun. I made it up so
Picasso would think we had the evidence we needed to arrest her
mother. The whole thing was a fucking ambush.

I'd hoped—hell, I'd wished with all my being—that the conversation would go a different way. That I'd find out the note in
the catchall book had nothing to do with the wives or the murder
of Oliver Lane. That somehow in some way her mother was innocent. That I'd been wrong about what I'd seen in Picasso's face.
But unfortunately it went exactly the way any good detective looking to solve a case would want it go.

Exactly the way I *did not* want it to go.

When Picasso asked me if her mother was going to jail, I could
have lied, but I thought she deserved my honesty. I'd already done
enough to hurt her.

"Probably," I said.

"Can't you stop it?" she asked between sobs.

"I wish I could, sweetie."

She didn't say anything for a while. She wiped the tears from
her eyes, calmed herself. I watched a series of emotions cross her
face. Then she said, "But what if she wasn't the one who did it?"

"They still planned it together," I said. "But it's possible the
judge will go easier on her if she gives up the shooter. Think she'd
do that?"

"There's a clearing in the woods near the lake."

"What?" I asked.

"At Rainy Cove Park," she said. "That's where they're meeting.
I followed them sometimes. I can draw you a map. That way you
can get there before them, and you can hear for yourself."

The Wives

It was as if there was an invisible magnet between us. When we were within arm's reach, we paused, assessed one another. Yes, these were the faces we remembered. These were the eyes, the ears, the lips we imagined as we lay in our pink-petaled baths.

Together we inhaled our scent, that heady combination of Diana's floral sweetness, Jewels's musk, and Bert's mountain air. Together we imagined lying naked on a cloud, basking in the nimbi only our particular triumvirate could birth. Together we released our bodies from their yearlong prison. Our shoulders dropped. Our chests collapsed. Our breath escaped. We extended our arms, entwined our fingers, raised our heads to the sky, and gave thanks for this day, this hour, this moment, this opportunity to reconnect.

This freedom.

And then we walked.

The path was the same as we remembered. There was the crunch of the twigs beneath our soles, the light openness narrowing to dense forest, the happy chirp of birds, the smell of wood and leaves, and yes there, barely visible through the trees, was the lake. We almost missed the fork. Could it be that no one had traveled our trail since? Was it possible that no soul had entered our magical piece of earth?

Diana tossed out the blanket she carried under her arm. It snapped, billowed, hovered, landed—the sameness of this small ritual was comforting. She smoothed out its corners while Jewels opened the picnic basket, extracted the plastic plates, silverware, and wineglasses.

"Champagne first?" Bert asked. It was the first words we'd exchanged in a long while.

"You bet," said Jewels.

The cork popped, flew in the air.

"Here's to getting away with murder," Jewels said. That high-pitched clink.

We sipped.

Diana unwrapped the saran from the sandwiches, balled it, tossed it on the blanket. "Egg salad," she said. "Hope that's okay."

"Perfect," Bert said.

"Just like that first time," Jewels said.

"Yes," Diana said. "I thought it was fitting."

The air was still, the dense woods silent as we ate.

We felt a soft breeze. Tree branches moved. Leaves rustled. We shivered.

"My mother used to say that when it gets cold, there are ghosts nearby," Bert said.

"Shit," Jewels said. "That's all we need. Oliver's ghost."

An owl hooted in the distance, then again. A haunting ethereal song chimed in on the third hoot.

"What is that?" Jewels asked.

"A whip-poor-will," Bert said. "Legend has it they can sense when a soul is departing."

"You're messing with us," Jewels said.

"No," Bert said. "It's true."

"Do you think it's Oliver's soul, that it's been here all along?" Diana asked.

"It was a breeze, not a visitation," Jewels said. "And a silly whip-poor-will doesn't mean a thing. Oliver is dead, and his body is in the ground in a cemetery in Hollyville."

After we ate, we placed everything but the champagne and glasses back in the basket, closed it, and as if on cue began removing our clothes. Shoes first, then skirts and blouses, and finally panties and bras.

We stood facing the lake, shook out our long straight locks, warmed our faces with the sun. Three blond goddesses of unique size and shape. We skipped into the warm summer water, splashed one another, dove below its surface, disappeared just long enough to cause any onlookers, or ghosts, concern, and then, in unison, popped our heads to the surface, smiling, giddy with joy, laughing with such abandon we might have been patients from a lunatic asylum. We swam: three sets of arms slicing through water, three sets of legs kicking up foam. After some time, we emerged, wet hair sticking to our heads and skin, strands falling over our naked breasts, winding through our bare armpits, the sun washing over us, fading us. Three heavenly messengers gliding through the air.

Back on the blanket, we retrieved the pink towels from Bert's woven bag, dabbed our skin, dropped our backs to the blanket and fell asleep.

In an hour's time, we woke. Renewed. Released. Reborn. We dressed, and only then, after all the preamble, did we begin to talk about what happened that day.

In keeping with the order of the wives, Diana went first. She began with where we'd left off the previous year, with the events that followed the murder. She detailed the arrival of the neighbors, and then the police. She summarized the questions she'd been asked, and her answers.

"I stuck to the story," she said, proudly. "Just like you said, Jewels."

"Well, that's good," Jewels said, smugly. "Since obviously Bert didn't get my message, or decided to ignore it."

"What do you mean?" Bert asked. "Was there another message? I just got the one message about the meeting being canceled."

"And you chose to ignore it," Jewels said. "What a surprise."

"I didn't ignore it," Bert said.

"Wait," Diana said. "So you did get my message, Jewels?"

"Yes," Jewels said. "And I passed it on to Bert."

Two sets of eyes focused on Bert.

"Why are you looking at me? I didn't do it."

"Are you certain?" Jewels asked.

"Yes, Jewels, I'm certain. I think I'd remember killing someone. Come on, Diana. Obviously it was you. You got angry when he told you."

"Told me what?" Diana asked.

Two sets of eyes looked at Diana.

"Seriously, Diana?" Bert said. "Why play dumb now? It's just us."

"I swear to God I didn't kill him," Diana said. "I wanted to, but I changed my mind."

Three long pregnant pauses.

"Well, one of you is lying," Jewels said.

"Maybe you're the one lying," Bert said.

"Me?" Jewels said. "How could I kill him? I was at a design charrette."

"But you weren't there the entire time, were you, Jewels?" Diana asked.

"What do you mean?" Jewels asked.

"Don't act dumb, Jewels. The police told me about the airline ticket and rental car. I know you used my name so no one would know it was you. Or maybe you were trying to set me up."

"Back up," Bert said. "What did she do?"

"Jewels rented a car the morning of the murder, and then flew back to Philadelphia in time to catch her flight back to Raleigh."

Bert looked at Jewels with surprise. "Is that true?"

Jewels didn't respond.

"She obviously didn't like that I called it off, so she took matters into her own hands," Diana said. "Clever, taking my driver's license, Jewels. When exactly did you do that? That last time we met? While we were napping?"

"Actually, I didn't take it. I found it. It must've fallen out of your bag when you got out that damn notebook. It was loose, right? I was going to say something, but then, yes, I figured it was a safety net. You know, like Oliver always said, a just in case. But I didn't kill the bastard. When I got there, the place was already swarming with cops and medics. I figured Bert had been there and gone already. So I left."

"You expect us to believe that?" Bert said.

"I don't care whether you believe it or not, Bert," Jewels said. "You tell me, Diana. Was or was not Oliver already dead at a little after eight? I would've gotten there earlier if it hadn't been for the ferry. I waited forever for the damn thing to show."

"The neighbors said they heard the gunshot at seven fifteen," Diana said.

"There you have it," Jewels said.

We ran the events of that day back through our minds. In that moment, we no longer knew who or what to believe. In that moment, we no longer trusted one another.

"What did you mean you wanted to kill him, Diana?" Jewels asked.

"What?"

"You said *you* wanted to kill him, as if you weren't going to wait for Bert. Why?"

"Because of Bert's message."

"What message?" Jewels asked.

"The one she left on Oliver's phone. When I heard it, I thought he'd played me. I was so mad at you, Bert."

"You were mad at me?" Bert said. "I was furious with you. I figured you killed him because he told you he was choosing me."

"If you were so pissed, why didn't you say so when we got out of our cars?" Diana asked. "Why wait until now, after we toasted, had lunch, swam?"

"I don't know," Bert said. "It was just so good to see you both. Here, listen, I . . . I saved the message. I was in the shower so didn't pick up." She fished inside her purse.

"Hey, babe. It's me. Listen, there's something I want to tell you. I had hoped I could say this in person, but I'll make up for it when I get back from this stupid board meeting. I promise. Anyway, I just wanted to tell you that I've been a shit. Fuck, I've been more than a shit. I want you to know that you and Isabelle are all that matter to me. All that ever mattered. Do you understand? I love you so much, more than anything and anyone in the world. And I'm going to change. I promise. From now on it's just the three of us. No one else will ever come between us." Pause. "I love you, babe. I'll see you in a few days. Kiss Izzie for me."

Just then, as if in warning, the whip-poor-will cried. Even Jewels looked startled and fearful, but in true form she collected herself.

"What I don't understand, Diana," she said, "is why after you heard that message, after you admitted you wanted to kill him, *why* you called it off."

"I . . . I don't know," Diana said. "I just thought—"

"Thought what?" Jewels asked.

"That I overreacted. Oliver had been so loving."

"Oh—my—God," Jewels said. "Seriously, Diana? Well I've got news for both of you. Oliver told me the exact same thing. That he was going to leave the two of you. He said it that previous Monday, the last time we had sex. Fucking amazing sex. Only I wasn't naïve enough to believe him. Oliver was a lying, cheating, controlling bastard who had to win. He was a sociopath, remember?"

"You had sex with him?" Diana asked.

"It was just sex, Diana," Jewels said. "Get over it."

Diana started wringing her hands. "But if none of us killed him, who did?"

Jewels twirled a lock of her hair. "Good question."

Bert smoothed her skirt. "Could it have been a burglar? Was anything missing?"

Recognition dawned on Diana's face. "The police didn't find Oliver's money. I just figured he'd forgotten to bring it."

"Wow," Jewels said.

"Yeah wow," Bert said.

"Wait," Diana said. "What about the gun?"

"What about it?" Bert asked.

"The police said they didn't find a gun. I'm sure I put it in the crawl space, on the shelf behind the little blue door like we said."

"Maybe they didn't look in the crawl space," Bert said. "Maybe it's still there."

"Do you think it is?" Diana asked. "Should we go back and see?"

"Are you sure you put it there?" Jewels asked.

"Yes," Diana said. "I mean, I don't know—"

"Think, Diana," Jewels said. "Maybe he forgot it or decided not to bring it."

"Yes," Bert said. "Maybe he left it somewhere. He was always moving it around."

"No, I'm sure he brought it," Diana said. "I remember putting it on that shelf in the crawl space. I did it right before I left to call you that night, Jewels. Oh God. Maybe I dreamed I put it there. Everything about that day is so cloudy."

"Why would you put it in the crawl space if you intended to call everything off?" Jewels asked.

"That's just it," Diana said. "I don't know."

"Well," Jewels said. "I doubt the police would've missed it if you had put it there, so obviously you didn't."

We sat for a while, watching the sun reflecting on the lake, listening to the song of the whip-poor-will, trying to make sense of what we'd just learned, coming to the grave realization that each of us had lived the past year thinking ultimately she had been Oliver's one and only. That each of us had been willing, even happy, to piss the other two away, all so she could have Oliver to herself.

"Well, I for one don't care what happened, or who pulled the trigger," Jewels said. "The endgame is still the same. Oliver is dead."

Those were the last words we ever spoke to one another. As if in acknowledgment, a gust of wind blew through the trees, swirled through our private clearing, upset the picnic basket, yanked the blanket from beneath us and all but sucked it into the air. Our champagne glasses shattered. Our hair and skirts flapped and waggled. The empty bottle started spinning, faster and faster, and then slowed, pausing for a moment in front of each of us, and finally stopping. In that moment, we felt a visceral sensation of diffusing, like a single atom splitting into three. We reached for our own bodies, touched a bare leg, shoulder, neck, face, experienced something we hadn't in nearly two years, that tingling awareness of skin touching skin.

Oliver had brought us together. Planning his murder had kept us together. We had believed his execution would seal us together forever. But ultimately, Oliver, not we, had won. He'd driven a wedge between us as final as his death.

Without so much as a glance at the others, we rose, gathered our belongings, and went our separate ways.

Kyle

The word *rendezvous* took one last spin through my mind and disappeared.

Mack and I had followed the map Picasso gave me. We arrived early, crouched behind the tree trunk, which may have been big enough to conceal Picasso but required some serious contorting on our part. One of my legs was cramped and the other asleep, but out of fear we might snap a twig or rustle the carpet of dry leaves beneath us, we'd frozen ourselves in position throughout the wives' meeting. Now we stretched, rubbed our legs, twisted our necks, brushed twigs and leaves from our pants. The sound of cracking bones joined that of the whistling birds.

"Christ," Mack said. "I'm getting old. And what was with that fucking wind?"

"Yeah, crazy," I said. "For a minute there I thought we were all going to swirl into the sky like Dorothy's house."

"Do you buy it?" Mack asked. "One of them could still be lying."

By all accounts the three of them were innocent. While Mack and I had both been wrong, our brains hosted different boxing matches. Mack's presented the renowned middleweights Confused Disbelief in one corner and Stubborn Resolve in the other. Mine featured championship heavyweights Total Relief and Sinking Gut.

"To the others?" I said. "Doubtful."

"Yeah, but what if they just didn't want to admit it to one another, or maybe whoever did it is in denial? Think we should take them in, question them separately?"

"Why?" I asked. "What do we have? No gunshot residue or blood splatter on the first Mrs. Lane, nothing that puts either of the other wives at the crime scene, and three admissions, heard firsthand by law enforcement, to planning the murder but not carrying it out. Why would they cop to the plotting and not the crime?"

"What about the gun?" Mack asked. "I searched that crawl space myself."

"What about it?" I asked. "Maybe there never was a gun. Who cares what happened to a gun Oliver Lane bought and registered ten years ago. He could've sold it, given it away, or it's still in one of their houses somewhere, who knows? I say the real perp had a piece on him when he arrived at the scene. He shot Lane, took the cash, and left with the gun."

"So *Murder on the Orient Express*? Jesus. What are the odds?"

We didn't talk during the drive back to Cooper's Island. We both needed to wrap our brains around what we'd seen and heard that day. It hadn't been what either of us had expected. I spent the time thinking about what was next, how Diana and I could get beyond all this. What the future held.

The sun was setting as we pulled onto the ferry. I left the car and found a spot at the railing to watch it. When I was kid, like every other kid, I hated Cooper's Island. I felt trapped by the water, but there was nothing like an Outer Banks sunset, nothing like that pink glow dropping over the deep purple water. Nothing like the momentary kaleidoscope of color that happened when the two met. I once asked my mother if the sun drowned when it went down. I figured a different sun rose every morning, and then it drowned too. I thought maybe that's where darkness came from, from the world's sadness.

"It doesn't drown," my mother had said. "It just goes to sleep."

"The sun sleeps in the ocean?" I asked.

"No," my mother said. "It sleeps in your heart."

Mack dropped me off at the house that once belonged to my father and mother, the house that held memories good and bad. I opened the front door to the same empty rooms, same bare floors and walls, same rickety table, same pair of wobbly chairs. I went to the refrigerator, grabbed a box of five-day-old pizza, smelled it, figured it would do. My trusty bottle of Redbreast sat on the counter by the sink. I started to take a drink from the bottle but thought better of it. The events of the day, however daunting, at least deserved a proper glass. I swallowed the shot in one gulp. The liquid burned in my throat, warmed my stomach. I poured another.

Sometimes the thing you wanted most in the world was to be a seasoned and smart cop, to find that other world you don't know is out there. Sometimes you wished you weren't so seasoned. You wished you didn't have that sixth sense that some cops call their gut. You wished that one final word wasn't still flying through your mind.

Picasso

I love you more than life itself: a phrase made up of seven words.

I can no longer think about Daddy without also thinking about this phrase. Which means I don't much like it, and I definitely don't trust it. In fact, the only way I can get myself to feel nothing one way or another about it is to break it down to individual words.

I: pronoun used by a speaker to refer to himself or herself.

Love: as defined earlier, an intense feeling of deep affection.

You: pronoun used to refer to the person or people being addressed.

More: comparative, implying a greater or additional amount or degree.

Than: conjunction or preposition introducing the second element in a comparison.

Life: the condition that distinguishes animals and plants from inorganic matter, including the capacity for growth, reproduction, functional activity, and continual change preceding death.

Itself: used to emphasize a particular thing or animal previously mentioned.

Individually each definition is simply factual, but put them together and, depending on who the initial speaker is (or was), the meanings of the words become vulnerable to manipulation. Which in my opinion is sacrilege. Words mean what they mean, and anyone who knowingly misrepresents their meanings obviously has no regard for truth or language. Coming from Daddy, the only true word in this phrase is *I*. Sometimes in my mind I play with this phrase; I fix the meaning by switching the words around. *I love life itself more than you,* for instance. That way I can pretend Daddy wasn't such a liar. But what if you can't really switch the words around? What if the phrase was shortened to its first four words?

I love you more.

I guess I should start with what happened the day before Daddy died. Daddy and I were working on the sand castle while Mama swam. Daddy was sweating. He wiped the back of his hand on his forehead. "Geez, it's hot out here. Run in and get us some Cokes, will you Picasso?"

Daddy had never even once called me Picasso before, and so I told him that.

"You're silly," he said. "I call you Picasso all the time."

"No, you don't," I said.

"Don't argue with me, kid," he said. He made the unsmile again, just as he'd done the day before, and the way he said *kid* was like I could've been any kid to him, definitely not his, and definitely not one that he loved more than life itself, more like one that annoyed him. I remember thinking about what Jewels had said about Daddy saying those same words to everyone, not just Mama and me, and what she said about him being a sociopath, and right then and there I believed with all my heart that he was. Then the unsmile was replaced by the charming smile, and like I always did, I questioned whether I'd seen it.

I ran as fast as I could up to the beach house, the sand burning the bottoms of my feet the entire way, rinsed off under the outside faucet—Mama hated it when I tracked in sand—and dried off with the towel Mama had left by the sliding glass doors. Instead of going straight to the refrigerator, I went to the bathroom. I used to have accidents a lot when I was little—the pediatrician said it was either stress or an undeveloped bladder—and even though I hadn't done that in a really long time, at least four years, that's what happened that day. I didn't make it on time. I peed on my favorite purple swimsuit, and a little on the bathroom floor. There was some Formula 409 under the sink; I sprayed it on the puddle and wiped it up with toilet paper. I had to flush the toilet three times because I used so much paper. Then I closed the sink drain, twisted the tap, took off my suit, dunked it a few times, wrung it out, hung it on the hook on the back of the door, and emptied the water. I figured if Mama asked about it, I'd just tell her it got full of sand.

Wrapped in the towel I'd brought in from outside, I headed to my bedroom to put on another suit but couldn't find one. Mama always packed at least three swimsuits for me, so I figured the other ones were probably in one of her drawers. The bureau in their room was one of those kinds with a mirror and six drawers, three on each side. I opened one of the top drawers first, then a middle and bottom one. Still no suit. I opened the other top drawer—

That's when I saw Daddy's gun.

I stared at it for a long time, thinking that maybe I should hide it so no one could use it on Daddy. I remembered from eavesdropping at RCP that Mama was supposed to put it in the crawl space under the house, and since she hadn't done that yet, after all tomorrow was Kill Daddy Day, I thought maybe she'd changed her mind. I decided to think more on all this while Daddy and I finished up the sand castle. My extra swimsuits were in the other bottom drawer mixed in with Mama's. I put on the brown one, headed to the refrigerator to grab some Cokes, and went back outside.

Daddy saw me and waved right away. "Hey, Portia (the satellite of Uranus that is seventh in distance from the planet; also the rich heiress in *The Merchant of Venice* by William Shakespeare)." He was his old self again.

He was digging in the moat.

I handed him his Coke. He drank almost half of it.

"It's really deep," I said.

"Climb inside it."

The water was clear up to my waist. "Cool."

Daddy was busy building up the walls, and I was working on the keep, when we heard Mama come up. We were so absorbed that we didn't even notice her come out of the water. Daddy talked to Mama for a while as I worked, and before I knew it Mama was yelling something at me from up on the patio. I couldn't really hear her over the sound of the waves, but I was betting she was mad I took her towel again.

Then Mama and Daddy disappeared inside the house. If it wouldn't have been for me just showing up a little later, I'm pretty sure there wouldn't have been any lunch.

Later that night, while Daddy and I were playing Scrabble, Mama started acting strange, like she told Daddy she needed to go into town because there was no salt at the beach house, but there was. I'd seen her shove it into the dishtowel drawer. Then she said she needed a new book, but she'd just started reading the one she'd brought along. I was pretty sure she was leaving so she could call Jewels. I started praying inside again, this time that no matter what Mama meant to say, that God would make her say "The meeting is off."

After Mama left, Daddy said, "Your mama's sure been lying a lot lately."

"What?" I was stunned.

"I used salt on my eggs this morning. Do you know where she's going?"

For the first time ever, I was really scared of Daddy. It wasn't just the unsmile. It was the way he looked, like he was a whole different person, the flat tone of his voice, and his eyes. The cold, blank emptiness of his eyes.

I shook my head, maybe a little too fast. "No, Daddy."

"I know all about her little meetings with Jewels and Bert." He started laughing, a laugh I'd never heard him make before. It sounded like a crazy person's laugh. "How long have you known they were planning to kill me?"

"I . . . I . . . They're not, Daddy."

It was like he didn't hear me, like he was so mad he couldn't hear me.

Then he said something really scary. "I don't think jail is good enough for your mother, do you? You and I will be just fine without her, right?"

He must have seen how scared I was then, because he changed back to himself again, and said, "I was just kidding, Perry Mason (a fictional defense attorney who was the main character in works of detective fiction by Erle Stanley Gardner; also a TV show that ran from 1957 to 1966)."

I couldn't sleep that night. I worried over what Daddy said. He hadn't said anything else about Mama after he called me Perry Mason, and he was completely back to normal Daddy when Mama got home, but I couldn't get that image of him laughing out of my mind. I knew I had to warn Mama, but since Daddy was next to her the rest of the night, I'd have to tell her before she went for her morning swim. I remember thinking it was good I couldn't sleep.

But I must've dozed off because I woke to the sound of the sliding glass doors opening and closing. I bolted to a sitting position, got out of bed, and since it was conveniently lying there in a ball on the floor, climbed into my brown swimsuit and headed down to the beach. By the time I got there, Mama had already swum out pretty far. I panicked. My thoughts were all over the place. What if I couldn't tell Mama about what Daddy said? What had Mama told Jewels? What if Bert was on her way to kill Daddy? What if she actually did and Mama went to jail? All I knew was that the first thing I needed to do was find that gun. Since Daddy was still in bed and I couldn't check to see if the gun was still in the drawer, I ran to the crawl space, hoping the entire time that I wouldn't find it there.

The gun was perched on a ledge next to a couple of old paint cans, a rusty hammer, and a beat-up kid's sand pail, green with a yellow handle. I reached for it, carefully wrapped my hand around it, lifted it from the ledge, closed the blue door, walked back around the house and through the side door, and went back into my room.

A few minutes later, Daddy's alarm went off. I heard him go to the bathroom to do his business, flush the toilet, head into the living area, then the gurgle of the coffee maker, the tap of a closing cabinet, the clink of the porcelain cup being set on the counter, the splash of poured coffee, the patter of his footsteps on the tile floor, squeak of the floorboard under the carpet, flip of the lock, and swishing of the sliding glass doors opening. I imagined him sipping his coffee as he looked out to the ocean and waited for what I'd always thought was one of his favorite daily activities: watching Mama come out of the water.

I tiptoed out to the kitchen; Daddy was standing by the sliding glass doors with his back to me. I checked the time on the stove clock. Ten minutes after seven. Bert would be there any minute. As stealthily as a ninja, I climbed up on the blue shell chair nearest the side door so I'd be as tall as an adult, held the gun with both hands, raised my arms, steadied myself, curled my forefinger around the trigger—

I couldn't do it.

All at once, as if they were fighting over which one got there first, the memories came. Daddy being home less and less. Jewels showing up at our door. She and Bert in the blue sports car in the church parking lot. Mama getting into the car. Their matching blond hair flying in the wind like wings as they drove away. The phone call from Jewels. The three of them swimming naked at Rainy Cove Park. That weird chanting they did. Daddy and I working on the sand castle. Me catching Daddy and Mama kissing and him asking me why I was standing there. Daddy calling me Picasso. Me peeing in my swimsuit. Me finding the gun in the top drawer. Daddy saying all those things about Mama when she went to call Jewels. That crazy laugh. The unsmiles. Me finding the gun in the crawl space behind the little blue door. Bert coming to kill Daddy. Mama going to jail. Me going to foster care. And then all these thoughts merged together into two words: *synchronicity* and *threat.* I mean, weren't all the events leading up to me standing there pointing a gun at Daddy's back obviously meaningfully related, and hadn't what Daddy said about Mama indicated that he intended to seek retribution? Maybe even physical retribution? A vision flashed before my eyes of Daddy's hands tightening around Mama's neck—

I remember feeling the tears tickling my cheeks before I even realized I was crying, and I also remember feeling trapped, like I had no choice, that *I* was Daddy's destiny, not Bert. And I remember I started praying to God, who by then I really hoped existed, to please, please make it all go away, turn back the clock, but he didn't. And then, for some reason, it was like I was a little girl again, like when I thought there were monsters in my closet or goblins under my bed waiting to devour me, and I knew with certainty that only one person could save me, so I called for him—

"Daddy," I said. "I'm scared." And I was.

"What are you doing up so early, Primrose Path (the pursuit of pleasure that brings disastrous consequences)?" Daddy asked as he turned. His eyes got really big.

And then, I *saw* it. Before it even happened, I saw me firing the gun, Daddy dying, my entire life after Daddy was dead, and I knew I was Daddy's destiny, and he was mine—

I pulled the trigger.

He held out his hand, as if it could block the bullet from hitting him, and said, "Don't—"

I almost fell back into the chair but caught myself, widened my stance for better balance. Daddy stumbled when the bullet hit him, reached toward me, took a few steps.

I shot him again.

A high-pitched screech, like chalk scraping against a blackboard, came from his mouth. Both of his hands pressed into his stomach as he bent forward. He stayed like that for what seemed the longest minute ever, staring at me in disbelief, and then he fell, quickly, body over knees, like an exploding building, and landed on his belly. I wanted to look away, but I couldn't because it was like his eyes had locked mine into position. Then he started saying that phrase, the one I don't much like, and definitely don't trust, but he only got out the first four words before he coughed up blood and stopped breathing.

It was like I was being given a sign, an it-will-all-be-okay sign, because even as Daddy lay dying, he'd lied to me, he didn't love me more than anything or anyone, especially himself, he didn't love me at all, and so right then and there I stopped being afraid and I did what I had to do.

I looked out the sliding glass doors; a cool breeze swirled past me. Other than the red speck in the ocean that meant Mama had begun her swim back to shore, there was no one in sight. I ran out to my sand castle. Stepped out of my swimsuit. Wrapped it around the gun. Burrowed them into the moat as far as I could—I remember thinking how lucky it was that since the suit was brown it pretty much blended right in with the sand. Jumped in after them in case any of Daddy's blood got on me. Got out. Filled the moat with sand. Ran naked to the outside faucet. Washed off my feet and ankles. Dried myself really well, especially the bottom of my feet. Went back inside through the sliding glass doors. Closed and locked them (later, I wondered why I did that). Stepped over Daddy. Took the money out of his wallet. Hid it inside the cardboard tube of one of the extra toilet paper rolls. Headed to the bathroom. The purple swimsuit I had peed on was still hanging on the door hook. I climbed into it, wiggled it up over my hips, stretched the armholes over my shoulders, and went back out to the living room.

Mama was standing in the doorway; her hair and swimsuit were dripping. I wondered why she hadn't grabbed the towel she left on the patio and then I remembered that I'd taken it. She looked scared and sad and I wanted to go to her, but I knew I needed to kneel down by Daddy. I knew that's what Mama needed to see, what she needed to remember.

"Daddy," I shook him. "I'm sorry, and I know Mama is too."

For a moment I thought maybe he hadn't died. Maybe God had answered me after all, maybe I was still in bed, having a bad dream, and any minute I'd wake up and Daddy would be standing over me asking me to go get ice cream, giving me his secret smile, telling me not to tell Mama, and I'd jump on his back, and he'd take me downstairs, and Mama would be there, and he'd hug her, and the three of us were a happy family, Daddy's only family.

Then the weirdest thing happened. It was like I left my body and watched everything from a distance, like it was a movie or TV crime show. The actress that was playing me called to Mama, but Mama was staring intently at the painting hanging over the fireplace, as if she was searching for Waldo or some sort of hidden message. A lady was there. She said something about hearing a shot. She walked over to the girl, bent to feel Daddy's pulse. She started talking to some man who had miraculously appeared, like the camera had stopped, stuck him there, and then went on with the scene. The girl got up and started walking toward the hallway, and even though by then there were five people in the room, including Daddy, my eyes followed her. She disappeared into the bathroom, reappeared carrying a heap of something white and fluffy: towels. She wrapped one around her own shoulders, then walked Mama to the sofa and draped the other over her shoulders. I remember thinking that was nice of the girl. At some point, two men in suits showed up. The older one told the girl she could go outside and play with her sand castle, and I could tell she was happy about that.

That was where I joined my body again, at the sand castle.

Even with the gun right there in the moat, I wasn't as nervous as I thought I would be when Detective Kennedy came out to ask me questions, and I was surprised how easy it was to lie. I think it's interesting that sometimes you don't really know yourself or what you'll do in a situation until you're faced with it. I could've lied to Detective Kennedy at the Dairy Queen, but I didn't. I wanted him to see and hear for himself that Mama wasn't guilty, even if that meant he'd know I was, because I knew that Mama could never have survived jail, she'd always been too fragile, and she definitely could never have survived doing murder. Murder changes a person; I should know.

Probably it has something to do with my age, but no one ever suspected me. No one tested my hands or clothes or body for blood splatter or gunshot residue. No one wondered what exactly I was doing at seven fifteen that morning. No one questioned why I was up so early when I never get up early. No one asked me if I knew where Daddy's money was. No one looked in the sand-castle moat for the gun. In Mama's *Taking Charge of Your Life* book, there's this chapter on following your life path; it says you'll know when you're doing that because things will just fall into place and you'll feel like you're flying through space on a magic carpet, untouchable, at one with the world. With the exception of the actual Killing Daddy part, that's kind of how everything felt that day, and in the days, weeks, and months that followed. Even though I worried a lot about the police arresting Mama and did whatever I could—manifest, pray, lie—to make certain that didn't happen, I never once worried about them arresting me. Because I believed what I saw right before I pulled the trigger, me growing up, going to college and the police academy, becoming a detective, getting married, and having a child of my own.

It's been two years since Daddy died. Detective Kennedy transferred to the Hollyville Police Department so he could live with Mama and me. He said one day, if Mama and I wanted to, we could move to Cooper's Island because it's a healing place. He and Mama got married not too long ago. Mama is pregnant again. I'm not sure how I feel about having a little brother or sister, especially since he or she couldn't possibly be as smart as me; smartness just doesn't come around twice in one family. Ryan Anderson and Kelly Morgan aren't girlfriend and boyfriend anymore. Actually, about a week ago he asked if he could walk me home. I said I'd think about it. Lucy Baxter and I are still best friends. Mama always says we're "thick as thieves." The police never did arrest anybody for Daddy's murder, and I didn't used to think Detective Kennedy had any idea what really happened at the beach house the day Daddy died, but then one night, while Mama was at a Junior League meeting, he and I watched a movie he rented. It was called *Murder on the Orient Express*.

After the movie was over, he asked me if I understood about consequences. As usual, Detective Kennedy didn't wait for me to answer before he added, "Just because there aren't consequences in the legal sense, that doesn't mean there aren't other ways to make amends."

"Like what?" I asked.

"Sacrifice," he said. "Think about it this way. When people do something wrong in the eyes of the law, they go to jail, and when they go to jail, what do they give up?"

"Their freedom," I said.

"And freedom isn't a minor sacrifice. Do you understand?"

"Yes," I said. And I did.

"But just remember," Detective Kennedy added, "everybody makes mistakes. The challenge is not to let them define you. You need to define them."

I considered what Detective Kennedy said, especially that last part, for a long time. I thought about all sorts of things I could sacrifice, mostly stuff that I didn't want anymore. I even thought about giving up spelling, but if I did that, who would win for my school? Then it came to me: my dictionaries.

A few days later, Detective Kennedy drove me to an orphanage in Charlotte so I could give my dictionaries to kids who didn't have even one parent, like I almost didn't.

"Is that all of them?" he asked after we finished unloading.

I was in a pickle because even though I'd told Detective Kennedy I would sacrifice every last one of my dictionaries, my favorite dictionary, the one Daddy had gotten me for my tenth birthday, the one that had essentially made me understand the value and meaning of words, the one that had helped me win all those spelling bees and therefore not only gave me purpose but made me a valuable contributor to my school and its success, the one I'd used to randomly zero in on words during those months Mama, Jewels, and Bert were plotting Daddy's murder, the one that all this time had safely hidden the money Daddy brought to the beach house, the one I could never ever imagine parting with, was still back home safely hidden beneath my bed. I weighed my options. I could either let my name define me, or I could define it. Just as I was about to answer Detective Kennedy's question, the woman who took the books from us came running out.

"Mr. Kennedy, you left this envelope in one of the books?" she asked more than said. "There's more than three thousand dollars in it."

Detective Kennedy looked at me; I swore I saw pride in his eyes. "Picasso?"

"I thought the kids could use some extra money," I said.

Last week Detective Kennedy suggested we spend Independence Day on Cooper's Island, and Mama agreed. We hadn't been to the Outer Banks since Daddy died. We're staying in the house where Detective Kennedy grew up, which isn't right on the beach but isn't far either. We've gone to the beach every day, and Mama's been swimming again, something she hadn't done since Daddy died. This morning Detective Kennedy asked me if I wanted to build a sand castle, and even though thirteen seems a little old to be doing that, I said sure. After a while we got to talking about Daddy.

"Do you miss him?" Detective Kennedy asked.

"Sometimes," I said.

"What do you miss the most?" he asked.

"That's easy," I said. "I miss our secrets."

He cocked his head. "Secrets?"

"You know, just everyday secrets, like don't tell Mama stuff."

"That makes sense," he said.

I don't know what made me want to tell Detective Kennedy this, maybe it was because Daddy was dead and I figured his secrets died with him, or maybe it was because Daddy never told me this secret, I figured it out myself, or maybe, plain and simple, I felt like I owed him something since he didn't send me to jail, but I said, "Oliver Lane wasn't Daddy's real name."

Detective Kennedy sat back, wiped his sandy hands on his swim trunks, and stared at me in disbelief. "What?"

"He kept this shoe box," I said. "There were all these important papers, letters, and pictures in it. Pictures of Daddy, but he had a different name."

"Do you remember the name?"

"Peter Ares," I said.

"Well, I'll be," he said. "Where is this shoe box now?"

"Under my bed." Then I smiled, coyly, and said, "I'll have to show you sometime."

The thing is, folks probably think that if you kill someone your entire life should be plagued by debilitating guilt, but in all honesty, it's not like that. There are definitely times I think about it, and when I do, I wish with all my might that none of it would've ever happened and, just like I did with the gun, that I could bury all those memories in the sand castle moat, and the salt water would wash them far out to sea where the sharks or the whales would swallow them. But the truth is, there's something about this whole ordeal that's slowed me down, made me see things more clearly, made me realize what's important and what's not, like, for instance, wasting my time tying to make Ryan Anderson or any other boy like me, worrying over the All That Girls, or planning mean get-backs. Besides, wallowing in my own self-imposed island of grief doesn't do me, or the world, much good. Instead, I need to concentrate on the future, how I can be the best person I can possibly be, how I can live my love for Mama and Detective Kennedy, how I won't tell rumors or lies, unless the lies are for art or altruistic reasons, and how I should never ever tell anyone that I love them more than life itself unless I *absolutely* (with no qualification, restriction, or limitation; totally) mean it.

Because even I must admit, without truth behind them, words are just a bunch of letters.

Acknowledgments

I am forever grateful to the novelist Ann Hood for her unwavering support, mentorship, and especially her encouragement. Fifty pages of this novel were initially workshopped in November of 2011 at Spannocchia, a sustainable farm in Tuscany, Italy, where Ann holds an amazing writing conference, and it was she who encouraged me to complete it. Thanks to the Wildacres Writing Workshop and the Tin House Summer Writers Workshop. Special thanks to the Bread Loaf Writers' Conference for its continual dedication to giving established and aspiring writers alike the time, space, and context in which to live their passions and dreams, and to the University of Washington's MFA in creative writing program for not only being stellar, but also for sticking with me while I juggled my educational requirements with the completion of this novel. I am grateful to all the professors and workshop leaders I've worked with over the years, including David Bosworth, Stacey D'Erasmo, Lynn Freed, Jane Hamilton, Ursula Hegi, Anne LeClaire, Joyce Maynard, Whitney Otto, Ron Rash, Helen Schulman, Karen Shepard, David Shields, Maya Sonenberg, Helena Maria Viramontes, and Shawn Wong. So many people had a hand in the development of this novel. Initial input from the members of my small, but so large, North Carolina writing group—Kristin Sherman, Toccoa Switzer, and Ann Tsoa—was invaluable, as were the late-night "craft" talks with them and conference roomies Ari Gonzalez Asendorf and Margaret Burton, and the healing and manifestation powers of my dear friend Roma Gutierrez. Thanks to my fellow MFA candidates Tina Cachules, Mickie Centrone, Morgayne O'Neill, Matt Perez, Tyler Scowcroft, Rachel Shields, and Dave Thomas for their input on portions of this novel during workshop. I owe so much to my husband, David. I can't imagine any partner being more supportive, understanding, and loving of another during the many "absent" hours associated with the writing process. Thanks also to my daughter, Madi, for continually bringing love and light into my life. As a single mom for many years, it often felt like it was just she and I against the world. And heartfelt thanks to my publicist, William Heus; my marketer, Judy Jacoby; my agent, Mitchell Waters, my biggest cheerleader and by far *the* best agent in the entire world; and my editor, Jenny Jackson, not only for her editorial wisdom and tireless commitment to making this book the best it could be but also for her seeming innate ability to make the editorial process engaging, enriching, and enjoyable.

ABOUT THE AUTHOR

Jennifer Murphy received her master of fine arts in creative writing from the University of Washington. She is the recipient of the 2013 Loren D. Milliman Scholarship for creative writing and was a general contributor at the Bread Loaf Writers' Conference from 2008 through 2012. She has lived and studied in North Carolina, Colorado, and Michigan, and now resides in Seattle, Washington.

3 1531 00418 5432